HEART OF THE OLD COUNTRY

Tim McLoughlin

Akashic Books
Brooklyn, NY

D0170446

Published by Akashic Books
©2001, 2009 Tim McLoughlin

Inside design and layout by Will Croxton

ISBN-13: 978-1-936070-00-8
Library of Congress Catalog Card Number: 2009928086
All rights reserved
Fifth printing

Akashic Books
PO Box 1456
New York, NY 10009
info@akashicbooks.com
www.akashicbooks.com

Excerpts from *Heart of the Old Country* appeared in an earlier form in *Confrontation* magazine.

For my mother and father

Acknowledgments

The following people have been instrumental in seeing this book into print: Henry Flesh, Kaylie Jones, Johnny Temple, and Renette Zimmerly.

Thank you.

"This very place which is banishment to you is home to those who live here."

—Boethius, *The Consolation of Philosophy*

Nicky Shades was maybe the best sewer-to-sewer football player I ever saw. Of course that was before he became a junkie. When I was a kid I would watch him and the rest of the older guys playing rough tackle on Sixty-ninth Street, black leather jackets and watch caps bouncing off car fenders and each other. No one got seriously hurt, stitches here and there but nothing to speak of. All of them seemed to play with the passion of pros, but Shades was Namath at the Super Bowl every afternoon.

Nobody was playing now as I turned and drove by with my father, and that was surprising, since it was perfect football weather. Overcast but not too cool, and the kind of cloudy that didn't portend a monsoon. I went down to Fort Hamilton Parkway and along it to the Keyboard Lounge, my old man's last stop of the morning.

"Five minutes," he said, getting out of the car.

I remained behind the wheel, just off the corner, and thought about watching Nicky play. When the game used to end, several of the players would stay and toss the ball around for a while. If Nicky was one of those who lingered, he usually invited me to join them. I'd go the distance until I swore my arm would fall off. Sometimes we'd keep throwing past dark, then I'd have to call it quits and head in for dinner. Shades never looked tired, and if he didn't run off immediately he was usually the last to leave. He was about four years older than me, which meant adult when I was fifteen. After he got jammed up and went away for a while we lost touch. I didn't run into him for over three years. That was why it was so shocking to see how he'd deteriorated. He'd probably started on smack in the football days. It would explain the black-lens aviators he was never without. But who knows? What was it at first, fashion or crutch? Anyway, by the time I came to drive for Big Lou's car service, Nicky was already pretty much a wreck.

My father, true to his word, stepped out of the bar within five minutes. I knew he must have hustled to come back that fast, and he was still sorting policy slips and cash as we pulled away. The placement of these scraps of paper in his shirt, pants, and jacket pockets represented an elaborate filing system which, although observed by me for years, I'd yet to crack. That it worked was clear, as I'd witnessed him fairly toasted more than once, getting every bet phoned in and all action correctly covered.

Sometimes I worried about my father. Since my mother died he seemed to have given up on women, and I'd developed a fear that he would grow old alone after I left. Whenever the urge struck, he took himself to a whorehouse in Coney Island, dragging me along if we were both drunk enough. Otherwise, his only social contact was with men. He was out on a disability pension from Sanitation, which he supplemented nicely by taking numbers in a few neighborhood bars. Every morning, seven days a week, he made the rounds. That was where the car service came in. My father didn't drive. He was paranoid that for the rest of his life the Sanitation Department beakies would be watching for a sign of miraculous recovery. So everywhere he went, he went by cab or with me. He was Big Lou's most dependable customer. He also tipped generously, though most of the drivers gave it back to him on a number. He usually completed the circuit by noon and dropped his receipts off with Lou's brother Tony, who ran the social club on Sixty-fifth and most of the neighborhood action as well. Then he'd hang around the car service for a few hours, playing cards and bullshitting. When I got my license he hooked me up with a job, which was how I came to see Shades again.

Driving car service was supposed to have been a summer job, but I angled such a good schedule at the castle-in-the-air university I'd started that I'd be able to work almost full-time every week through fall. Going to college had been my idea, and with the exception of my high school guidance counselor—who probably got a kickback—nobody gave a shit. My father thought I was wasting my time and going into debt, but he wasn't in a hurry to see me leave the apartment, so my being a student kept me poor enough to suit him. Gina lost her mind over the idea of not being able to get married right away. Pretend I got drafted, I told her, but the girl had no sense of humor. It was a stall and she knew it, but she let it go for the time being. I figured I was good for about a year. If the school thing panned out I could always finish up part-time at night.

Gina lived with her mother in a two-family up on Twenty-first Avenue. We started going out when I was fifteen, and a year later the old woman who was renting the second floor in their house died. Gina's mother kept the rooms empty and said that they were for us when we got married. They had been vacant for three years and I could feel the weight of them over my head when I ate dinner there. Once we tried setting my father up with her mother, but that was a disaster. It was just as well. If it had worked out, I figured I'd have the two of them to contend with when I tied the knot.

"What are you thinking about?" my father asked abruptly, almost as if he knew.

"You and Gina's mother," I said. "Just picturing the two of you as a couple."

He snorted. "That was one historic fuckin' meeting, hah? Her house looks like a church. I'd have to go to confession every time I farted. How could a person live like that?"

I dropped my old man off, accepting the dollar and a quarter commission on the call. When I first began driving for Lou, my father insisted that he would pay and tip me like he did the other drivers. When I told him to fuck himself, he tried to at least pay the fare. I hadn't planned on taking anything. Ultimately, we settled on the commission Lou would take from the ride, so in a sense we both saved face.

I pulled a U-turn and headed for the store. It was Friday afternoon and the next day was one of my every-other-Saturdays off. I looked forward to sleeping in. Shades was parked in front of the car service, hood up as usual. Even if there was nothing wrong with his car—and that was rare—leaving the hood up kept him from getting tickets in the bus lane.

I knew Nicky was supposed to be cured, but I'd seen right off that it didn't matter. After he was released on parole the last time I'd heard that the state sent him to Florida for free to enroll in some experimental program, but that first day at Lou's I was stunned. The years of junk were written all over him. Still in the dark glasses, thank God. I didn't want to think about what Nicky's eyes looked like. His face had become tighter—skeletal—and the cords in his neck were prominent from the years of working out. The rest of him just looked used up. If I hadn't known him I would have guessed he was in his late forties. He was twenty-three; that made the two of us and a guy called Little Joey about thirty years younger than almost all the other drivers. It was a typical car service crew, evenly split between retired and retarded, with a few degenerate gamblers thrown in. Surprisingly, no drunks, but then maybe they'd hired me for my potential.

Nicky and I had never been friends, but our acquaintanceship was renewed over the first couple of weeks I was driving. We discussed mutual allies and enemies; who had married, moved, or died; who was on the way up and who was a loser. These were ambitious judgments for two guys with ten-year-old cars shuttling old women to their bingo games for two bucks a pop minus commission. The irony wasn't lost on me, but Nicky was always so serious when he spoke that I didn't bring it up. He never talked about being a junkie either, so I hoped he might be temporarily straight. He was able to get to work on time anyway, something I wasn't all that good at.

Around mid-summer, Little Joey, Nicky, and I began stopping off at Peggy's, a gin mill on my father's route, for a few beers after work. Little Joey wasn't dazzling company. He was aggressive almost to the point of being nasty, probably because he was short and, at twenty-one, nearly bald. He had been laid off from a damn good job as a paper handler at the Daily News and had a bad attitude about the nickel-and-dime money that driving brought in. But we were the three kids and we were sort of thrown together. Besides, Joey loved baseball, and since it wasn't a big betting sport, no one in Lou's except me would discuss it at any length. Relationships have been forged on less.

Gina wanted to go shopping along Fifth Avenue that Saturday, and all my excuses were so dismal that I had to tag along. I didn't know anyone who did anything in the daytime, and figured I'd have to work on that. I swung by her house around noon, fifteen minutes later than I had promised. She was waiting on her stoop with the shocked expression of a bride left at the altar. Since I'd known her, Gina had never managed to be on time for anything. Not school, not any of the jobs she'd lost, and certainly not any of our dates. The only exception was shopping. For shopping she was on time— if not early—and responded to any delay with the understanding of a drill sergeant. Even though I usually arrived early for just about everything except work, I could never resist sitting in the car around the corner from her house until I was at least ten minutes late for our shopping trips. There was no way it balanced out all the time I spent waiting for her over the years, but it made her a basket case, and I took some satisfaction in that.

I stopped at the pump in front of her building and got out, opening the trunk to toss in the several handbags that she seemed unable to do without, but which she never wanted to carry from store to store. She came around to the back of the car and put all her bags in except the one containing her pumps. She'd have to put them on before venturing into any of her regular haunts. She stood up on her toes and I bent down a little and we kissed. Gina was exactly five feet tall and I was just a shade over six. Kissing standing up was awkward if she wasn't in heels, but she wore them almost all the time. She even had a pair of high-heeled slippers. She owned sneakers, but only wore them to and from places—yuppie style—and always changed before we got out of the car. I couldn't even get her to keep them on when we visited her brother in Staten Island and just sat around the house.

We kissed until she couldn't stay on her toes anymore, then I closed the trunk and we got in the car. She began lecturing me about the importance of hitting the stores early on a Saturday. I raised the volume on the radio and nodded my head vigorously whenever she paused to take a breath.

As soon as we were moving she slipped out of her sneakers and began rustling around in her bag for her shoes. She was wearing black jeans and a black denim jacket that was fashionably baggy to the extent that it would have been large on me. The bottom half had dozens of holes the size of half-dollars, each hole ringed in brass. Her bag matched the jacket exactly, except the holes were on the top half of the bag. Probably took a lot of testing in some design house before they realized that everybody would lose their change otherwise. The bag was large also, and glancing over as we drove it was impossible to tell where the jacket ended and the bag began. I reached across and poked a finger through one of the holes in her side and Gina let out a squeal. She came off the seat a few inches and scuttled as far away from me as she could. Gina was about the most ticklish person I'd ever met.

"Stop it," she said, trying to be serious while stifling a giggle.

She kept her eyes on me while she finished changing into her heels, and as soon as we hit a red light she tried to get even. We tormented each other that way for the ten-minute ride to Bay Ridge, and by the time I found a meter and parked, my side hurt from laughing and we were both teary-eyed.

The shopping strip ran from Seventieth to Ninety-fifth, more or less, and we'd worked out a game plan over the years. I'd drive to Seventy-fifth and park there. Gina would shop the five blocks downtown of the car and I would sit in the nearest bar and have a few beers. When she was ready, I'd throw all the shit she'd bought into the trunk, drive five blocks further, and repeat the process. There was usually a ball game on in the bars and I could count on catching it from beginning to end, minus the five or ten minutes of shuttling the car. It's known as the art of compromise.

The sky was starting to cloud over and the wind was kicking up a bit when she pulled me out of the third place. There were only two innings left so I was going to try for a ten-block jump and hope to make this stop the last.

"Remember that place?" Gina asked, giving my arm a squeeze.

"What place?" I said without looking up from arranging the trunk, which had seemed empty at the beginning of the expedition.

"That place," she said, pointing across the avenue dramatically with her left hand extended in front of my face. I looked.

"Sure," I said. "It used to be Ernie's. It was a decent club. Jesus, it looks like they're turning it into a Chinese restaurant. This neighborhood is starting to suck."

"It was where you first kissed me. Do you remember?"

I closed the trunk, walked around to my side of the car, and opened the door.

"Gina, I don't remember what I had for lunch yesterday." I got in, reached over, and unlocked the door for her. Her expression hung somewhere between a pout and a snarl.

"You're such a goddamn romantic. It was our first date. You took me there after the movies. I was impressed cause you knew everyone and nobody proofed us. You kissed me up against the—"

"Jukebox."

"You remember! You just gotta be a bastard about it, that's all." She put her head on my shoulder and locked her arm through mine as I pulled into traffic.

At moments like that I knew I could rule the world if I wanted the job. Holmes himself had nothing on me in deductive reasoning. Ernie's never had a pool table or a real dance floor to speak of. No video games. What would I back her up against? Bar? Too crowded. Ladies' room? No class. Phone booth? Always occupied. Jukebox? Bingo. She almost had me wishing I really remembered.

"Tell me about your first kiss," she said.

"What's to tell? It was great. You were really hot that night."

"Not *our* first kiss, your first kiss. The first girl you ever kissed."

"You serious?"

"Sure."

"Gina, I have absolutely no idea. That's like asking me about my first beer."

I got shot down on my ten-block jump plan, because just then Gina saw a shoe store that she had to "stick her head in." I double-parked and told her I was timing it.

I had lied through my teeth about not remembering my first kiss, but she was walking on clouds about the jukebox thing so I didn't see any reason to start telling the truth. Besides, it might've led to something resembling conversation. I had had a first, and then a first, now that I thought about it.

Just before my fourteenth birthday I asked Donna Vitale out on a real date. A going-to-the-movies date. She accepted. We'd go to the Fortway because it was within walking distance. We settled on a day that was probably a Saturday, and fell a few days after I turned fourteen. I didn't go to school on my birthday. Never have. I was sleeping late and my mother came in and woke me around ten. She said my father was on the phone and wanted to talk to me. I picked it up from the bed.

"Hey, big shot. You feel any older?"

"Hi, Pop."

"Happy birthday."

"Thanks."

"Whattaya doing today?"

"Nothing. I got nothing planned yet. Everybody's in school."

"Come on down to the depot. I wanna take you to lunch."

"You want me to come to the depot?"

"Take your lazy ass outta bed and come down here. Me and Chuckie wanna take you to lunch. I can't take my kid to lunch on his goddamn birthday?" He sounded drunk already. I checked the time again. Must have been his day in the union office.

"Yeah, sure, I'll come down. When should I meet you?"

"You should meet me when you get here. Come on down." And he hung up.

I was out of bed and hunting through clothes the next time the phone rang. I picked up. It was my father again. "Take a shower," he said.

"What?"

"Take a shower. It's hot out today; take a shower."

"I take a shower every day. What's wrong with you?"

"Nothin's wrong; it's hot out. I wanna make sure you take a shower."

"So I don't smell too bad around the garbage?"

He hung up. Even at that age I should have known better. My father was very sensitive about being in the garbage business. He liked the Sanitation Department to the extent that he loved the politics, titles, and being involved with the union. But he was a real dandy. Never wore his uniform to work. He always left the house in a sports jacket and slacks, with the collar of a lightly perfumed shirt rolled down over the jacket. He carried his uniform—cleaned and pressed undoubtedly to military standards—in an opaque garment bag and changed at work. I never saw my father's hands dirty. That impressed me as a kid, but later I realized he must've been deadwood to work with. He hated picking up garbage and hated being reminded that it was what he did. I think it was why he ultimately faked his injury.

I caught a bus to South Brooklyn and got there around noon. The depot also housed the union offices and one day a week my father hung around doing shop steward business, which, as far as I could tell, meant doing nothing at all. Chuck Davis, "Chuckie D," was my father's partner. Two shop stewards per day were assigned to the union office on a rotating basis, and my father and Chuckie always got the same day. Chuckie was a black version of my old man, which was probably why they got along so well. He was heavyset, with a short, tight afro and a salt-and-pepper goatee. He was every bit the Beau Brummel my father was. It was a good thing they were both union reps, because if they ever had to work on the same crew, nobody's garbage would get picked up.

I'd been to the office once or twice before so I knew my way around. They had a big-boned Polish blonde out front who was a receptionist and secretary. Behind her desk was a doorway that led to an inner office with two more desks and chairs, where the reps conducted all that official union business, and a sofa, for the official union naps. The blonde waved me in and I found my father and Chuckie, as I'd expected, half-crocked. Chuckie was at his desk; my old man was sitting on the sofa. They both had paper cups with ice, and a bottle of Wild Turkey stood on the desk in front of Chuck.

"Suzy," my father yelled out to the girl, "bring us another cup a' ice."

"Bring two," Chuckie said, "one for yaself." He winked at my father.

They both got up and belched happy birthdays at me while simultaneously shaking my hand, slapping me on the back, and punching my shoulders. I was tense and embarrassed. They hunkered back down in their seats and Suzy came in with two cups of ice. She was chewing a fist-sized wad of Bazooka bubblegum and the sweet smell of it was so powerful that it cut through the bourbon stench that hung in the room.

"You guys are makin' it a real party," she said. "Thanks for the invite. I was gettin' a complex sitting out there alone."

"You never had a complex anything," my father said, laughing. "We were just waitin' for the birthday boy."

"Oh fuck you," she said, giggling, then walked over to me with the cups and handed me one. I took it, then looked over at my father.

"It's okay," he said, nodding to me. He turned to Chuckie. "I only let him have beer before." Chuckie grunted approvingly. "I think we can let you try some good bourbon; just don't like it too much."

Chuck reached over and filled my cup and Suzy's. I was perched uncomfortably on the edge of my father's desk, and Suzy was standing very close to me. She hadn't stepped back after handing me my cup and she hadn't said a word to me yet.

"You ever tried bourbon before?" Chuckie asked.

"No," I said. My voice sounded a little hoarse. The smell of the liquor was mixing in my nostrils with Suzy's gum and making me kind of nauseated. I had nothing in my stomach and I'd assumed I was coming here for lunch.

"Well," Chuckie said, raising his cup, "it's a good day for firsts."

"Cheers," Suzy said.

We all emptied the plastic cups quickly and Chuckie refilled them, killing the bottle.

The Wild Turkey wasn't so bad going down. My old man seemed disappointed that I didn't gag, but then I'd been lying about never having had it before. Just the one cup gave me a buzz, though. Chuck stayed on his feet after pouring the second round. He tossed his back before the remains of his ice could have begun to cool it. My father followed suit, then stood too.

"Looks like we're dry," he said. "That's no way to run a birthday party. Poor planning, right Chuck?"

"Piss-poor planning, man. No wonder this union's going down the fuckin' toilet." They both laughed.

"We're gonna get another bottle an' bring back some sandwiches. You two drink slow; this stuff makes you loco." He and Chuckie left, giggling and wheezing.

The situation was fairly obvious.

"How long . . ."

"About an hour," Suzy said, smiling at me as she unbuttoned her blouse. "Plenny a' time."

I made myself throw down the second bourbon. I remembered hoping she'd spit the gum out.

I couldn't work myself up to getting angry with my father about it, but lunch left me somewhat depressed. And concerned, of course. If sex made me feel this way, then maybe I was a psycho and would end up a fag or a priest. I thought that the experience would completely destroy my excitement over my upcoming date, which would have to be a letdown now. I was relieved to discover I was wrong. My night out with Donna Vitale was filled with all the thrills and awkward moments that someone without my hour's worth of worldly experience would have gone through. When I walked her home that night I got a kiss. So I had a first, then a first.

Funny thing, though, my memory of Suzy, the chunky sofa gymnast, didn't do anything for me. But Donna, in her hallway that night, with one kiss, could still get my dick stiff as a diamond drill. Just went to show what Gina knew. I was a goddamn romantic.

She emerged from the shoe store then, remarkably carrying only two small bags. She tossed them over the seat into the back as she climbed in and slid over next to me.

"What's the matter?" she asked, resting her hand on my thigh, perilously close to that memory hard-on. "Whatcha thinking about?"

"What am I thinking about?" I yelled, pushing her hand away. "I'm thinking about where the fuck I'm gonna park this car when we get to Ninety-fifth Street. Do you see this traffic? If you could drive I wouldn't have to do this shit."

She put her hand back in her jacket pocket and moved to her side of the car, sullenly staring straight ahead. I turned the radio on. Loud. If I hurried, maybe I'd catch the last inning.

Chapter 3

The following Monday morning three things were fighting for my attention: pain, the dream, and the telephone. The dream, unfortunately, was being edged out. It involved Lisa from the paint store and was erotic in nature. I tried to keep it but the ringing became more and more intrusive. Eventually I realized I was awake. With consciousness came pain, ebbing in slowly at first, but soon swallowing me completely. I reached out and grabbed the phone.

"Mikey. Seven o'clock."

"Oh God, no," I moaned.

"Up, Mike. Let's go. You up?"

"I'm up."

"You're not up."

"I'm up, I'm up." I wasn't up.

"Come to the window. Wave to Stix."

"Lou, I can't come to the window. I'm in the kitchen. I'm making coffee."

"You don't know how to make coffee, you lying prick; come to the window. Wave to Stix."

"Okay. Hold on."

I swung my legs around and rested my feet on the floor. My stomach started to shimmy and I had to remain perfectly still for a few seconds. It subsided. I tried standing and then, tentatively, walking. At the window, I pulled the shade up and sunlight streamed in. The effect on me was vampiric. Across the street on the opposite corner I saw the scarecrow outline of Johnny Stix waving his hand slowly over his head like he was signaling aircraft. I inched the window open, stuck my hand out, and shook it weakly. He saluted, then turned and walked around the corner. I collapsed back on the bed and snatched up the receiver.

"Okay?"

"Okay. Stix seen you. You're up. Now c'mon, let's go. I got two guys out and Manhattan calls are gonna start rolling in. Come make some money."

"You don't need money when you're dead."

"That's what you think." He hung up.

I put my left arm over my face and lay still. By doing that I managed five more minutes of relatively passive pain before I hiccuped, and felt the shaking and throbbing begin. This was a bad one. No solid food today, I thought, bracing myself. I raced down the hallway, bounced violently off the bathroom doorjamb, and made the bowl with two seconds to spare. It pays to train.

Half an hour later I staggered around the corner to Big Lou's, my sociology textbook under one arm. I'd recently taken to carrying a schoolbook into work now and then, but as yet I hadn't found any reason to open it. Though I would have denied this to anyone who asked, I was already feeling that college held little attraction for me and that it was more the idea of school that had been appealing.

My shift started at eight, so I thought I'd have a few minutes to pull myself together. As soon as I walked in, the glare from the naked bulb that hung over the card table caught me at just the right angle to set off a small explosion in my head, and I thought I might lose it again. I knew I'd be blinking the image off my retinas for the next twenty minutes.

Lou's had been there, in one incarnation or another, for as long as I could remember, and it still looked like a place you'd use temporarily while setting up a real car service. Painfully cheap, pale green woodgrain paneling had been thrown up over the crumbling plaster walls, which showed through at the seams and corners where the particleboard was starting to crack and disintegrate. There had never been a shade or fixture over the light that hung from a wire, and what chairs and tables there were seemed to be of the sort that get older and older without ever achieving the charm of antiques. In contrast to all this was Lou's desk. It was stunning and ridiculous at the same time. It easily occupied a third of the floor space in the store, and looked like a football field done in mahogany. He'd bought it some years back from one of the rip-off furniture places on Atlantic Avenue downtown, and they had to remove one of the storefront windows to get the damn thing in there. Lou sat behind it, booking three-dollar calls and ordering pizzas, all the time acting like a nineteenth century railroad baron.

When he saw me, he began struggling out from behind the desk and reaching in his pants pocket at the same time, which meant I was going to be sent out for coffee. Lou was massive, and watching him try to get around his desk in a hurry in the close quarters of the store was usually amusing. He stood about six two and weighed well over 220. He wore his curly black hair fairly long and had a woodsman's bushy beard. The overall effect inevitably invited jokes about Lou Albano, the old-time professional wrestler. Big Lou didn't mind at all. He seemed to like it. Sometimes, after a few drinks, he'd hang rubber bands from his beard like Captain Lou used to do before a big match. Then he'd take turns holding everyone in the bar in headlocks, including the women.

Lou always ran a tight ship at the store, but I had the feeling that Tony, being neighborhood poobah, was a little embarrassed by his kid brother. He didn't seem to think Lou was serious or presentable enough for a right-hand man, someone who could be groomed to fill his shoes. Even though Tony was fairly young, I occasionally wondered who would take his spot when he retired or died.

I was trying to maintain my equilibrium in the doorway when Lou got over to me and handed me five dollars.

"Go around the corner; get some coffee for the guys. It's on me."

"Lou, I'm dying here. Nicky didn't go? Where is he?"

"Shades didn't even have money for gas this morning. Anyway, he went to King's Plaza. He won't be back for an hour. C'mon Mikey, before we get busy."

Mornings, Nicky was broke about half the time. The way you could tell was that if he had money in his pocket, nobody else could

24

buy breakfast. Coffee, rolls, even an egg sandwich; whatever anybody wanted, Nicky had to pick up the tab. It got annoying but it was just the way he was. "Nigger rich," Little Joey called it. Joey managed to come up with an anti-black sentiment to cover just about every character flaw known to man. I got a big kick out of him pacing the store, pulling on his dick, and spitting in the corners, all the while lecturing me about what a bunch of animals spades were.

Four drivers were playing brisk at the card table in the back. Fat Sal was partnered with Danny, a born-again Christian who only drove seasonally when he was laid off from his job at an air-conditioning place. They fought so loudly that sometimes I thought they had to be playing different games.

"Leash, you cocksucker, leash! You unnerstan' English? LEASH!"

"I got no leash. You take a load or I throw trump."

"Big trump?"

"Enormous."

"Throw the load."

Danny threw the load and it was picked up immediately by the other team.

"Your mother's cunt," Sal said, and threw in his hand.

"You said throw the load."

"That's cause you got no goddamn leash, you useless fuck."

Sal laboriously stood and paid off the other team. Anybody who played partners with Danny paid off double if they lost because he didn't gamble. If you won, you won double, but I didn't see where the incentive was for Danny to put his heart into the game. He didn't drink either. He was probably allowed to screw his wife, as long as he didn't enjoy it.

I took the coffee orders and left. When I got back the calls were coming in. I dropped off the coffees, took mine with me, and went to work.

By early afternoon I felt almost human. The calls had slowed to a nice steady pace with about a half hour between each run. I was resting with my eyes closed, listening to Danny preach loudly at Sal.

"God's not gonna care that you had a heart attack behind the wheel in the Battery Tunnel. He's not gonna care that you couldn't get to confession in time."

The phone rang. "Car service," Lou barked, before he had the thing halfway to his mouth.

"He's not gonna care that you *meant* to straighten out; that you didn't know you were gonna die."

Lou hung up. "Mike," he said, "that was Shades. He's stuck in Sheepshead Bay. Emmons Avenue just off the belt. He wants you to give him a boost."

I knew that would kill the rest of the afternoon. I paid Lou my commission and put my jacket on.

"When you die, all that counts is the state of grace you're in right then."

I walked out and turned to pull the door closed behind me.

"You see, when you die . . . when you die . . ."

"When you die," Sal screamed suddenly, leaning into Danny's face, "God says Fuck You."

Shades was sitting in his car reading an old TV Guide when I arrived. I pulled a U-turn and parked nose-to-nose with him for the boost. It wouldn't take at first, so we left the wires hooked-up and let it charge for a while. Finally it turned over.

"All right," I said, letting my hood drop. "I'll follow you back in case it goes dead again."

"I don't want to take it through the street. I'm gonna run it back and forth on the highway a few times to let it take a charge."

"What am I gonna do? Follow you?"

"Come with me. Leave your car here. I'm not gonna stall out on the highway, man."

We ran Nicky's car up and down from Sheepshead Bay to Starrett City about six times, then rode back to where my car was parked. Nicky killed the engine and started it three or four times just to make sure. Having done all those important, intelligent things, we left both cars there and went to Joe's Clam Bar for dinner and a few beers.

We both had salmon, and an order of raw little necks as an appetizer. Nicky had a shot of Johnny Walker, but I stuck with beer until some real food arrived. My father had told me years earlier that hard liquor caused raw clams to congeal and harden in your stomach. I didn't know if it was true or not—or even why that would be a bad thing—but the image was disgusting enough to keep me clear of the combination.

"Cutting back?" Nicky asked.

"Just till I get something solid in me." I was too embarrassed to mention my father's clam theory.

"Lou say anything about my commissions?"

"Yeah," I said. "He says don't worry about it. You can even up when you see him. And he said the last one is on the house, because you broke down."

"No shit?" Nicky brightened visibly. "I guess that's another round on me. Lou is all right. Too bad his brother's such a scumbag."

"Tony?" I was a little surprised. "I didn't know you didn't like Tony."

"I didn't say I didn't like him. I said he's a scumbag," he said evenly.

"He seems all right to me."

"Yeah, he's a fuckin' prince. You weren't too thrilled he took the television from that poor fuck with the kids."

"That's collecting," I said, suddenly sounding to myself like my father. "It's just the nature of the game."

"Then the nature of the game," Nicky said, shrugging, "is being a scumbag." He popped a sauce-drenched clam into his mouth.

While I thought that one over, the waitress arrived and set our dinners down. If taking that television made Tony a scumbag, just what did it make us? It was the first job I'd ever been asked to do for Tony, and as far as I knew, the first for Nicky as well.

We'd been approached by Lou to pick up the set from a guy down the block who owed money. I never found out if it had been a gambling debt or a loan, but given the gentleman in question it could easily have been either. Lou came to us with the same solemn look and tone of voice he used for anything more important than sending out for coffee, and asked if we could do Tony a favor. He explained that this poor guy was out of work and had made an offer, and that Tony was generously accepting the TV as payment.

Nicky agreed immediately and I agreed more or less because he did. We took his car that afternoon and drove down to the address on the corner that Lou had given us. I rang the bell and we were buzzed into the hall. We walked up two flights, and an apartment door was opened by a dark-haired woman who looked like she'd been frozen in time around 1964.

"We're here . . ." I started.

"For the TV. I know," she said.

She spun around and walked back into the dark apartment, a blur of beehive hair and cigarette smoke, and left us standing in the open doorway. Nicky shrugged at me and we followed her down the long hallway. She walked into the kitchen, which was a mess, and we were at her heels before we realized it.

"Not here," she said, annoyed. "They're in there." She gestured through the doorway, though not in any specific direction. We went back into the hall and stopped for a second to get our bearings.

"This is a little fucking weird," Nicky whispered. "We shoulda brought miner's hats."

All the rooms were off the main hall, and there was only one, farther than the kitchen, with an open door. It didn't seem any more promising than the rest of the gloomy place, but we walked in anyway and we found the TV. It was on, and there were two little kids sitting on the floor watching a Scooby-Doo cartoon with the sound off. Behind them on a sofa was the guy who owed Tony. He was snoring and he reeked of booze. The shades were drawn and the room was bathed in that bluish television light. One of the kids, the girl, was obviously retarded. She stared directly at me with her mouth open, a strand of drool from her lower lip trailing into her lap. The boy never took his eyes from the set.

I wanted to take Nicky and get out of there, but he seemed resolved to do the job. Actually, he looked furious.

"This is it, right? This must be it," he said loudly.

I didn't know if he intended to scare the kids but he certainly scared me. The guy on the couch woke up for a few seconds and sort of mumbled at us.

"S'good," he said. "Tellim s'good; good picture." He gurgled a bit, then went back out. I looked at the picture. It was a new-enough set to be color but it was showing only black and white, and one antenna was broken off halfway up.

"C'mon," Nicky said. He almost jumped over me to get in front of the set, then picked it up by himself while it was still on and took a couple of steps. "C'mon. Get the cord. Let's go."

I walked over, past him and the kids, to the outlet near the floor. I unplugged the set and Nicky went out the door like a shot. I watched the cord drag along in front of the kids and snake slowly through the doorway; then I was alone in there with them and it was even darker than before. The girl still looked at me and the boy continued to stare at the spot where the television had been. I walked around behind them and followed Nicky out of the apartment, leaving the door open. He was almost running and I thought he'd trip over the plug, but he made it down the stairs. I got in front of him and held the hallway doors. We stowed the set on the backseat. When Nicky was starting the car I tried to talk to him.

"This is fucked-up. How can we do this?"

He looked at me, and for a second I thought he was going to swing at me. "What?" he screamed. "What? Forget about it, okay? Just fuckin' forget all about it."

I didn't forget about it, but I was smart enough not to press the issue. I'd never seen Nicky so enraged.

When we got back to the store he brought the TV in and Lou placed two twenty-dollar bills on the desk. Shades took one, and when I made no move, he took the other. He never offered it to me and I never asked for it, but I knew it found its way onto bars where he was paying and I was drinking, so wasn't it the same thing? Two days later I saw the television sitting on the trash outside Tony's club.

A day hasn't passed since then that I haven't thought about that cord going out the door, and how, for just a few seconds, I was part of the group in the room watching as it happened.

We finished our dinner in silence, and when we were done Nicky ordered another scotch. Bolstered by the food, I switched over to Jack Daniel's. The place was almost empty and we weren't holding anyone up, so we sat for a while and ordered a few more rounds.

"What set you off that day with the TV?" I asked.

Nicky shrugged and let out a small chuckle. "I don't know, man," he said, signaling the waitress to bring another round. "You were pretty upset too."

"I was upset, but you were nuts."

"Yeah, well, it's just that—you know—what are you gonna do? You gonna take those kids and adopt them? Cause otherwise you gotta forget it. We can't do one fuckin' thing that'll make a bit of difference."

The new round arrived and Nicky tossed his down. I sipped mine.

"I can't even go fishing anymore," he said quietly. "I used to love to fish with my old man. But it's been too long now; it's no good. I tried again last year with him out here," he said, gesturing out the window at the bay. "It made me sick. Fish suffocating, dying, taking hours to go. All over the boat. I couldn't look at anything else.

"It's bad to see too much. It ruins things for you."

We left Sheepshead Bay after dark and wound up in Coney Island. There's a bar in the B.M.T. station at Stillwell Avenue. Coney Island is the end of the line for a lot of trains and a lot of people, so the crowd was pretty strange. Actually, it reminded me of the bar in Star Wars. It was a good place to drink for a long time without spending much money, which was what we did. A group of pimps were playing joker poker on a TV screen suspended over the bar. They were passing the remote back and forth and alternately cheering or cursing in impressively flowery language. Every few minutes a whore walked in, bored or tired, and pestered them. They'd either yell and chase her right out, or set her up with a drink first. By the time we left some of their girls were looking pretty good.

I tried to talk Nicky into going to the house my father used, but he was reluctant. He had some coke, so we did it up, and soon I was drunk and wired and horny. We stopped at the light on West Fifteenth and Mermaid, and I swear I saw the most beautiful girl who ever walked the streets in Brooklyn. From across the intersection she was a double for Whitney Houston. I was hanging out the window, screaming. She smiled and waved but Nicky kept going. I started to protest, then realized that he was even further gone than I. He hung a left on Neptune and another on West Seventeenth and circled back. Coming down Seventeenth between Mermaid and Surf, Shades decided it was time to test the car's maneuverability, and turned the street into an Olympic slalom. He weaved in and out around parking meters, jumping the curb repeatedly and scrambling my already-punished brain. We turned back onto West Fifteenth, and my dream girl was now in front of Dempsey's Crown Bar. She sauntered over to my side of the car. I smiled up at her and only slowly realized that I was looking at a monster. From across the intersection at night she was a doll. Up close she was meant to be seen from across the intersection at night. I shrieked and rolled up my window. Nicky drove away and we left her standing at the curb cursing us.

"No more stunt driving," I told Nicky. "We're both too fucked-up. Pull over by the bodega on Sixteenth. I'll get us a six-pack and we can drink it driving home. I think it's time to call it a night."

He managed to get the car something like parked in a spot on the corner. I abandoned any notion of retrieving my vehicle that night, and was calculating the number of tickets it would collect by the time I was mobile the next day. Shades bought the Schaefer—he was paying for everything again—and we went back to the car. It had been my intention to drive, but I was pretty fuzzy, and Nicky got behind the wheel before I realized it. A station wagon pulled up behind us just as the engine turned over. Nicky put the car in reverse and accelerated into it so hard that his sunglasses were thrown off from the impact. I didn't know what was more shocking, the crash or seeing Nicky's naked eyes. I wanted to cover them. Even in the darkness of the car the whites glowed a sickly junk-yellow, like old newspapers. I leaned over into the back to find his glasses, and through the rear window I saw the largest black man on the planet getting out of the station wagon.

"Nicky, put it in gear. Drive. DRIVE! Get us the fuck outta here. This guy's gonna kill us."

Shades put the car in drive and floored it. We surged forward, ripping the bumper off the station wagon, traveled about ten feet, and stopped. The engine died. The black guy was approaching Nicky's door.

Shades looked at me, shrugged, and got out. I reached under the seat and felt ashamed as my hand closed around Nicky's tire iron. I opened the door and stood up. We were a hundred percent wrong, but this guy was going to get hurt before either of us.

"I hope you got about five hundred dollahs," he bellowed. "I hope you got it in cash in your pockets right now or I'ma take it out your white ass."

"Listen," Nicky said calmly. "I got no money. My friend's got no money. We fucked up. We shouldna tried to take off. Now, we can roll around on the ground and get all messed up, or we can split the cold six I got on the front seat and forget the whole thing. Whaddaya say?"

"Okay," he said, so quickly that I had to look back and forth from him to Shades a few times to make sure I'd heard correctly.

I was standing half behind the rear passenger side of the car, keeping the tire iron out of sight. I was suddenly aware that I'd been holding my breath, and allowed myself to exhale while Nicky got the beer off the front seat.

The behemoth turned to me. "You can put the crowbar away now; no point in *any* of us gettin' hurt."

31

"Glad you feel that way," I said, trying to sound casual. My pulse was racing and my hand shook when I tossed the tire iron into the car through my open window. I walked back to find Nicky and the giant sitting on his mangled hood drinking beer.

"Mike, this is Leonard. Leonard's decided not to kill us. We're gonna have a few beers and be good friends and all go home."

"Swell," I said, breaking a beer loose from the pack. Leonard still had the piss scared out of me and I wasn't at all happy about having put down the tire iron. We each drank two beers and made some meaningless drunk conversation with one another, and when I finally thought we might leave alive, Nicky insisted on going back into the bodega for another six. At that point I decided that if Leonard didn't kill him, I would.

When he came out, I noticed for the first time how really unsteady on his feet Shades was. For a moment I didn't think he'd make it all the way over to us.

"You better not let your frien' drive home," Leonard said. It occurred to me that maybe he really didn't intend to tear our heads off.

"You all right?" I asked Nicky. "Why don't you lie down in the car. I'll drive home in a couple of minutes."

"I'm all right. I'm fine." He broke a can off the new six and dropped it while handing it to me. "I'm sorry, Mike. I'm really sorry. I thought I had it—you know—under control."

"It's okay; don't worry. I had too much already anyway." I handed Leonard the rest of the beer. "I think I better get him home, Leonard. I'm sorry about what happened here."

"Sonny," he said, "tomorrow if I see you or your frien' you're jus' two more assholes and I'm the nigger's gonna cut your throat. Tonight, though—tonight we're frien's."

His eyes were red-rimmed and the pupils were the size of pinheads. He held out a hand Fay Wray could have slept in. I shook it and felt like I'd put my fingers in the space between two bricks in a wall. Whatever universe Leonard was visiting, I was happy that it made him a peaceful beast. I was also happy that we wouldn't be there when he returned from the trip. I took the keys from Nicky and Leonard deposited him in the passenger seat. He pulled his car perpendicular to ours, completely blocking Mermaid Avenue, and gave us a boost. I was able to locate Drive on the first try, and we were off.

Shades passed out within five minutes and I damn near followed suit. It was one of the roughest times I've ever had driving home. I parked halfway down the block from Nicky's building and tried to roust him, but he was dead to the world. I walked around the car and opened his door from the outside. He tumbled out onto the sidewalk and hit his head on the curb, giving himself a nasty gash right over the bridge of his nose. That sort of brought him around.

"Jesus, Nicky, help me out a little," I said, trying to hoist him up from under the arms. He was mumbling and he'd started to cry.

"You shoulda left me back with that big jig, man. You shoulda left me to die."

"You don't want to die. Sal says when you die, God says fuck you."

Nicky was still crying when I got him to his building. I dragged him up too many steps and had his keys out when his girlfriend, Louise, opened the door. I was very shot, and I'd had all the surprises I felt I could handle, so seeing Louise pregnant nearly pushed me over the edge. Nicky hadn't said a word about it in the months we'd been hanging out.

She helped me walk him to the bedroom and sit him on the bed. Louise was from Colombia, and looked to me like an American Indian. Her sharp, angular features, which had always appeared stern, seemed even more so in contrast to her rounded belly. She didn't say anything to either one of us. I stood there while she wet a washcloth and went over his most obvious abrasions. She usually seemed to be about to scold Nicky, but now she looked more sad and tired, which only made me feel awful.

There wasn't anything else I could do, and the booze and exertion were taking their toll. I had a four-block walk ahead and I knew I wasn't up to it, but I wouldn't crash there. I didn't want to see Nicky licking his wounds and Louise being self-righteous first thing in the morning. I tried to sneak out while Louise was in the bathroom rinsing the washcloth, but Shades reached out and caught my arm as I turned. He had stopped crying and was just sitting, zombielike. I had thought he was out again. He pulled me very close—uncomfortably close—to those naked, sunken eyes.

"You know what?" he whispered conspiratorially into my ear. "God already told me fuck you."

The room started to spin and I yanked my arm free and ran out.

Sal had just explained to me that flies shit and throw up every six seconds. We were brisk partners, and as we played we watched them land on the white styrofoam coffee cups and rub their legs together. Sal counted.

"...four, five, six; that's it. The cocksucker just shit in your fuckin' coffee." And he'd wave them away, laughing hysterically. It was pretty distracting, but Sal and I were still a good team. Except for my father, Sal was the best brisk partner you could get. Brisk required only two things: basic common sense, and a thorough knowledge of your partner's personality. We worked well. Danny and Little Joey were playing against us and they didn't work well, but at least they were quiet, so Sal's play-by-play of insect bodily functions was the only noise in the place. Big Lou was behind his desk, either watching the game or napping; it was hard to tell. The rest of the drivers were out on calls or off. It had been slow. I was recovering from the previous night's debacle with Nicky. He'd had the common sense to bang in sick. My father once told me that if you couldn't make it into work because of a hangover, you had a problem; but if you managed to drag yourself in, no matter your condition, you had it under control. So there I sat, a person clearly in control, unable to escape the feeling that I was sweating blood.

When the phone rang for the first time in an hour, Lou stared at it briefly, like he'd forgotten it was there. He picked up on the second ring.

"Car service," he screamed. It always looked like he was juggling the receiver and about to drop it, even after it was safely nestled against his shoulder.

"Yeah sweetheart, no problem. Right now. How far ya goin', baby? It's six dollars, Eileen. He'll be right there. I don't know, hold on." He put a hand over the mouthpiece. "Who's up?"

"I am," Danny said.

"You ain't up," Sal said. "You just got in. I'm up." He started to lurch out of his chair.

"No, I think I'm up," Danny said, then jumped up ahead of Sal and walked to the desk.

"Eileen," Lou said, "it's either Danny or Sal. Yeah, they both got green cars. Be outside in two minutes. Right now, he's leavin' right now." He hung up. "What the fuck is this?" he yelled. "I got four guys an' I can't find out who's up?"

"I'm up," Sal said, approaching the desk and standing next to Danny. He reached toward Lou for the call slip. "I been sittin' in that chair for forty-five minutes. This fuckin' nitwit just came back fifteen minutes ago. Look at the sheet." Sal took the call slip from Lou's hand. "Whoa," he said. "Zak's wife. No wonder this prick wants the call."

"I didn't know it was Zak's wife. I thought I was up."

Joey and I looked at each other and smiled. Not only had Danny not been up next, he was behind the two of us as well. His total infatuation with Eileen Zaccaro had been in bloom since he got lucky with her once back in mid-spring.

Lou came over and sat in for Sal and we split the next four games down the middle. Then the phone started ringing and we got a flurry of short calls. It always amazed me how quickly two hours could slip by while I mindlessly covered the same ten square blocks with a dozen different disabled senior citizens. It was like they worked in shifts and relieved each other for breaks and meals. If one old lady wanted to leave church early, she had to wait until I brought another one to take her place. They all called around the same time, and usually stopped just as abruptly.

When the next lull set in I came inside to find my father talking with Lou and Sal and a couple of the other old-timers. I didn't see

Danny pull up, but he walked in about a minute behind me, so he must have parked down the block.

"Hey Dan-O," my father said. "Sal was just tellin' me he got the blow job of his life from Zak's wife. He says she could suck-start a B-52."

Danny walked by as if he hadn't heard him and sat in front of the TV, which was going with the sound off. The other drivers laughed, but nervously, and nobody else would pick up the joke. Eileen's husband, Philly Zak, was an absolute animal. He worked sanitation, like my old man used to, and they'd locked horns a few times. As a union rep, part of my father's job was to intercede on behalf of every misfit and fuck-up who had a problem with a foreman during his shift. Zak had a problem about once an hour. He'd been lifting weights for better than fifteen years and looked it. He was a bodybuilder gone mad, pumping himself up to the point of appearing misshapen. He had a foul personality and a short temper, but he was a simpleton and, according to my father, easy to confuse. He worked part-time for Tony, sometimes as a leg-breaker or collector of bad debts, but mostly just as a gopher. Everybody but Zak knew that Eileen banged anything that moved, crossing gender lines and raising a few questions about species, but few people talked about it openly besides my old man. I couldn't say that I'd ever heard him mention Eileen to Zak's face, but I'd been in Tony's club while both of them were present and my father was joking about her loudly enough to make me nervous.

"C'mon, Danny," my old man continued, "we'll call her up, have her come in here, she can do all of us. She'll love it. We'll call Zak; he can watch. If you want, you can bang him in the ass too—you know— a bonus. Two for one."

"Enough," I said. "Jesus, give it a break already."

My father smiled up at me, but he stopped talking. The drivers by the desk stood uncomfortably and drifted over to join Danny by the television.

"You know, Vinny," Lou said quietly to my father, "you really ought-ta watch that shit. Philly's a crazy fuck, an' you push it sometimes. You really push it."

My father leaned forward a little and spoke as softly as Lou had. "Zak's a crazy fuck. And he's tough. But he ain't so tough that if Mike comes up behind him one night and whacks him in the back of the head with a baseball bat, he won't crack open like an egg. Zak ever touched me, Mike would do that. He ever touched Mike, I'd do it. So what's he got? He ain't got dick. Zak's not tough to anybody with an ounce a' fuckin' brains, which means that around here," he glanced at the group huddled in front of the TV, "he's plenny tough." He stood to leave. As he was going out the door he called over to Danny. "Wait here, Dan-O, I'm gonna go find her right now. I'll tell her to powder it up good so it don't smell too much like Philly." He roared with laughter and walked out. One of the drivers raised the volume on the television. Lou looked at me and shrugged, then he started laughing too. After a few seconds, so did I.

Later in the afternoon when the original brisk crew was back at the table, Danny spoke up out of the blue in the middle of a game like we were hearing his confession.

"You know; I don't do this sort of thing. I been faithful to Marie since I found Jesus. It's just that with Eileen, there was something. I sensed something. I really felt her reaching out."

"So you hadda bang her," Sal said.

"She's looking for something. All these affairs. Being married to someone like Zak. She's trying to find answers; break out of her life. She just doesn't know how to go about it."

"The way she walks around," Sal said, "I figure she knows how to get exactly what she wants. You just gotta justify fucking around so you say she needs you. What'd God do, tell you ta bang her an' bring her back into the fold? Did you dip your dick in holy water? Listen to me, kid. Right now you're walkin' around with a clear head. Everybody can see inside. If Zak sees inside he'll drop you off a fuckin' pier. Snap out of it. You did her, an' now it's over." He lowered his voice. "Everybody knows you only go around once with Eileen."

"She's like a disposable douche," Little Joey whispered, giggling. "You can't use it again."

Sal ignored him. "A coupla cops maybe she does regular. That's it. Everyone else—you're a stranger later. It's just how she is."

"She wants help," Danny said.

"You're gonna be wantin' help, you dopey cocksucker," Sal yelled. He got up from his chair. "Don't you see what she done to you? Don't you see it? You never felt like this before? What are you, sixteen? This is what they do. It's what they do to men. It's the cunt—makes you crazy, makes you stupid. Jesus, don't you know?" He walked around to the side of Danny's chair. "It's that little triangle a' hair," he bellowed, making an upside-down triangle in front of his own crotch with the thumbs and forefingers of both hands. "That little triangle is more powerful than a fleet a' fuckin' tanks. Armies go to war for it. Kings give up their thrones. Countries fuckin' fall. For that little goddamn triangle. So who are you? You're just one more."

"He's right," Lou said from his desk. "He's absolutely right, Danny. Listen to him for Chrissake."

"It doesn't feel like that," Danny said. "You think I don't know? I know how stupid it sounds. What can I do?" He threw his cards in and dropped his head into his hands. Little Joey looked at me and made a face.

Sal reached down and grabbed a handful of Danny's hair. Slowly, he pulled Danny's head back until he was able to look straight down into his eyes. "You're gonna live with it," he said. "Just like every other miserable fuck. Just like me."

Danny never mentioned Eileen in front of me again. For the next week or two I assumed he'd cooled it. Then one afternoon I spotted him talking to her in front of the candy store on the avenue. From where I sat in my car it was fairly obvious that they were arguing. By the time the light changed and I pulled away, she'd walked off around the corner of Sixty-ninth Street, leaving him standing under the awning of the store, calling after her. When I got back to the car service Lou told me that Eileen had called him. She'd asked that he not send Danny for her anymore. She said he was bothering her.

"How the fuck do I tell 'im that?" Lou asked me.

"You'll think of something," I said. "You're a born diplomat."

Personally I didn't understand Danny's fascination. For one thing, his wife, Marie, was no slouch for looks and seemed to be tolerable company; though over the long haul you can never tell. She had dealt well with the born-again shit, but after all, it kept him home nights.

I'd had Eileen in my car a few times and I couldn't honestly say any sparks flew. She had a nice body, but with too much of everything for my taste. Big tits, big ass, big hair. Sex appeal, yes, but frighteningly aggressive. There'd be no seduction with Eileen; she'd rape you. The first time I drove her somewhere she licked her lips and played with her brassy blonde curls a bit, but it all seemed rather perfunctory, and when I didn't rise to the bait she was content to act like I didn't exist. That was the way all our future trips went.

Little Joey said I was chickenshit, afraid of Zak. Joey wanted to bang her in the worst way—he was hung up on the older woman thing—but he was scared to death of Philly. Zak certainly crossed my mind, but I wouldn't have let that govern what I did. It also bothered me a little that my father had fucked her; but again, I don't think it would have stopped me if it were something I really wanted to do. I disliked her overall attitude, which reminded me of Zak. She lived right down the block from the car service, but would never walk to the store. She would call, and a driver would have to get in his car, maybe turn it around, drive three hundred feet or so, and pick her up. As often as not you'd have to turn around again to take her where she was going. I just couldn't see it, but evidently Danny could.

It was early twilight, with maybe fifteen or twenty minutes left on the day shift, when the phone rang. I was talking with Lou and Sal and Nicky. Little Joey was stuck taking Penny the waitress to her diner on Staten Island, so he'd be gone until almost seven. Nicky and I were trying to decide whether to stop off or not, which meant we would; the only question was for how long. I was up for the next call and whatever I drew would determine what we were doing.

Lou spoke in an uncharacteristically low voice, and when he hung up the phone he didn't say anything. I walked over to the desk.

"They asked for Danny," he said.

"Fine by me," I said. "I'd rather settle up now and split."

"Yeah, O.K." Lou said. He seemed distracted.

"What's the matter?"

"Nothin', I guess," he shrugged. "That was Eileen."

"Zak's wife? She asked for Danny by name?" It had been about a week since she had told Lou not to send him anymore.

"Yeah. I tole her he was picking someone up at Methodist an' it'd be a while—she says no problem. He can ring the bell when he gets there."

"Sonofabitch," Nicky said.

"That fuckin' holy roller prick," Sal laughed. "He finally wore her down. Maybe I should get fuckin' born again."

"Yeah," Nicky said. "I wouldn't mind reading the Bible with Eileen."

I paid my commission and ran upstairs to change my clothes and check in with my old man before I went out. Nicky hung around in case he could squeeze in another short call. Sal paid up when I did, but he always stayed by the store until his wife called from the subway so he could pick her up on the way home. My father was snoring to wake the dead on the couch in the living room. The tape in the VCR—Charley Varrick—was still going, so he couldn't have been out all that long. I wrote a note and taped it to the television screen so he wouldn't bring any food in for me. Then I changed and ran out. Danny was getting into his car as I turned the corner. He had an armload of packages and waved to me from behind them, car keys in his mouth.

Sal and Nicky were still inside. Lou was packing up to turn everything over to the night dispatcher. Shades hadn't caught any calls, but he didn't seem to care.

"So, what are we doing?" I asked Shades.

"I don't know," he said. "I just called home. Louise is cooking."

"Yeah?"

"Nothing. She's cooking, that's all."

"What does that mean? You don't want to stop off?"

"No. No, we can stop off. I told her we were stopping off."

"So what's the problem?"

"No problem. I didn't say there was a problem. I just said she was cooking."

"What are you telling me she's cooking for? I'm not eating at your house."

"I feel a little funny going out—you know—when she's cooking."

"Nicky, make up your mind. You're either a scumbag or you're pussywhipped; either way you'll be miserable."

The door swung open and slammed against the radiator. Pete the night dispatcher ran in screaming. His face was flushed and he was out of breath. "Jesus," he wheezed. "Jesus Christ. Get down there. They're killin' Danny."

Shades was out the door before I was out of my chair. I followed as quickly as I could, and behind me I heard Lou struggling to get out from behind his desk. It was almost dark and I couldn't see clearly down the block, but I saw a car double-parked by Zak's house. Its lights were on and it had to be Danny's. As I ran, the lights flickered in front of me, and I realized people were moving back and forth across them.

By the time I was close enough to see what was happening, Nicky was there. Danny was on the ground in the street, lying in a fetal position in front of his car. Three men stood over him. One of them was Zak. I didn't know the other two, but they were both roughly Zak's size and shape. One of them, about my age and with red curly hair, was kicking Danny in the head, leisurely, as if it were just something to do. Zak stood by, looking on appreciatively. He was breathing hard, like he'd already had his workout. The third guy was older, bald, and wearing a lot of scar tissue around his eyes that a pair of black-framed Clark Kent glasses did little to hide. He had his back to the others and was face-to-face with Nicky. His arm was half-extended, palm flat against Nicky's chest. Shades was yelling quite a bit, but I didn't see him try to get around the guy.

I was moving at a good clip and decided to try to dodge the bald man. I never saw him move, but his free hand snagged my jacket collar and held me in place while my feet spastically ran out from under me. Then he let go and I landed hard in a sitting position at his feet. His other hand was still on Nicky's chest. Lou and Sal slowly trotted up behind us.

"Stop," Nicky screamed. "Enough, man. Enough . . . you got him, man. You got him. That's plenny; let him go for chrissake."

Danny looked like this had been going on for much longer than I knew it could possibly have been. Looked like hours—maybe days. His nose was definitely broken; it was spread across his face. There was a lot of blood, and one eye was already swollen shut. He was conscious and seemed to be looking at me, but I didn't know whether he could actually see anything. Sitting on the ground I was just about at eye level with him. He was trying to talk, but he couldn't unclench his teeth. I realized his jaw was broken. Whatever other damage he'd sustained was hidden by his clothing. He'd lost a shoe. On the ground between us was a bouquet of flowers and a bottle that looked to be wine or champagne.

Sal and Lou stood next to Shades. The bald guy had taken his hand from Nicky and was watching the three of them. Sal reached down and helped me to my feet. My tailbone was killing me, and I knew I wouldn't be sitting much for a few days.

"Fuck these guys," I whispered to Lou. "Between us at least we can make it cost them."

"Stay put," Lou said. "Zak wouldn't do this without he clears it by Tony first. Anyway, it's over now. It's done." He raised his voice and yelled over to Zak, "Right, Philly? It's done."

Zak shrugged. The red-headed kid stepped back. With a graceful sweep, Zak scooped up the bottle.

"No," I screamed, lunging forward again.

The bald guy had me before I'd moved six inches, and he held me in place. Zak hefted the bottle by the neck and stepped in toward Danny, bringing it down across his forehead and raking the top of his head with the jagged edges. As his arm completed its arc, he let go of the remains of the bottle, which sailed a few feet and crashed on Danny's hood.

Zak looked at Lou. "Yeah," he said. "It's done."

Danny was trying to scream through his clenched teeth, but the sound came out a loud horrible buzz. It had been champagne, and when the white foam subsided, blood mixed with the stuff and ran down his face from above his hairline as though someone had opened a faucet. The bald guy stepped back and Sal ran over to Danny, who had both hands up to his head.

"Don't touch it," Sal said. He grabbed both of Danny's wrists and held them out, away from his head. "You still got glass in there. You're gonna make it worse. Don't touch it. We'll take you to a hospital."

Zak and the other two started to walk back into Zak's house. The young guy kicked the flowers. The front door was open but the outer storm door was closed. Standing behind it, framed by lighting far inside the house, was Eileen.

"You're an asshole," I yelled at Philly's back as he started up the steps. He stopped and turned to look at me. "A total asshole. You're the biggest asshole on this goddamn block. Everybody knows it too. You're fucking retarded."

The other two looked at Zak for their cue. Lou moved vaguely in front of me, half protective, half making sure I didn't try to get near Zak. Philly extended his arm toward me and pointed, making a gun out of his thumb and forefinger. Then he jerked his hand up slightly at the wrist, mimicking a shot.

"Someday," he said.

"In your dreams, you fuckin' freak."

"Someday," he said again. Then he turned and the three of them went inside. I stood staring at the door.

"C'mon," Lou said. "Best thing we can do is help Danny."

Shades ran down the block and drove his car back. Lou turned off Danny's lights and locked the doors to his car. Danny had his keys on him somewhere, but nobody was going to look for them. Sal was trying to get him to sit up and I went over to help. Danny was such a total mess that there seemed to be nowhere to grab him. He was covered with blood, and by the light of the streetlamp I could see glass shards glistening in his black curly hair.

Shades pulled up and somehow we hoisted Danny onto the back seat. He made the buzzing sound again. I noticed that the foot without a shoe was turned at a bad angle.

"I'll take Sal," Lou said to me as I closed the back door. "You ride with Nicky. We'll meet you at Lutheran emergency room."

"All right," I said.

While I got in the front seat Lou and Sal stood for a moment, looking at Danny through the open car window.

"He shoulda listened," Lou said.

"Yeah," Sal said, wiping blood off his hands with his handkerchief. "But it's that little fuckin' triangle."

We drove off.

Chapter 5

I remember the night I realized Nicky was going down the rabbit hole. It was about two weeks after Danny had gotten worked over, and only a few days after the hospital let him go home. Afternoons were getting darker and a little cooler and homework had become a reality. None of the Martians who were my classmates could be relied upon to intelligently relate anything of importance I might miss, so I was forced to attend most of my classes. I was thinking about this injustice, and the horror of possibly having to write a term paper, while I was returning to the base from what Lou had promised would be my last call. It was six o'clock, and as I pulled up to the store the streetlights flashed on, making the unlighted areas between them seem unnaturally dark and bleak. Lou was standing in the middle of the street in his navy windbreaker, waving his arms like a lunatic. His hair and thick beard, combined with the agitated gestures, made him look more like a religious fanatic than a pro wrestler. I rolled down my window and braced myself for the sob story.

"Mike, gimme ten dollars and we're square for the day." He pushed a piece of paper into my hand as he took the bill. "An' here— go get this lady at Victory Memorial an' bring her to her daughter's on Sixty-six Street. It's three dollars. Please Mikey; she's an old lady—got

44

a walker—so help her in and out, okay? Last one a' the day. I tole her ten minutes. Go, don't make the old lady wait." And he was gone, lumbering back inside before I could argue. I was in the middle of a U-turn when I heard his voice from the doorway.

"Shades says to meet him an' Joey at Peggy's. He says eat first cause they went to get dinner."

I waved without stopping and took off to get the crippled woman Lou had marooned God knew how long ago. The phrase "ten minutes" from him was truly scary. I didn't know how he got away with treating customers like that. Lou had one of the oldest gypsy outfits in Brooklyn. A storefront car service tends to operate with the stability of a massage parlor—the greatest expense being the phone. Any two guys who rent a store and get a phone are entrepreneurs. They put a sign in the window and start taking walk-ins and phone calls. Cops don't get involved because the licensing and insurance violations fall under the domain of the Taxi and Limousine Commission. In this part of town the T.L.C. is treated like Internal Revenue in the Ozarks, their last agent probably killed and eaten in 1949. But Lou was no fly-by-night, and that's because he had a lock on the geriatric set. They all loved him for letting them ride on credit. He even cashed social security checks. Every place made big money at night, but the oldsters—home to bingo, to the bank, church, post office, and doctors, lots of doctors—that's a lucrative day trade. Other joints joked about it, but they would have killed for the old people action. Old people wait for you. You can tell them there won't be a car for a half-hour and it's no problem. Your late-night club-hopper is having coke convulsions and calling six other places if you make him wait two minutes.

I rescued the woman, who wasn't nearly as helpless as Lou described, dropped her off, and hunted up some dinner. My old man was going to his in-laws' house in Red Hook; I could eat alone in peace. He had asked me to join him, but I'd declined, and he wasn't very surprised. He knew the place just plain scared and depressed me too much.

As far back as I was able to determine, Red Hook had always been a slum. It used to be a white slum; now it was a mostly black and Hispanic slum. It had grown more violent over the years, much like the rest of the planet, but it hadn't been a rose garden to begin with. In the '40s the city built a massive housing project in a loose sort of semi-circle across the peninsula. This was done, according to a 1939 newspaper article that my uncle had clipped and saved, to "rehabilitate the deteriorating area." What it accomplished was to triple the population of the same sort of people who were already poor and overcrowded. The neighborhood got much worse.

On the water side of that moat of public housing, between the projects and Erie Basin (invisible except from the air), was about eight square blocks of buildings and a few stores. Within that tiny area a handful of old-time Red Hook natives, most of them Irish, hung on like some fishing village in Derry. My mother's people were among that group. Their lives revolved around the Church, the liquor store, the Knights of Columbus, and the V.F.W. Up and down the narrow streets men stood in doorways and sat on stoops. Young and old were virtually indistinguishable, with sunken eyes and broken teeth, drinking their beer in the shadows of the monolith the city had thrown up to cut them off from the world in the name of urban renewal. Our trips there had always fascinated me, but as I got older I found them disturbing as well. The ride through the labyrinthine drives and underpasses of the projects seemed endless; then we'd emerge on another scene of hopelessness that looked like it would never change. The tiny strip of land could disappear for a hundred years and then return and no one would realize it had happened. Not the inhabitants and not the rest of the city. It was *Brigadoon* by Stephen King.

Since my mother had died my father had avoided going out there almost as fanatically as I, but I thought maybe that was changing. His need for an ongoing connection to her—any tie to when we were whole—must have been even greater than mine. At least I had Gina, and could cling to that illusion of stability. Whatever his reasons, I was glad he hadn't pressed me on it.

I picked up some pizza and brought it home, then wondered why I hadn't taken it straight to the bar instead. I wolfed it down, stuffed the trash in the freezer to avoid attracting bugs, and was back out the door in ten minutes.

Nicky and Joey were at the rear of the bar when I arrived. They were watching a game of eight ball with mild interest. As I reached them, someone called out from one of the booths.

"Hey, it's Mikey—half man, half mick. How the hell are you?"

I took a lot of ribbing because my mother had been Irish. I waited until my eyes focused in the gloom so that I could identify this asshole. When they did, I knew he wasn't someone I had to take any shit from.

"I'm good, Florio, how are you? Bring any candy to the schoolyard today?"

"Up your ass ya shant fuck." He started to come out of the booth, but when one of his friends grabbed his arm he took the excuse and slowly sat down, mumbling into his drink. I hadn't moved.

Last year, Jay Florio got caught in the Dyker golf course parking lot getting a blow job from Phil Delfini's thirteen-year-old sister. Phil beat him half to death and didn't let him show his face on Eleventh Avenue. For some reason that had made him sensitive. Sometimes I wished someone would kick me off the avenue. Maybe then I would get my life in gear. Maybe not.

Joey relaxed in the corner and put down a pool cue I hadn't seen him pick up. He looked disappointed. What a sweet kid he was.

"Sorry guys," I said, "no excitement tonight."

"You shoulda cracked the prick," Joey snarled.

"Another time, a different mood—maybe. Who knows?"

Little Joey looked at me for a moment, assessing this. He was trying to figure whether I was genuinely indifferent or just chickenshit. Then he shrugged, coming to some decision. "Fuck 'im. The prick's already in exile. Let him live out his miserable life." He turned his back on Florio's booth and downed his mug of beer. That apparently cleared me, so I waved the bartender over and took a seat. All this time Shades had been sitting quietly, watching as though bored or half-asleep.

"What's the matter, Nicky," I said, "are we acting like kids? You embarrassed?"

He looked at me and didn't speak for a few seconds, as though he were hearing in slow motion. Then he made a dismissive gesture with one hand. "Hey, no," he said. "Live and let live, you know?"

I, for one, did not know. I didn't know what the fuck Nicky was talking about. Gary, the bartender, got down to us, and I ordered three beers.

"Nick's not drinking beer tonight," Gary said, pointing to the half-empty glass in front of Shades.

"I didn't realize," I said. "Okay, two beers, and a rum and coke."

"No rum, just Coke," Gary said.

Nicky was on a nod. I turned to little Joey and he rolled his eyes. "Been like that all night," he said, with his who-gives-a-fuck shrug. I felt like I was in a class for slow children. Even Gary looked at me like I was stupid. No rum, just Coke, and passed out at seven-thirty. I shook my head. Nicky had once again taken up residence in Dreamland.

The next day was so lousy that it made the night before seem pleasant by comparison. My car broke down; the exhaust system fell out. When I got to work I found that Shades hadn't come in or called. Lou gave me Nicky's house car to drive while my heap was being repaired, so I had the thrill of riding in a real deathtrap with no lights or radio.

Early in the afternoon I was coming back empty when some brain-dead Romeo in a white Trans-Am jumped the light on Bay Ridge Parkway and almost totaled me. I had to stand on the brakes and wrench the wheel. We only missed by a few inches, and of course he took off. As I was trying to calm myself I noticed that, along with all the other debris shaken loose, two wallets had slid out from under the front seat. I left them there and drove back to the base. After I parked, I straightened up the mess and brought the wallets in with me. I told Lou the story and we looked through them together. They both contained plenty of IDs, but no money, and they didn't belong to anyone we knew. I left them with him and took another call.

When I returned to the store I heard Lou raging before I cleared the doorway. "Goddamn junkie sonofabitch. I'll kill the dopey fuck." He was stomping around the office waving the two wallets in one fist. "He's a mugger, a motherfuckin' mugger." The other drivers were sitting quietly, afraid of being accidentally swatted by one of Lou's flailing paws. He turned to me as I sat down. "Mike, I called one a' the guys whose wallet this is," he bellowed. "The chink. The guy can't hardly talk English, but he tole me that somebody stole his wallet yesterday. Somebody in a cab called the poor fuck over to the window for directions, then put a knife to his throat an' robbed him. Somebody with sunglasses. Robbed a guy inna street. From one a' *my* cars. You know where Shades is today?"

"No," I said honestly.

"Neither does his girlfriend. I just called there. She says she threw him the fuck out two days ago cause he sold her TV an' stereo while she was at work. Listen to me, Mikey. When you see that junkie bastard tell him he's fired. Tell him he ever comes near my store or one

48

a' my cars I'm gonna have his legs broke. This is my business. This is my business, an' he can't fuck with my business. You tell him, Mike. When you see him you tell him."

"I'll tell him, Lou." I stood and walked outside. I felt unbearably depressed. Little Joey had pulled up across the street and was sitting in his car smoking a joint. I got in and he passed it to me.

"What's up?" he asked.

"I guess you heard Nicky fucked up."

"Big time," he said, exhaling.

That weekend we got an unexpected blast of Indian summer, and I had to go with Gina to a barbecue at her brother's house on Staten Island. Most of her family was there and it was about as much fun as root canal. I was a veteran of these get-togethers, so I knew what to expect; I started drinking before I had my jacket off. There were relatives I knew, and other people I'd never seen but who couldn't have been any other creatures but relatives. Then, of course, there were the friends. Victor, Gina's brother, was a CPA who watched golf on television and dreamed about moving to New Jersey, but all his friends weren't quite as exciting. They sat in lawn chairs in the tiny backyard, airing their spare tires by lounging in running suits that were two sizes too small. One day I would have to find out if clothes dryers were that much hotter on Staten Island, or if this was a fashion statement.

Gina spent most of the day in the kitchen with the women and I spent most of the day alone, avoiding the morons in the yard and the gaggle of children and dogs that periodically charged through the rooms. After bolstering myself with a half-dozen beers, I risked a brief foray out back to steal some food. As I passed the doorway to the kitchen I heard Gina's mother's gratingly familiar sing-song voice.

"Jesus was killed for thirty pieces of silver. My Henry was killed for eight dollars and forty cents."

This was a litany I'd heard often—almost every time I walked through the door at their house, which was why I tried so hard not to. I would have been more than happy to give her the eight-forty to shut the fuck up, but I didn't think it would work.

I did find it impressive that she was capable of making a connection between her husband—a deadbeat gambler and bottomed out alky who owed everyone from here to Jersey—and the son of God. I'd asked around about Gina's father when the two of us first started dating. My father remembered him and was able to fill me in on the details.

The eight bucks and change part was pretty much correct, story being that he'd been caught cheating in a poker game, and that was the size of the pot. The guy who did it had to take off; my father thought he'd moved to L.A. Gina was ten when it went down, and I was sure she had no idea what had happened. Her brother would have been about seventeen then, certainly old enough to pull a trigger. But he was probably already a suit-and-tie-loser-boy-rodent in training, and far enough down the food chain already to be worthless. I'd never talked to him about his father and I never would. Whenever Gina mentioned her old man it was like he'd won the Nobel Peace Prize, but that was how it should be. I wouldn't fuck with that illusion, even when she got me really pissed.

When I stepped into the yard Victor was prodding hot dogs with a fork and talking to his friends about one of their group who had been fortunate enough to have missed this particular soirée.

"He's a bum; the man's a bum," Victor said. "Don't get me wrong—he's a nice enough guy, but he's got no ambition. He's the kind of guy who's content to sit back and make his sixty grand a year. He doesn't want to move—to grow. My opinion, a man like that really isn't thinking about his family. Hey Mike, come on over, have a frank. You know the guys."

The guys smiled and grunted, and I smiled and grunted. I had no idea whether I'd met them or not. They all looked alike and I suspected their heads were interchangeable. I took a hot dog and tried to slink away, but somehow I got sucked into the conversation.

"So, Mike," a guy introduced to me as Leo started, "you live on the Island?"

"No," I said. "I live in Brooklyn."

"He's over by Mom and Gina in Bensonhurst," Victor added.

"Bay Ridge," I said.

"Bensonhurst," Leo said. "That's the heart of the old country. Time to immigrate, kid. Get away from the niggers and spics and the hebes that sold us out to 'em. Move back to America."

"Yeah?" I said. "Immigrate is such a code word for run away. I should move to this radioactive swamp, and raise kids that glow in the dark? Leo, tell me—where do you buy bread?"

"Bread?"

"Yeah, bread. I buy my bread at Santo's on the avenue. When I go up there Sunday mornings the old man's been making it for five hours, and the whole store and half the block smells like fresh bread. Where do you buy your bread?"

"At the mall."

"What does it smell like?"

"What do you mean, what does it smell like? I don't know. It smells like mall."

"Exactly. This whole fucking island smells like mall."

"Hey Mike, chill out," Victor said, giving me what was probably a stern look for a CPA.

"I'm fine," I said, grinning and taking a beer from the cooler they had out there. "Hey, Victor doesn't mind venturing into the urban jungle for stuff he can't get at home." Victor looked like he was going to ·burst a blood vessel. Six months ago, I'd walked into the 49street Cafe in Sunset Park and caught him cuddling up to his Puerto Rican girl-friend. Ever since, the time I was forced to spend in his company had been a little more tolerable.

"There's nothing wrong with the neighborhood, Mike," Victor said, forcing a smile. "Nobody's saying there's anything wrong. Don't be so defensive. It's just that a guy—you know—should try to better himself. Don't you wanna do good and buy a house? You don't wanna be upstairs forever, living over Mom, after you and Gina get hooked. Believe me, you don't really want to raise your kids there."

"You're young," Leo said. "Maybe you should forget Staten Island altogether. There's no Staten Island people left anyway. It's all Brooklyn people now. The Staten Island people are all in New Jersey. That's what you should do—jump straight to Jersey."

"Where are the Jersey people?" I asked.

"Pennsylvania, mostly."

"Maybe we should move to Wyoming and wait for everyone to catch up with us."

"Out west is nice," Leo agreed enthusiastically, happy that we were all friends again. I'd had as much as I could take, so when Victor's wife came out to clear the used paper plates and cups I gave her a hand and got back in the house.

I managed to leave shortly thereafter without having to talk to anyone else, a major victory. Gina was a little pissed about our abrupt departure, but deep down she knew her brother was an asshole, so I don't think she took it too hard.

I was starving. Since the food had been guarded by the Sears Roebuck army I'd only had the one hot dog all day. We drove over the bridge and stopped for dinner, then caught a movie at the Alpine. We'd been together all day and half the evening. It was making me feel old and domestic.

The movie was *Hellraiser II*. It wasn't bad as horror flicks go, but I felt distracted. The show ended at ten minutes to eleven. I was supposed to meet Joey and a few old high school friends at Peggy's at midnight. I started yawning but Gina wasn't buying it. She said that she wanted to talk. I parked along Shore Road. We started fooling around, and before long she had my defenses down and bird in hand. As she ducked her head in my lap I checked my watch. I had time, but just barely.

When she was finished, I put the car in gear before zipping up.

"I thought we were going to talk."

"I enjoyed this conversation," I said, as I pulled into traffic. She wasn't amused.

"You're taking me home?"

"It's late, honey. I have to be at work at eight tomorrow morning and I still have homework due on Tuesday."

"You're full of shit. You don't want to talk because you know what I want to talk about."

"It begins," I said, sighing. We were across Fifth Avenue and making good time.

"When are we gonna talk? Are we ever gonna talk? When the hell are we getting married?"

This was not on my agenda for tonight. "Gina, we've been over it a million times. Let me see how school works out this semester. When I get my grades I'll make some sort of decision. Right now I'm making a hundred and a half a week part-time and I can't even think about getting married." I made the light on Eleventh Avenue.

"Your father could get you into Sanitation."

"I don't fucking want to be a garbageman. I don't know what I want to do."

"You know you don't want to get married."

"Bullshit. I do want to."

"My mother says we can live rent free until you get a job if you want to stay in school, so there's no extra expense."

Jesus Christ. That threw me a curve. I didn't think the old bitch would stoop that low. Next thing she'd be telling me she had cancer and wanted to see her only daughter married before she died. "You know I'm not gonna take something like that from your mother. When we move up there, it'll be when I can pay a fair rent." Fifteenth Avenue.

"She's not getting anything with the rooms sitting empty." She raised her voice.

"That's her goddamn choice," I yelled back. Seventeenth.

"You just don't wanna marry me. You don't wanna get engaged. You don't wanna do anything. You just wanna go to the movies once a week and get your dick wet in the backseat of the car." She was screaming in my ear. "So until you're ready to talk commitment, until you're ready to talk serious, don't talk to me at all."

"Fine. You got it," I said as I stopped the car. Twenty-first Avenue. She jumped out, slammed the door, and ran up her steps. I checked my watch. Eleven fifty-five. Close.

I got to Peggy's about ten minutes late. No one seemed crushed. We played a couple of hours of uninspired poker that I turned a small profit on, then cruised out to Nathan's for chili dogs at about two-thirty. After everyone left I drove around drunk for an hour or so, wondering if I'd see Nicky sleeping in some doorway. No one had talked about him in Peggy's. It was as though he'd fallen off the planet. Eventually I went home, parked half on the sidewalk, and crawled to bed.

Within an hour I was jarred awake by a sound that was all too familiar. A car down on Sixty-ninth Street had plowed into something. I dragged myself over to the window, but I couldn't see a thing. I had parked just off Eleventh, and that seemed to be the direction the sound had come from. I dressed as quickly as I could, which was not quickly at all. I was in that hideous state of waking up still drunk. I think I preferred hangovers to that terrible disoriented feeling. Before I left I looked into my old man's room, but he hadn't come in yet. I went downstairs and made my way to the corner.

There had been an accident all right—a classic—but my car was okay. A brand new Buick Regal, candy-apple red with Connecticut plates, had been driven straight into the brick wall of the old apartment house on the corner, next to the bus stop. Nobody was in it and the driver's door was hanging open, so I guessed no one was hurt.

A group of people from the after-hours on Seventieth Street was already there and speculating about how it happened. Apparently nobody saw the driver leave. I figured that he had stolen the car and thought it wise to get clear of it before the cops arrived, which they did while we were standing there. They talked to a few people and wrote some things down, but they didn't seem awfully excited. They left after a few minutes and the crowd dispersed, each person looking longingly at the car and wondering how soon he could sneak back for the radio, tires, or battery. The cops were probably wondering the same thing.

I was wide-awake by then, though still buzzed. One of the bouncers from the after-hours, who I knew to say hello to, invited me back for a nitecap, and since the alternative was going home to sleep, I accepted.

I left during twilight because I hated to step from a bar into sunshine. It killed my whole day. As the door closed behind me the blasting dance music was reduced to muffled thumping. They'd done a good job soundproofing the place. When I was halfway down the block I heard different music, farther off but not muffled. I was at the corner when I realized it was coming from the wrecked car. I couldn't believe no one had lifted the radio yet. I started to cross the intersection toward it, then saw that somebody was in there. Approaching from the back, I was almost up to the still-open driver's door before I saw that it was Shades. His right arm was draped casually over the steering wheel and his left leg was out of the car, foot on the sidewalk, pumping up and down to the music. He had it cranked all the way up. His head was tilted back against the headrest, and he was screaming along with the song, that "you gotta fight for your right to party."

I knew he hadn't seen me, and I really wasn't up to finding out what his story was right then, so I left him there and went back home, just beating the sun.

Chapter  7

Though I didn't see Nicky over the next few weeks, I don't think a day went by that I didn't hear his name. He was spotted all over the neighborhood by drivers and customers. He was reported to be skulking around on Thirteenth Avenue—shoplifting, begging, even collecting bottles and cans. Each new story portrayed him in a more derelict condition. At first I went out of my way to look for him, but as time passed, I avoided areas where he'd been seen. The person described was more and more removed from anyone I could think of as Shades. I found myself wondering if there was someone who resembled him staggering about while the real Nicky was safely tucked away at a Daytop Village somewhere.

Gina still hadn't cooled down. She was really putting the screws to me this time. She wouldn't talk to me unless I was talking marriage. If I hedged at all she hung up. Two weeks was her average for this sort of thing, but so far she showed no signs of giving in, and this was a new record. Her mother was probably pumping her full of all kinds of wonderful advice. I was thinking of poisoning the old bag's cat.

Anybody can Monday-morning quarterback, but I'd always suspected that Gina and I would have been history ages ago if my mother were still alive. I'd sort of come to terms with that, and with the role we had in each other's lives now. Interestingly, it was the same thing that kept me ducking the marriage. When my mother got sick and then died I spent a long time thinking about how she'd lived her life. She had never traveled farther than from Red Hook to Bay Ridge— except for two trips to New Jersey—and it didn't seem fair, let alone satisfying. When the time came for Gina and me to plan our wedding, I'd developed a strong interest in a college education.

It was when my mother was in the hospital for treatments that my father and I first began communicating by not communicating at all. During her bout with cancer we raised telepathy to a high art. Commenting briefly, glibly; saying what we liked and didn't like about the neighborhood or the planet, we expressed what we did or didn't like in each other and in ourselves. My father, for example, never told me outright that he despised Gina, and he never would. But it was abundantly clear to me that he thought she was a whining bitch. I didn't so much disagree as feel that it was none of his business, which was after all a more defensible position.

I wished to hell I'd asked my mother's advice more when she was alive, because she'd always been so direct with me. I wasn't nearly grown-up enough to ask her opinions back then, and she was altogether too smart to offer them unsolicited.

Thanksgiving came and went with little fanfare. I had no interest in dining in Red Hook, and my father must have felt the same way, because he didn't press the issue. We made reservations at Lento's on Third Avenue and ate turkey and pasta. Ours was the only table with fewer than six people. If my father noticed or cared, I couldn't tell, but it depressed me.

One Friday morning early in December my father was waiting for me in the kitchen. I was already dressed and had my books, planning to eat a quick breakfast before school. Seeing him sitting there shocked me. We probably hadn't occupied that room at the same time in years. I hadn't even known he was home. He must have waited quietly for some time while I was getting ready. He looked old. His face and hair seemed the same shade of gray, like cigarette ash. He'd always been a big man, but I could see his face starting to hang loose, the cheeks dropping into the beginnings of jowls. I felt like I was looking at his father. Maybe I felt like I was looking at me. I shivered.

"Sit down," he said. I did. He looked at a point on the wall over my head and spoke. "Last night I spent most of the evening in Tony's club playing cards."

"Have any luck?"

"Enough. I was up about four hundred at one o'clock. That's when Nicky Shades comes in with a monster fuckin' gun and holds the place up."

I stared at him, waiting for the punch line. He kept looking at the wall.

"Tony was there," he said. "Shades didn't wear no mask—just robbed the place like it was an A&P." My father looked down at me, nodded once, and stood. "I wanted you to hear it from me because I was there." He walked past me and squeezed my shoulder, then took his jacket off the hook and went out the door. I watched him until he left, and then I moved to his chair and looked at his spot on the wall, waiting for an explanation.

I sat in a class called Sociology of Deviance, staring at the spiked green hair of the mutant in the seat in front of me. I was trying to concentrate on the lecture and not think about Nicky or anything my father had told me that morning. I hadn't been all that tight with Shades, so why did I care? I wanted suddenly to be like Little Joey—just blow everything off.

The class concluded and I started gathering my books. The green porcupine turned to me and handed back the pen he'd borrowed.

"Thanks, Mike," he said. I nodded. "Want to grab a brew at the Pub before you push off?"

"No thanks," I said. "I want to try to clear the bridge before rush hour." I'd gone out a few times with people from this class, to have a couple of drinks or get stoned in the park. I didn't find them offensive; I simply had nothing to say to them. They were mostly from East Cupcake, Long Island, and talk always seemed to focus on socialism, feminism, or, insanely enough, the subject matter of the lecture we'd just left.

"A couple of people are gonna stop off. Cat Woman's gonna be there." He nodded toward Kathy Popovich, the most attractive girl in the room. She was, as always, dressed completely in black.

"Well," I said, "she's got the body, but I still can't hack this bullshit." I gestured at the class in general.

"She has her own apartment," he said, raising one eyebrow.

Maybe Green Hair wasn't a total hamster. I trailed along.

The Pub was a dreary plastic excuse for a bar as far as I was concerned. Each social group down there staked out its own quadrant. Much as a prison dayroom will have its black, white, and hispanic sections, the Pub was split into preppies, jocks, and punks. There wasn't much, geographically speaking, for normal people to do except sit alone. Then again, there was no overwhelming reason for normal people to be there at all.

The group I entered with went catatonic at the prospect of having to make a decision. After pulling each other in different directions for a while like an amoeba trying to reproduce, they settled on two large tables at the fringe of the punk district, but near the preppies. Keeping their options open.

I don't know if it was because of the tension I'd been feeling about Shades, or if I was just mellowing with old age, but I enjoyed myself. There was something refreshing about hanging out with people who spoke in complete sentences. I discussed urban decay with Kathy Popovich, and found that by smiling and nodding my head at appropriate moments I could appear quite well-informed.

"It's devastating," she said, "the kind of environment these children are growing up in. Nightmare conditions that you and I couldn't imagine."

"Absolutely," I said, smiling and nodding.

"It's no wonder they turn to violent crime. And do you know what's at the root of it?"

"Racism?"

"Education!"

Shit. I was going to say education. "Education, sure. But I mean, it's really racism in the broadest sense."

"Yeah," she said. "I think I know what you mean."

Kathy Popovich was majoring in anthropology, and when she looked at me I felt like I had a bone through my nose. After chatting with her for a while I took a shot and asked her out. She told me that she was planning to see a midnight movie in the East Village on Saturday, but that I was welcome to join her. It certainly wasn't what I would have picked, but whatever got me in the ballpark.

"Sure," I said. "What's playing?"

"*Satyricon*. A Fellini film."

"I've never seen it."

"You'll love it. Fellini presents such a unique world view."

"Sounds great. Should I pick you up?"

"What for?" She laughed. "I live ten blocks from the theater. I can walk. I'll meet you there."

"What time?"

"Let's say eleven. I don't know what kind of line there's going to be."

"Afterwards maybe we could grab a drink?"

"Maybe," she said, and smiled.

A few minutes later I excused myself and left. On the walk back to my car I picked up a copy of the Village Voice. I figured I might be able to rake enough horseshit out of it by Saturday to get laid.

Friday night some of the guys on the block had a fire going in the trash can in front of the fruit store. They huddled in the doorway, or moved from one double-parked car to another, socializing. I lifted a bottle of Wild Turkey from my old man's stock and joined them. I didn't stay too long. Winter was setting in.

Saturday was dreary but profitable; I was in my car most of the day. My last call was an airport run and I didn't get back from JFK until six-thirty, a half hour after my usual quitting time. The night dispatcher was on with two drivers. The day crew had gone home, and it didn't look like there was enough coverage, but that wasn't my problem. I turned in my commission and got my ass out of there before anyone tried to push calls on me. I was getting in my car when I noticed that Lou was still hanging around. He was sitting in his Caddy, parked in front of me, warming it up. He slid his window open and waved me over.

"What's doing, Lou?"

"Get in a second, Mike; I wanna talk to you." The door locks popped open loudly. I got in and tried to close the door as gently as possible. Nothing intimidated me like a new car. "Mike," he said, "I gotta ask you a big favor tonight."

I thought of the two-man night crew I'd just seen and started to make my excuses. My date with Kathy of the Unique World View And No Roommate was for eleven, and I couldn't let myself get stuck working a double.

"I need a driver tonight."

"Lou, any other time but tonight. I got a date. This girl lives alone."

"I wouldn't ask, it wasn't important."

"There must be ten guys you can call to drive tonight."

"I don't want you to drive here," he said impatiently. "I want you to drive me somewhere."

That was new. "Why don't you want to drive?"

"It looks better I get driven."

"This isn't one of those guinea things where I'll catch a bullet in a seafood restaurant?"

"Yeah," he said, "that's it. We'll go out inna blaze a' glory with clam sauce on our chins." We both laughed. "Will you drive?"

He wasn't going to tell me what it was about. "What time?"

"Ten o'clock."

"How long?"

"Twenny minutes. No time at all."

I gave in. "Okay. But I really have to be on the road by ten-thirty."

"Piece a' cake."

I was showered, shaved, and dressed for my night out when Lou turned the corner and stopped in front of my building. He awkwardly slid over and I got behind the wheel. There was a mountain of a guy in the backseat whom I didn't know. Lou introduced him as Edward and he grunted at me. I smiled as politely as I could.

"We got one more stop," Lou said. "Pass by the store."

When I pulled up, Little Joey strutted out and climbed in the back with Edward. Joey and I looked at each other with equal surprise.

"Lou," I said, "what the fuck's going on here? Am I driving you somewhere or are we having a reunion?"

"I asked you to do me a favor," he said. He didn't look at me or Joey. "You gonna do it or you gonna ask questions?"

"No questions," I said. "But please drop the Don Corleone. You sound silly."

Lou grinned, but then looked back to see Edward's reaction. He was looking out the window as if he were alone in the car. Edward definitely had me worried.

Following Lou's directions, I drove under the El tracks along New Utrecht Avenue to Sixty-second Street. We parked across from the subway station, in front of the mouth of an alley that ran between a deli and a video store. Every shop on the block was closed and the place looked deserted. I glanced back at Joey and realized he was frightened. He looked like a dwarf next to Edward.

Lou told me to cut the lights. We sat that way, in silence in the dark, for about fifteen minutes. Then two people turned the corner from Sixty-third Street and walked down New Utrecht towards us. They looked completely bombed, weaving and tripping and mostly leaning against each other to stay upright. As they drew closer I saw that one of them was Shades. The other looked like a hippie, with long hair pulled back in a ponytail. When they were next to the car the rear door opened and Edward got out. I tried to say something then, but I couldn't. I felt like one of Edward's huge hands had my throat squeezed shut. The guy walking with Nicky suddenly straightened up and veered away from him. Nicky practically collapsed into Edward's arms. The hippie walked over to the car. Lou handed him an envelope and he turned and ran back to Sixty-third and out of sight. Edward was walking Nicky down the alley. Lou got out of the car and stuck his head back in the window.

"Joey, I want you to walk around the block to Fourteenth Avenue. You stand at that end a' the alley. Nobody comes down the alley, you unnerstan'?"

Joey stepped out of the car and began walking around the corner. After he'd gone a few feet he started running. Lou turned to me.

"Keep the motor running. Lights off. Keep your eyes open. Hit the horn twice if there's trouble."

As he was turning away I tried to talk again. My throat still hurt and his name came out in a stage whisper. He turned back.

"I know, kid. You gotta be on the road by ten-thirty."

He walked to the back of the car and opened the trunk. I thought for a moment they were going to throw Shades in, but when I looked down the alley, Nicky and Edward were disappearing behind a dumpster. Nicky seemed to be talking to him. They looked like old friends. Lou slammed the trunk. He walked down to them with something bulky under his coat. They all moved out of sight around the bin.

I wanted to move, but I couldn't seem to take my hands off the steering wheel. There wasn't anything I could do, I told myself. I was a driver. I couldn't stop them.

Overhead, I heard the roar of the B train approaching from downtown. It passed and continued south to Coney Island. I closed my eyes and tried to will myself onto it. Nathan's, chili dogs, whorehouses. As the sound faded, I thought I heard another screaming that lasted a few seconds longer than the wheels on the rail marking the turn at Fifteenth Avenue. I looked down the alley, but saw nothing. I hoped I was mistaken.

About five minutes later Lou stepped out and trotted to the car. He was getting in next to me when I saw a flash of light—fire flaring from behind the dumpster. Its glow framed the mammoth shape of Edward as he plodded down the alley toward us.

"Go," Lou said, the second Edward slammed his door.

I pulled out, keeping the lights off. I made a right at Sixty-third and another at Fourteenth.

"The fuck you going?" Lou screamed.

I didn't answer. I just pulled up at the other entrance to the alley. Little Joey ran over and jumped in.

"Oh," Lou said. "Yeah, right."

His hands were shaking. Joey was bouncing up and down on the backseat. I drove away. After three blocks I turned the lights on. I looked at Edward and saw that he was staring out the window again, impassive as when they picked me up.

I went totally numb. That must have been the way Edward felt all the time. Me and Edward. Maybe we'd become buddies. Physically I was calm, and I seemed to be outside of the car watching this scene from a distance. I glanced over at Lou. He turned his face away quickly, toward the window. I knew better. He'd never find what Edward saw out there.

We dropped Little Joey off. He bolted without saying anything. I drove back to my building.

"We'll talk tomorrow," Lou said, but he didn't meet my eyes. I got out, and he slid over in the front seat and drove away. Edward never turned his head from the street. I watched their taillights vanish over the hill on Twelfth Avenue.

I stood there alone on the sidewalk for a few minutes and tried to orient myself. My block looked different. The buildings were unfamiliar and everything seemed to be at crazy angles, as if I were looking down at the street from a great height. I leaned against a parked car and took several deep breaths. That made me much more dizzy at first, in a blinding wave, but it receded almost immediately and in a minute or two the whole thing passed. I looked up and down the block, but there was no one around. A couple of people passed by up on the avenue, but nobody turned down the street.

It suddenly popped into my head that Nicky was probably alive, and needed my help. I ran to my car, started it, and headed back to New Utrecht. They probably roughed him up good, I thought. He had, after all, robbed the club. That couldn't go unanswered. They had to send a message. That was why that guy Edward was there. He was a leg-breaker if I'd ever seen one. Lou probably couldn't do it. No more than Little Joey or I could have. He could've slapped him around some. He was pissed off enough about the cars for that. But I doubted he could have broken anything or really hurt him. So they brought that scumbag Edward. He did the number on Shades. I looked at my upholstery. Nicky would make a real mess of it on the way to the hospital.

I parked this time on the Fourteenth Avenue side of the alley, where Little Joey had been stationed, and on the opposite side of the street. As I got out of the car I noticed a faint smell of smoke lingering in the air, and a slightly visible haze at the mouth of the alley. There were no flames that I could see. I hadn't thought about the fire, and I didn't let myself think about it much now. It was another message, just one more scare tactic.

Whatever occurred had been obscured from my line of vision while it was happening by the large green dumpster that was halfway down the alley. I assumed that meant that it had been in full view of Little Joey from the other side. When I approached from that direction, however, I discovered that there were two steel doors recessed a good four feet into the wall next to the dumpster. There was nothing to be seen from where I stood, so Nicky was either in the trash bin or in that doorway. I moved further slowly, my feet making exaggerated crunching sounds on the broken glass and other debris that covered the ground.

"Nicky?" I whispered. No sounds but city noises. In the distance another B was moving up from Fifty-fifth. I went past the doorway and had one hand on the dumpster lid when the smell hit me. I turned back to the doorway and saw him crumpled in the far corner. He'd been out of my line of sight until I'd moved past him.

We used to have an elaborate fireworks show on my block every year on the Fourth of July. Recently it had degenerated into twenty little displays outside people's houses, but it used to be a fairly organized—if not well thought-out—event. One year, when I was maybe ten, Stevie Bosco's father John walked into the middle of the street and dropped a mat of firecrackers into a burning wooden crate. He then produced a can of lighter fluid from his back pocket and, swaying drunkenly, squirted a stream of it into the carton. I remember his screams when the fire ran up his right arm. Other men, including my father, had been heading toward him to pull him away. As his arm, then his electric blue Hawaiian shirt, went up in flames, they stopped moving toward him and backed off. The mat began exploding and he was thrown to the ground. Once he was down the men approached him again. They rolled him around and poured soda on him until the fire was out. He lived, and didn't even look that bad after five or six operations. He had to wear a rubber shirt, like a scuba diver's outfit, for about two years. I never forgot the smell in the air that day. It was sickening. I smelled it again in the alley, a hundred times stronger, and I knew Nicky was dead.

I resisted the impulse to gag and the impulse to run away. His legs were tucked under him, out of sight, arms at his sides, palms up, like he was praying or asking forgiveness. His eyes bugged out wildly, making me wonder if he'd been throttled, and all of him below his head had been burned. His imitation leather jacket had melted open in spots, revealing either a dark shirt or charred flesh. Wisps of smoke still rose around him as if he had dry ice in his pockets. I leaned in more closely, then leaped backward, lost my footing, and fell. I wound up sitting on the ground facing Nicky. I quickly pushed myself across the concrete with my feet until my back touched the wall on the other side of the alley. I braced against it and stood up, then froze there and stared. Shades looked more indistinct from that distance. More acceptable. Only dead.

Nicky's eyes weren't bugged out. His sunglasses had been removed, his eyes torn out, then the glasses replaced and the eyes set on top of the lenses. This was a message, a personal touch—specific punishment for a guy called Shades. Tony must have wanted that very clear. I hoped to God they'd killed him first.

Another train approached. I started shaking. At first it was just my arms, then my chest and shoulders. It seemed that the louder the noise of the train got, the more intense my trembling became. By the time it came to a stop at Sixty-second, my body was wracked and I didn't trust my legs to support me if I moved off the wall. The B seemed to sit in the station a very long time, and I felt naked and spotlighted in the protracted silence. The shaking wouldn't stop. When the train finally began to pull away I pushed myself off the wall and stumbled back toward my car.

The first time I tried mescaline I'd gotten marshmallow feet, the sensation that my legs were boneless strips of rubber and that I had powerful springs on the soles of my shoes. That was how I felt moving out of the alley. When I reached the curb I ran across the avenue to the car. I must have looked like the first lungfish trying to evolve. I'd left the door unlocked, which was good, because I wouldn't have dreamed of screwing around with the key. I sat there for about ten minutes before I began to feel the shakes diminish and I regained some control over my muscles. As soon as I could I pulled away and drove down the avenue eight blocks. Then I parked again and waited until the shuddering completely stopped. I looked at my watch. Eleven o'clock. Kathy was on line for her movie.

I pulled out and began driving again, aimlessly at first. I found myself heading toward Manhattan, but before I hit the highway, I turned around and drove straight to Gina's house.

I had to lean on the bell for two minutes before she came to the door.

"I knew it was you," she said. "My mother's got people over."

"Fuck your mother's people." I reached behind her and pulled the door to the apartment closed. I walked her farther out into the hallway, over to the stairs leading to the empty second floor. I started to pull at her clothes.

"What's the matter with you? Are you stoned? Knock it off!" She grabbed my wrists and was trying to hold them against either side of her waist.

"Nothing's wrong. This is gonna be our apartment." I kept my hands where she held them and picked her up, carrying her up the stairs. "We're gonna try it out, that's all."

"No," she said, trying to squirm free. "My mother . . ."

"Fuck your mother," I hissed.

She put her hand over my mouth, but she stopped fighting. We got to the top and sprawled on the floor in the dark. Her blouse ripped coming off. After I yanked at her jeans a couple of times she unzipped them and I got them down. She was dry and the position was awkward, but I managed to get in and we fucked on the landing, my forearm cushioning her head from the wooden banister. It seemed to go on forever but I just couldn't come. After a while Gina started to cry. Finally she pushed me off of her and rolled away from me into a ball. I couldn't see her clearly, it was so goddamned dark up there.

"Are you all right?" I asked.

"No," she said. "What's wrong with you?"

"You want to get married? If you want to, we'll do it. Pick out a ring tomorrow."

She lay there sniffling in the dark for a long time. "Okay," she said.

I stood and pulled my clothing together. I ran down the stairs and heard her calling after me just as I cleared the door.

Chapter 9

My father came into my room and woke me up late Sunday afternoon.

"Lou is looking for you," he said.

I must have slept for sixteen hours. I felt like everything had been a dream, but I was still in Saturday night's clothes.

"Pop, there's something I have to talk to you about."

"No," he said. "There isn't." I didn't like the way he looked at me.

"I have to talk to someone. I can't talk to Gina."

"Later," he said. "Get changed. Go see Lou. We'll talk another time."

He left the room. I stared at the posters on my wall. Paula Abdul. House of Pain. Had I put them there? How long ago? When was I a kid? I changed my clothes and left.

Lou wasn't in the car service. The dispatcher said he was at his brother's club. I got the same feeling from the dispatcher that Lou had given me on the ride home the night before. Distance. I walked around to Sixty-fifth Street.

Lou and Tony were watching a football game at the bar while a table of old men passed money back and forth over a lackluster game of poker. Half of them were watching the TV too. There were five phones on a shelf along the back wall. Tony got up to shake my hand. Lou smiled and nodded, but he still wouldn't look directly at me. "Let's go in the back," he said.

We sat around a coffee table in Tony's office. I'd never been in the inner sanctum before. It was invitation only. Tony poured Chivas on the rocks for the three of us without asking. Lou looked like he was going to speak, but Tony cut him off.

"Sometimes my brother can be very stupid," he said. "I didn't intend for him to involve you in this. But it happened. These things can work out for the best. I hear you kept your cool. I hear that, except for Edward, you were the *only* one who kept his cool." He looked at Lou, who was staring at the floor. "Your asshole friend Joey is shooting his mouth off up and down the avenue. Makes himself sound like Al Capone. One fine day I'm sure he'll occupy his own dumpster."

"What did you want to see me for, Tony?"

"To thank you, kid. You did Lou a favor. You did me a favor. I know you liked Shades, but you knew it had to happen. Your father's been making the rounds for me for a few years now. He's good people. I always figured you were good people. But to me you were a kid. I was shocked when Louie brings you in on this. Now I'm shocked again you act like more of a man than my brother.

"So I want to thank you. By way of thanks I'm offering you work. Lou and I have a messenger service. Lou always said you're his best driver."

"See, the way it works," Lou jumped in, "is, you drive to Tarrytown and pick up a package from this nigger. You bring it . . ."

"African," Tony interjected.

"What?"

"He's an African."

"They're all Africans."

"This one's from Africa. He's Ethiopian."

"You pick up a package from this Ethiopian nigger an' you bring it to a hebe in Borough Park."

"What is it?" I asked.

"No questions, Mike," Lou said.

"Is it dope?"

"No questions," Lou repeated.

"Take it easy, Lou," Tony said. Then to me, "It's not drugs. There's no drugs."

"What then?"

"No questions." It was Tony's turn. "You do it two days a week. The days vary. The pay is eight hundred a week cash. You should be able to live pretty well unless you start putting bets in with your father." He smiled.

I stood up. "Is there anything else?"

Lou looked at me. "You takin' the job?"

"I'll let you know."

"You'll let us know! You little prick. This is . . ."

Tony held his hand up and Lou stopped talking as if someone had unplugged him.

"Take your time," Tony said. "The job is yours if you want it. Play your cards right, kid; someday you could be a made man."

The guys on the corner greeted me that night with a kind of formality I felt I'd have to become used to. I nodded briefly, and passed a bottle around. I would be a visitor from now on. I would not be part of this crowd anymore. And, as little as any of the individuals meant to me, the idea still made me sad.

Nobody said anything as I approached the trash-can fire with my school books under my arm. My new status would make any eccentric behavior hip. One by one I fed them into the fire. I thought about my classes. Kathy Popovich. *Satyricon*. In the last book, *Sociology of Deviance*, was my tuition receipt. Fifteen hundred dollars. By waiting this long I couldn't withdraw and get a refund. Fuck it. I dropped the book and receipt in and stood there, leaning forward, feeling the heat on my face. I'd make fifteen hundred in two weeks working for Lou's brother. Soon I'd make it every week. In cash. Nothing that school could do for me now.

Chapter 10

For the next four days I didn't leave my room except to go to the bathroom or take some food from the kitchen. I spoke to no one. I slept fitfully, an hour here and there, more in the daytime than at night. Whenever I dropped off I would plunge back into the same long dream. I was alone in the pitch-dark listening to indistinct voices, unable to make out any words, though the inflection changed often. Sometimes there were several voices, and I thought I was the topic of conversation. Other times it was one voice that I was certain was talking to me, teasingly out of reach, and I'd wake up with a longing I couldn't identify. Sometimes I cried.

The phone in my room was unplugged, so I would hear the other one ring dimly out in the kitchen. My father answered, and I could tell from his muffled tone whether it was personal or just someone making a bet. He never came into my room, but he kept the refrigerator stocked with cold cuts and potato salad—something he hadn't done in years—so I knew he was worried about me. Later I found that he'd screened calls for me during that time. He made excuses to Gina, who was used to them, and to Lou, who called only once.

We finally sat down and talked on the day I came out. It was cold and raining hard outside, and I figured I could go out briefly without seeing anyone. I was starting to go stir crazy, and took it as a sign that whatever had kept me locked in was passing.

My father came into the apartment while I was getting dressed. I'd showered and shaved while he was making his rounds. He didn't hang around the car service much anymore. I heard him sit on the sofa in the living room and rustle the paper. I finished dressing, walked out, and sat in an easy chair opposite him. He put the paper down and looked over at me.

"Back in the world?"

"I think so."

He nodded. "You were gonna get sick if you kept eatin' that shit three meals a day. Your asshole must hate you already."

"It does. Thanks. You're the one who brought it all in."

"Complaints? I didn't see you doing any shopping. I shoulda let you starve. I notice you ate it."

"What are we talking about here, Pop?"

"Cold cuts and your asshole."

"Why are we doing that?"

"I don't know. I thought you wanted to."

He smiled; so did I. Then we started laughing. Then we talked about school and work and the neighborhood and generally avoided discussing my having become a recluse. Finally he asked me, "Are you going to work for Tony?" I said I wasn't sure.

"I think you should."

"Why?"

"To show that you're not running away. The way it all happened—with you involved—was fucked-up. But Lou and Tony, right now, they think you're cold-blooded, a stone motherfucker. Tony don't know you enough to know any better. Lou should, but Lou don't know anything good enough to tell Tony he's wrong. Now is when you show your face just a little. Work for Tony for a while and you drift on to something else. Back to school or whatever you want. Just don't suddenly disappear because of this."

"You're worried about yourself," I said. The words came out as I thought them. "This is about you. I'm in the middle of this shit, and you're afraid that the guys in the club will think your son's a pussy."

He looked down. I felt bad that I'd said it, but worse because it was true.

"Why don't *you* just quit?" I asked.

"What am I gonna do? I'm gonna move to the suburbs and take up gardening? This is what I do. I hang around. I nickel and dime."

"I can't work for Tony after what happened to Shades."

"Grief's a funny thing. I didn't want to do *shit* after your mother died; just sit around. But you do one little thing, then two, and by the time you think about it there are these whole new routines you got worked out. It ain't the same. For me it won't ever be the same, but," he shrugged, "you get used to things. You know that. You had to adjust before."

"That's not what I mean," I said. "I mean what Tony did to Shades. To have him killed. To . . . I don't even know if you know what happened. It's not grief. This isn't like Mom. Tony killed him, and I should go work there?"

He sighed. "Act of God, act of man, what's the fucking difference? Your mother is as dead as Nicky Shades, and I wish I had someone like Tony to blame. I hope you're not stupid enough to feel guilty, cause you couldn't help Shades anymore than I could help your mother. If you want to blame somebody you can blame the guys who did it a little. Blame Tony a little. And blame Nicky Shades the most cause he did it to himself as much as if he stuck a gun in his mouth. Never forget that.

"Why don't you take this job for a coupla months, then tell Tony you're not interested anymore. Don't give up your edge."

"I don't have to live my life impressing the street corner ginzos. That's your story, not mine." I stood up, took my coat and an umbrella, and walked out.

It was a great exit line, and because it was so good I felt particularly stupid at the door of Tony's club half an hour later. Asshole that I was, all the things my father had said were in fact important to me.

When I was younger, ten or twelve, I used to think Tony was the boss of the whole world: that he ran everything, had connections in Washington and on the west coast, probably Europe too. The day my father told me that Tony's territory ended at Sixteenth Avenue it was like discovering there was no Santa Claus. Even the Old Man, who I eventually met and actually picked up and drove to Tony's club once, only had Coney Island to Sunset Park. There was just too much land, too many people, too much action in the world. I accepted the fact that I would never ever fathom what the real movers and shakers might be like.

A funny thing happened as I walked through the door of the club, though. I became that stone motherfucker. I squared my shoulders, and maybe even swaggered a little. After all, I was the guy with the balls to keep Tony waiting four days for an answer on an offer that half the mopes on the avenue would kill for. If he thought I was the goods, then I'd let him.

The scene in the club looked exactly as it had when I'd been there last. If they weren't the same old men in the same clothes playing the same poker game, you couldn't have proved it by me. But there was no game on TV. Instead they had a soap opera on and were watching it as avidly over their cards as if it were football. I wondered if they'd found a way to bet on it. I glanced at the screen. A honey blonde in a nurse's uniform was telling a guy in a suit that she'd slept with his boss, but had done it for *him*, to advance his career.

"Butana," one of the old men yelled at the set, and spit ceremoniously on the floor.

The door to Tony's private office opened and Zak came out. He looked at me with no sign of recognition, turned, and went back into the office. Ten seconds later he opened the door halfway, stood in the jamb and snapped his fingers once, dramatically, then pointed at me and gestured with his head toward the inner office. I leaned against the bar and stared at him. He glared at me and snapped his fingers twice more, quickly.

"You must have mistaken me for the bartender," I said. "I'm not him. I'd like to see Tony if he's got a minute." I smiled politely.

Zak got that wild look in his eyes and I thought I could see his nostrils flare. For a moment I was afraid I'd been outrageously stupid, even for me. Then I heard Tony's voice, low and well-modulated, from behind the door. Zak shuddered and swallowed. "Come in," he managed to rasp.

"Thank you."

I inhaled and squeezed sideways around his bulk in the doorframe. He didn't move an inch for me and I felt his eyes boring into my back as I walked to the chair opposite Tony's desk and sat. Tony looked at Zak and nodded. Zak left the room and pulled the door closed behind him. Tony reached across the desk and extended his hand. I shook it.

"How come you torment Zak like that?" he asked.

"I don't know. I don't like him. He's an ape. I don't like the way he treats people."

"He doesn't like you either. And he doesn't like your father. He don't think you should get this job."

I didn't say anything.

"What do you think?" he asked.

"I don't think you got here," I said, glancing around the office, "by listening to guys like Philly Zak."

Tony smiled. "I assume you're here because you're accepting the job."

"Yes."

"You took a while."

"I thought it through."

He looked at me, not speaking, and I got the feeling that he was weighing me. I sat in one of his small manicured hands, while in the other he held things that he considered important as values, to see how I balanced out. I couldn't begin to guess what those things might be. It felt like two hours passed. He stood, so I did.

"Zak's right about one thing," he said. "You're very much like your father. I'm glad to have both of you with me."

He extended his hand again, and again I shook it. I wondered how many times a day you had to shake this guy's hand.

"Come by tomorrow morning about nine-thirty. I'll have Lou show you the run. He's been covering, but he likes to stay by the store."

He walked me to the door of his office and we said goodbye. I beat him to the punch by extending my hand first this time. He looked surprised, then pleased. No grass grew under my feet.

Zak stood outside the club, sheltered from the rain by the leaky awning. I stopped in the doorway long enough to get my umbrella open. He regarded me menacingly, but he didn't look really angry, just dumb and mean. As I walked away I looked back at him over my shoulder in the rain. He hadn't moved, just continued watching me, perfectly still, a rock formation in a sports jacket. I'd been generous to call him an ape. He was a fucking dinosaur.

The next day was my first run, and it was fairly uneventful. I rode with Lou in a car I'd never seen before to a nice house in a suburb of Tarrytown, where I rang a bell and met an Ethiopian. He was tall and bony, almost to the point of being emaciated. Looking at him, I kept thinking about the famine over there. His name was absolutely unpronounceable, and after I tried it twice he told me to call him Todd. There was a Todd in his name somewhere anyway. He and Lou obviously didn't get along, and each did their best to stare the other down for the whole six minutes we were there. Todd left the front room and returned shortly with a small brown knapsack. He held it out to Lou, who ignored him. I took it. Todd was being polite enough to me, so I didn't see any reason to follow Lou's lead. I shook his hand as we left.

When we got to the car Lou suggested I drive, so I'd get familiar with the route. The knapsack lay on the seat between us, and neither of us ever referred to it. I had heard other people in the house with Todd, but I hadn't seen anyone else. No questions, I told myself.

Lou and I bullshitted amiably, as though the night with Shades had never happened. He was apparently over his embarrassment, and was back to looking at me when he spoke. We talked about horses, sports in general, and real estate, guessing the prices of different houses we passed.

"How come you don't like Todd?" I asked him.

"Uppity jig. I don't trust him. He thinks cause he ain't from here it means he ain't a nigger."

"Why do business with him if you don't trust him?"

"We hafta do . . . sometimes you gotta do business anyway, with people . . . hey, whattaya think that one goes for?" He pointed to a white columned house with shutters and a fieldstone chimney. "Gotta be half a mil."

"Half a mil easy," I said. Evidently we were finished with our conversation.

When we arrived back in Brooklyn, Lou directed me to a wood-frame house in danger of imminent collapse in the middle of Borough Park. Hasids in black coats and furry hats and their wives in gaudy jewelry and wigs, trailing a hundred kids, were all over the streets. It was like a constant rush hour. We couldn't have stuck out more in Bed-Stuy.

"This neighborhood gives me the creeps," I said. "It's like Invasion of the Body Snatchers. Nobody's looking right at us, but I know everyone's watching us."

"It's okay," Lou said. "Everybody watches, but nobody sees a thing."

The drop-off took less time than the pick-up. We opened the splintering front door and stood in a damp vestibule, looking at a second door made of steel that would have seemed more appropriate on a bank vault. There were four bells set into the crumbling tile wall to our left. Lou rang all of them.

"Only one works," he said, "but I can never remember which one."

The door was opened by a short Hasid with red hair and beard. He looked about fifty. Behind him stood a tall, skinny kid in his mid-twenties with thick glasses and a yarmulke, but without the rest of the costume. He looked like someone whose lunch money you'd take.

"Go ahead," Lou said. I handed the bag to the older one.

"Only give the bag to this one," Lou said. "Nobody else."

"Or him," the Hasid said, indicating the younger guy.

"Or him," Lou repeated, annoyed. "Anyone else?" he asked. The Hasid shook his head. "Okay, then that's it." They went in and closed the door. We left.

"I told some a' the guys I'd bring lunch back to the store," Lou said, as I was driving down Fiftieth Street. "You mind if we go by Five Brothers, get some potato an' egg heros?"

"No, I don't mind," I said. I looked at my watch. The round trip with stops had taken three hours and forty minutes and I'd made four hundred dollars.

Five Brothers was a deli by the docks in Sunset Park. Borough Park, all Jewish, is right up against Sunset Park, all Spanish, and the number of children in both neighborhoods was staggering. As we drove past Maimonides Hospital, on the line between the two areas, I stopped for a red light. To our left was some sort of clinic entrance that must have been maternity or ob-gyn. Dozens of women—all very pregnant and each with several small children—lined both sides of the alley leading to the double glass doors; a battalion of baby carriages bobbed up and down, it seemed to me, to the same beat. Lou looked past me down the alley.

"South Brooklyn breedin' war," he said. "Whoever wins, we lose."

"Tough call," I said. "Hasids smell like shit and they're arrogant, but my old man's taxes don't pay for their kids."

"Yeah, an' who ever heard of a Hasid mugger. That's a funny picture—you know—a Beard mugger."

The light changed and I drove on. At Five Brothers Lou ran in for the sandwiches. When we got back to the car service I had a quick cup of coffee just to show my face, then left. Lou walked me out.

"Next run's Tuesday, Mike. Just you. Come see me about nine-thirty, pick up some car keys, an' you're off. After the drop, park the car around where you found it, gimme back the keys, then go see Tony an' get your eight bills. Simple as 'at."

"I don't take my car?"

"You don't never take your car, my car, or anybody else's car. See me inna morning. I give you keys. I say something like, 'There's a blue '85 Buick on Ovington.' You take that. When you're done, park it back on Ovington, bring me the keys. Got it?"

"Got it."

"Good. Welcome to the club."

It felt like he was pronouncing sentence.

Chapter 11

When I left the car service I went up to the apartment and straight into my room. I closed my door, although I had no idea whether my father was home. I sat on the bed for about a minute and then stood, walked to the bookshelf, and turned on my radio. I had one of those ghetto blasters that looked like it had eight cylinders and an automatic transmission. The sound jumped out like a physical thing, and I immediately turned it down. I must have been in a pretty good mood the last time I'd played it. Now, nothing sounded right. After trying a half-dozen stations I turned it off. I looked through my tapes, but it seemed like my own taste in music had turned to shit as thoroughly as that of every dj in New York. I glanced quickly around the room. It looked stupid: childish and small. I opened the door again, but I still felt closed in. Walking through the living room to the kitchen for a drink, I realized that I felt like I was inside the car service. Caged. Nothing was any different up here than it was down there, and suddenly I needed to be someplace where it was different. I walked all through the apartment. My father wasn't home. I considered heading over to Gina's, but I knew I would feel the same way over there, and then I'd have to contend with her trying to figure out what was wrong. There was no way I could explain anything to her because—aside from the fact that I didn't have a terrific handle on things myself—she was a part of that whole car service world out there that had me boxed-in. I couldn't expect her to see it any more than Lou or Little Joey would.

Then I thought of Kathy Popovich. It had been almost a week since I'd stood her up at the movies. Since I'd spent an afternoon bullshitting with her in the Pub. I felt like it was last night and last year at the same time. Nicky was alive then, and I was still, in some sense, a college student. The school stuff I could do without. I'd been kidding myself from jump. But the atmosphere—the conversation—was what I missed. And now I felt like I'd miss it for the rest of my life. I looked at my watch. Sociology of Deviance would let out at a quarter to four. If I didn't mind paying to park in a lot I could make it easily. I changed my shirt, splashed some water on my face, and left.

Traffic was nonexistent on the Gowanus at three o'clock, and by three-thirty I handed the car over to the custody of some surly third-worlder in a lot. I hated lots, and usually left for class early enough to secure one of the dozen legal parking spaces on the street in Manhattan. Giving my car keys to a stranger felt like wife swapping.

If I waited outside the building, I ran the risk of missing Kathy if she chose a different exit. On the other hand, if I waited right outside the classroom, I might bump into some of my former classmates or even the instructor. I'd come this far, so there was little point in playing it safe.

The class ended a few minutes after I arrived. I positioned myself about fifty feet down the hall and pretended to study a flyer on the bulletin board. It was about nuclear power being the ultimate evil, and how if we got rid of all of our atomic weapons so would everyone else. As nearly as I could determine, whoever wrote it was serious. Kathy walked out of the room with two other girls and went down the stairs at the opposite end of the hall. I let a minute pass so anyone else who might want to talk would have drifted off; then I went down the stairs as quickly as I could. I caught up with them on the corner, waiting for the light.

"Kathy?" I said, walking up behind her. If she hadn't been in the middle I would have approached from the side and just quietly asked to talk to her, but now I was going to have to do the casual-encounter-on-the-street bit until we could talk privately.

"Mike." She turned around. "Where the hell have you been? Are you okay?"

"Yeah . . . um . . . I'm fine." There was no question that I was a smooth operator. The only thing left for me to do was to look down at my shoes and drag one toe across the pavement while thrusting my hands in my pockets. It was pretty rare for me to go into brainlock like that. Luckily, I didn't have to think of anything for a moment, because she turned to the two other girls and promptly excused herself. They crossed when the light changed, and we walked back toward the school.

"I didn't mean to pull you away from your friends," I said. "You didn't have to do that."

"I hardly know them. We were only going to do a little window shopping. On my budget that's just torture. Anyway, what's going on with you? I was pissed off Saturday when you didn't show up. Then you missed two classes in a row and I got worried. My friend in the bursar's office gave me your phone number, but when I tried it I got some Chinese lady and she'd never heard of you."

"I must have given them the wrong number."

"You wrote your own phone number down wrong?"

"I have a small problem with voluntarily giving out information. I'm working on it. It's why I took a deviance class," I said, smiling.

"Why haven't you been in class?"

"I'm cured?" She didn't laugh. "Look, it's a fairly complicated story. I'll try to tell it if you want, but it's cold out. I came to apologize for not showing up Saturday. You want to get some coffee or a drink and we'll talk?"

"All right," she said.

We were walking into the Village and I figured we could hit one of the cafés on Bleecker where you can drink liquor or coffee and they don't chase you off if you linger. We talked about trivial things on the way and after a couple of blocks she slipped her arm through mine. I was very cool about it. Not once did I yell yippee out loud.

"I really am sorry about Saturday," I said, as our drinks arrived. She had a cappuccino and I had black coffee and an amaretto.

"What happened to you anyway? I mean, I was with a couple of friends, so don't think it was anything tragic, but I was annoyed. Then after a while I got worried."

"Well, I certainly didn't mean to upset you. I didn't even connect not showing up for the movies with not showing up for school or I would have gotten in touch with you. I haven't been thinking straight lately." I didn't know where I was going with this, but it occurred to me that she was being really decent about everything and maybe I could stick fairly close to the truth. "Saturday night a friend of mine died."

"Jesus, I'm sorry. My God, no wonder you haven't been around."

"We weren't that close. I mean we were, but I hadn't seen him for a few months. We'd drifted a bit; I didn't know it was going to happen."

"How did he die?"

"He was killed."

"Christ, that's terrible." She put her hand over mine on the table. "Of course you couldn't know it was going to happen. You can't let yourself get into feeling guilty about something like that. It's this damn city."

At that moment I wanted to say that I could know it was going to happen because I drove the car carrying the people who killed him. Because I saw him going downhill and didn't do anything about it. Because after it happened I chose to go to work for the guy who set it up. Because I'm a soulless scumbag. "Yes," I said. "It's this damn city. Parts of it anyway."

She sipped her cappuccino. "Did he get mugged? Was it crackheads? The news makes it sound like Brooklyn is crawling with them."

I had to laugh. "Have you ever been to Brooklyn?" I asked.

"Once. I dated someone who lived in Brooklyn Heights."

"Brooklyn Heights is not Brooklyn," I said. "It's a little piece of Manhattan they keep on the other side of the bridge so people from Manhattan can take a cab over, put one foot down, and say they've been in Brooklyn."

"I see. Good you're not defensive."

"Not a bit."

She smiled. "What is it about the outer boroughs that makes people so protective of their little enclaves?"

"Maybe it's phrases like 'little enclaves'."

"Sorry."

"No. That's okay. They're not offensive to me. The more people who think that way, the safer I feel."

"From whom? Manhattanites?"

Tim McLoughlin

"Manhattanites?" I asked. "There are ten Manhattanites in all of Manhattan. The rest of the people who live on this rock, by and large, are assholes from Cleveland who got off a bus half a year ago and pay a million dollars a month rent to share a rat-infested two-bedroom in alphabet city with three strangers. They ride the subway at night, get mugged, give money to the bums they promoted to homeless when no one was looking. In other words, they do all the things that real New Yorkers never do. They stand on endless lines for movies and restaurants like this was Moscow or something. And when they finally get into a club after it's not hip anymore they say, 'Well, it used to be great before the people from the outer boroughs started coming'."

"I'm from Cleveland," she said.

"What?"

"I'm from Cleveland."

She was staring at me with an absolutely blank expression. Mentally, I cut my tongue out and fed it to wolves. I knew this sticking-close-to-the-truth shit and speaking openly was going to be a mistake, but I didn't think I'd bury myself before we'd finished coffee. "When I said Cleveland I wasn't specifically—"

"I'm joking."

"What?"

"I've never even been there. I couldn't resist." She began giggling.

"You've never been there?" I wanted to choke her, but I was laughing too.

"Nope."

"Where are you from?"

"Philadelphia."

"A trick to see if I'll say bad things about Philadelphia?"

"No. Philadelphia, really. Does your formula still apply?"

"No," I said, considering my words carefully. "Philadelphia's close enough to New York. Aside from that, it's almost like a real city by itself."

"Well, we lived in the suburbs."

"Aha. That's not what you said."

"Everyone talks like that. If you live in Brookline or Quincy and someone asks where you're from, you say Boston."

"Are those places in Boston?" I asked.

"Just outside."

"Well, are people who say Boston lying?"

"Of course not," she said.

"Okay, that proves my point."

"What point?"

"People from the outer boroughs are the real New Yorkers." I smiled and held my hands out, palms up.

"Touché, and who cares? No more geography. Did you want to talk about your friend?"

"No," I said. "That's the last thing I want to talk about. I just wanted to let you know why I wasn't there Saturday."

"Don't worry about it. You can copy my notes from the last two classes. I'm a manic note-taker so it's almost as good as being there, except for the spelling."

"Thank you." Somehow I felt that this wasn't the time to tell her that I was dropping out. It would lead to the kind of questioning and conversation that would ruin the way I was feeling. This wasn't the same as when I avoided conversation with Gina. That was usually because it was too much hard work and her range of interests was limited, even by my standards. I didn't want to get into anything deep with Kathy because I was afraid it would break the mood.

I wasn't sure why I liked her. Sometimes she was witty and fast enough to make me keep my guard up. Other times she'd lapse into the airhead college student drivel that the rest of the class seemed to favor. They formed all their opinions based on other people's theories, and had little or no experience with life in the real world. That had always infuriated me, but now, listening to Kathy, I realized hers was more a sense of innocence than ignorance. It was appealing. Maybe it was her humor, or that she didn't try to come off like she had all the answers. Then again, maybe I just wanted to sleep with her more than I wanted a VISA gold card, and I would have made excuses for devil worship.

We talked about the class and about world events—two subjects she showed vastly too much interest in. After an hour or so I suggested we go to dinner.

"Not here," I said. "These places are great for dessert and coffee, but they really aren't for dinner. I know a couple of spots in Soho or Little Italy. It depends on what you want. We can go into Brooklyn if that's all right with you. I'm more familiar with places there."

"Mike," she said, "I can't afford to eat dinner out. I can barely afford the cappuccino."

I was confused for a moment. "I asked you to come for coffee, and now I'm asking you to come to dinner. I don't expect you to pay for anything."

"Oh no," she said. "That's too much money."

"It's no money at all. Listen, I told you I'd be there Saturday and I wasn't. Let me buy dinner. I'll feel better."

"Are you sure you want to do this? You don't have to make anything up to me."

"Of course I'm sure. I'm starving."

"All right."

When the check for the drinks came we did another Miss Manners tug-of-war. I'd never been out with a girl who tried to pay for anything. I didn't mind the idea as long as what we could do wasn't strapped to her budget. If it was, we'd probably be eating White Castle on city buses in the future. My father said there was nothing worse than being poor. He said it often. I always figured he was right, but I really didn't know. I never saw my parents fight about money, or even discuss it. If I needed cash for anything when I was a kid, my father would peel it off the roll he always carried, and I was set. When I turned fourteen he insisted I get a part-time job. Going out takes money, he'd said. And you'll be wanting to do plenty of going out. He hadn't been wrong. I'd worked part-time ever since, full-time during summers. When I started driving, I was good for seventy-five a day off the books, and I was working four days a week. My old man paid a whopping two-seventy a month for our six-room rent-controlled apartment, and he wouldn't take a dime from me, so whatever I earned was pocket money. If I lived on my own, like Kathy did, I'd probably be broke, too. As it was, I had the best of both worlds. My father and I both lived on our own. We just did it in the same apartment.

Kathy and I settled on Little Italy and she let me pick the restaurant. It wouldn't have been a very long walk, but it was getting damn cold out, and besides, I kept hearing the car calling to me the farther we strayed from the lot. I suggested that we pick it up and drive downtown. I knew it was sufficiently past rush hour and that I'd get a spot.

"You drove in?" she said. "God, I haven't met anyone who owns a car since I moved to New York. Maybe you *are* rich."

I was going to point out that I'd never met anyone who took public transportation until I started college, but thought better of it. One of us was emerging as fairly provincial during the course of the evening, and I had a nagging suspicion it was me.

We parked on Hester Street and walked to Tommaso's on Mulberry. My father had worked with Vincent, the owner's son, in the Sanitation Department. We were seated promptly and had red wine and cold antipasto brought to us before we ordered. Tommaso's wasn't one of the more famous places on the tiny strip, but it was one of the few family-owned spots that had survived. It was nestled between two newer, glitzy cafes that lived off the tourist crowd.

"I like it here," Kathy said. "I've only been to the area two or three times, but it's so colorful. I wish I knew more places down this way."

"There aren't really that many more places," I said. "Little Italy is only about three square blocks these days. It used to be everything above Canal and south of the Village, including Soho. The Chinese came up from the south, and the yuppies and artists moved in from the north and the west, and bingo, you're left with four restaurants, a couple of social clubs, and a souvenir store that sells Mussolini t-shirts and 'Kiss Me I'm Italian' buttons."

"Really? That's so sad."

I shrugged. "I guess. Everything changes, though. The Chinese pushed the Italians out. The Italians must have pushed somebody else out when they got here, though I can't imagine who. In fifty years, people will be sitting on this spot in the last Chinese restaurant talking about what a shame it is that the Orientals were driven out by Croatians."

"Probably," she said, laughing. "That doesn't make it seem so pessimistic." She looked around the dining room. "It still bothers me a little. I know everybody moves to the suburbs in a few generations and we all become generic Americans, but there seems to be such a thinning of ethnic culture when that happens. And what if they don't want to move? Are businesses and storekeepers actually forced out?"

"I don't know for sure. My father says it doesn't happen like that very much. He says that whatever the Chinese got in this neighborhood they paid for, and probably much more than it was worth. From what I know of people, anybody who can, sells out the minute somebody waves money under their nose, and they jump at the opportunity to become a 'generic American'."

"Awfully cynical outlook," Kathy said. "Probably too true. But what about the old people? The ones who live forty or fifty years in places like this. Can they handle the change? And the younger ones who just don't want to go, or don't have the education and skills to—I don't know—assimilate, I guess. I think about people like that: the hangers-on. You know what I mean?"

As she stared at me over her wine glass I had to remind myself that Kathy Popovich knew virtually nothing about me. Did I know what she meant? I couldn't have known any better if she'd said, What about guys like you, Mike? What happens to you in this changing society? Because clearly you're the kind of loser who'll never be able to adapt or move on.

I looked back into her intense brown eyes and assured myself that it was I who was always making those accusations; I who felt that my chunk of the planet was being eroded from under me and that I was as ill-prepared to deal with it as any seventy-year-old gindaloon on Mott Street.

She smiled suddenly. "Hey. There's no right or wrong answer. I was just thinking out loud. Are you in there?"

"I'm sorry. I guess you struck a nerve. I worry sometimes. I mean, about my father."

"Oh, I didn't realize. Do you have older brothers and sisters? Are your parents elderly? I always assume that everybody's family is like mine. Just conceited, I guess."

"I think everyone does that. My father is fifty-one. I don't have any brothers or sisters."

"Fifty-one. He's a very young man. My father is fifty and he's more like an older brother to my sister and me sometimes. She's twenty-five. My parents took us both to see the Rolling Stones at JFK stadium when I was ten. He still sends tapes of any new bands he thinks I might like, but frankly I think he's trying to steer me more to jazz and some of the experimental, intellectual stuff now. I really feel dumb next to him sometimes."

"I feel dumb next to my father quite often," I said. "Enough that it's become a comfortable feeling."

"Yeah, I know what you mean. Is he a young fifty or an old fifty?

I mean, did he ever take you to concerts or anything like that?"

"No. Nothing like that, really." I decided not to mention that he'd taken me with him and my mother to see Frank Sinatra at Carnegie Hall when I was six. They dressed formally and were even able to rent me a tiny tuxedo from a place on Thirteenth Avenue that stocked a few of the small suits for ringbearers at weddings. I'd always thought it was fairly silly, but now, hearing Kathy's story, I thanked God that I didn't have hip parents who did embarrassing things like take their kids to rock concerts. If my father and I did occasionally relate as brothers, it wasn't because he was a young fifty-one; it was more that I was a very old almost-twenty. "He took me bowling a lot. We were in a father/son league."

She rolled her eyes. "An old fifty."

I rolled mine. "Yeah."

Dinner arrived and we continued to make small talk through the meal. Kathy was a tough person to get a handle on. Sometimes she was out in space, sometimes right on target. The hard part was figuring which was the personality trait and which the aberration. I decided to keep playing both sides of the fence until I could sort it out.

After dinner I hung back and let Kathy steer the conversation on the walk to the car and the drive to her apartment in the East Village. We wound up on social issues again and, following her lead, I passionately endorsed affirmative action, racial quotas, abortion rights, and threw in what little anti-nuke rhetoric I'd gleaned from the poster at school. There was a sticky moment when she began talking about Israel. I knew she was Jewish, so I almost instinctively went for the poor, suffering Tribe surrounded by enemies. At the last second, though, I decided that she had, after all, voluntarily moved from some middle-class suburb of Philly to Manhattan, so instead I rambled about the land-hungry oppressors of innocent Palestinians. I was tense for a moment, but she joined in almost immediately and sang the praises of some Arabic-sounding "freedom fighter" I'd never heard of. It was a judgment call and it had been close, but it left me with the kind of giddy exhilaration I'd felt once at Belmont when I picked the winners of the first three races, knowing there were six to go.

We parked a couple of hundred feet away from Kathy's building. It was a faded tenement-looking thing, which, I was surprised to realize upon closer examination, looked more like where I lived than I cared to admit. As we were approaching, a woman who'd beaten me to a closer spot was getting out of her battered VW Rabbit. She locked it up and walked away. When we passed the car Kathy slowed, then stopped. I followed her gaze to the rear side window and saw a rather elaborate version of a tellingly popular sign. It was hand-lettered and read: No Radio in Car or Trunk. No Spare Tire. Windows Broken Twice. Trunk Broken Into Three Times. Nothing of Value. You Got it All.

"Shit," Kathy said, "that's horrible."

"It's sickening," I said.

"Yes." She looked over at me. "It is."

"How can anyone let themselves be reduced to that? Groveling, begging people not to steal from you. She probably jogs wearing a t-shirt that says I've been mugged twice and raped three times—nothing of value left. If I were stealing radios I'd break that window for the time I lost reading the sign." I stopped before I hyperventilated. "No radio" signs were a pet peeve of mine.

"I was thinking," Kathy said slowly, "that it's horrible that our society is so degenerate that we have to live like that. I wasn't really thinking about blaming the victim."

Shit. Major fuck-up. It was probably the t-shirt remark. I had to retreat and regroup. We couldn't argue now. I was almost in the goddamn apartment.

I struggled for a nice even tone, something like a radio dj. "Of course the main problem is people stealing radios, not people putting signs in their cars," I said as I tried to get her walking forward, toward the door again. She moved, but hesitantly. "It just bothers me to see people degraded by begging criminals not to assault them."

"Even if that's true," she said, "you know it's overly simplistic. And 'criminal' is such a vague term. There are many kinds of people who commit crimes, and many different reasons."

Tell me about it. "Do you think that matters to the woman who's had her windows broken and her trunk popped?"

"Probably not. Maybe it should, though. Besides, you didn't have much sympathy for that woman a minute ago. You were making fun of her."

"I have plenty of sympathy for people who are victims. I just don't approve of advertising it. People who victimize other people aren't going to feel bad for you because you list your previous record of assaults on your car window. It just means you're an easy mark."

"It means you're weak?"

"Exactly."

"So this is about weakness. You shouldn't let people see you as vulnerable, whether you are or not?" She stopped at the foot of her stoop, then stepped up on the first step and turned to face me at eye level.

I knew what my answer was, but I didn't know what answer she wanted. "I'm not sure," I said.

"Well," she smiled. "I'm glad there's something you're not sure of. Would you like to come up for a little while?"

"Sure," I said. I decided to keep my mouth shut more often.

Inside the first doorway all similarities between her building and mine ended. They had probably been identical at some point in time, but while mine had become a little shabby, this had become a slum. The inside hallway door had been removed and the hall stank of piss. There was graffiti on the walls that continued up the stairwell, and, though the mailboxes were intact, they looked like they'd been shelled for several days.

My apartment was in an eight-unit building that was structurally the same as Kathy's: four stories, two apartments per floor. Each apartment ran front to back—railroad rooms. We were on the third floor, right. My room was in front on the street, and my father's was in the back. Between us was enough room for a landing strip. Kathy's building appeared to have been haphazardly chopped into about thirty units of randomly picked sizes. She lived on the fourth floor, of course, and took the stairs at a near sprint.

I tried not to seem openly exhausted, and waited patiently for my heart rate to stabilize while she opened the dozen or so locks on the dented metal door. She wasn't winded at all. It occurred to me that if I did manage to get her into bed she'd probably kill me.

The last lock clicked, and she swung the door open to total darkness and went in. I stood in the doorway until she turned a lamp on. The apartment was small, a room and a half, but had three windows over the street, so it didn't feel closed-in. It was furnished sparsely and—I was a little taken aback—plainly. It looked a bit like my apartment. It looked like an older person lived here. Kathy, with her all black outfits, black hair, and occasionally, black nail polish, seemed to me a little more bohemian than this.

Kathy made make-yourself-comfortable and don't-mind-the-mess noises while she took our jackets to a closet. I moved to the bookshelves to see how her reading tastes ran. The decor had thrown me, but the books were reassuringly predictable. School texts mixed in with the obligatory pop-psych and paperback feminist stuff. A few science fiction novels, most of them dragon-and-castle looking fantasies. No mysteries, no spy stories.

I liked to read, but almost never did. For someone who didn't accomplish anything by the end of the day, I seemed to be busy an awful lot. When I did read, it was mostly spy stuff. My father read a lot of it, and I read what was around the house and got hooked. It was the only way I could stand hearing about places that weren't New York without them seeming boring.

Behind me Kathy put a record onto a turntable which was part of a sound system that looked like it had been thrown together out of spare parts. The sound was decent though, and the music was familiar, but I couldn't quite place it. She went over to the kitchenette area.

"Would you like something to drink?" she asked.

"Okay. Anything you have besides scotch," I said. "Bourbon's great and anything else is almost as good."

I turned from the bookshelf to see Kathy standing in front of the refrigerator holding a container of orange juice in her left hand and a bottle of ginger ale in her right.

"I was just going to have some juice. I didn't think you'd be up for any more alcohol. I may have some vodka, though, if you want to mix it with the o.j."

The only thing I wanted to mix vodka with right then was an ice cube and the inside of my mouth, but I declined entirely and had a glass of ginger ale instead. I'd been hitting it very light all evening, but if Kathy thought I wouldn't want another drink it was because she thought I'd had enough already. I'd picked that less-than-subtle hint up from Gina over the years. Kathy brought the drinks to the sofa I was on and sat with me. I assumed it was a pull-out bed, unless she slept in the bathtub.

"What record is this?" I asked her. "It sounds like something I've heard, but I'm not sure."

"It's Dire Straits. The album is called *Making Movies*. It's their third. I'm sure you've heard it; there were several singles off it that did very well."

"I heard something by them. Didn't they do *Sultans of Swing* a long time ago?"

"Ages ago. Even this is a couple of albums old now."

"I don't follow music much."

"What do you listen to?"

"Whatever's on the radio when I'm working. I'm usually behind the wheel all day. I listen to oldies, rap, a little heavy metal, some old disco."

"What about folk or jazz? Is classical out of the question?"

"Only if there's a quiz. I'd probably like it, but I've never heard much of it."

"Hmm. I see I've got my work cut out for me," she said, leaning forward a little as she put her glass on the floor.

This, I thought, was a reason for optimism. It sounded like being told there was a future here, beyond this night. I scared myself by deciding I liked the idea.

"Well," I said, ditching my glass as I leaned the rest of the way to her, "if there's that much work to be done you'd better get started."

It was one of those slow motion, you-definitely-see-it-coming kisses. She narrowed her eyes to slits, but kept them open enough that she wouldn't miss my mouth. I put my hands around her waist and she rested hers around the back of my neck, half-cupped. Her nails—covered that evening in clear polish—moved in small circles beneath my shirt collar at the top of my spine. The touch was so light as to be almost nonexistent, and in fact I gently arched back a couple of millimeters to assure myself that it was her I was feeling. We kissed like that for a long time without moving. I tasted the orange juice in her mouth and something stronger, sharper, on her tongue. Peppermint. She'd speared a lifesaver or tic-tac while she was getting the drinks. It reminded me of Gina because she popped them constantly before we kissed when she was lying to me about quitting smoking. I was pretty sure that Kathy didn't smoke. Last minute nerves, I supposed. While it was comforting to know that she had them too, I also realized that I was nowhere near as spontaneous as I'd thought.

She moved her hands around to the front of my throat, still keeping her fingers under my collar. Then one hand moved up along my cheek with that same tantalizing, barely grazing motion, while the other moved down slightly and began unbuttoning my shirt. I slid a hand around her back, and after some searching, up under her black turtleneck. She stopped unbuttoning and both her hands lay motionless, flat against me for a moment. She drew back a little and we disengaged from the kiss.

"It's romantic as hell," she said, gently removing my hand from under her shirt. "But the way this thing fits it'll take until dawn."

She crossed her arms in front of her and held the bottom of the turtleneck in her hands, pulling it off inside-out. Underneath, she was wearing what appeared to be a small man's athletic undershirt. I'd never seen her in anything white before. It softened her and made her look a few years younger. I leaned forward again as she draped her shirt over an arm of the sofa, but she put a hand up, stopping me.

"Your turn," she said.

I quickly unbuttoned the rest of my shirt, failing miserably at not gawking at Kathy's breasts. When I started to slide the shirt off my arms I turned a little so that I was facing her directly, my right side almost pressed against the fabric of the couch. This was always when I was at my most self-conscious, especially with a girl I didn't know very well. My tattoo was high enough up my right arm that even as early as September it could be easily concealed by clothing, so I didn't think Kathy had ever seen it.

In the past it hadn't posed much of a problem with girls in Brooklyn or Staten Island, but it was inevitably the kiss of death with girls in Manhattan. Even the real artsy ones—and I was assuming Kathy fell comfortably into that category—only liked "new wave" style tattoos: small, Day-Glo colored things that looked to me like skin diseases from Star Trek. Mine was a cross done in black, with no other colors used at all. Two small birds held a ribbon over it that read "In Memory of Mom." I got it a week after she died. My father never said one word about it. Gina said it was sweet. Apparently in Manhattan it was about as hip as spats.

My intention had been to kill the lights in Kathy's apartment before we got this close, but then I hadn't counted on her making most of the moves and me just keeping pace. I got the shirt off without a problem, but I couldn't stay in the one spot all night. Kathy had slid down into a half-prone position opposite me. I was beginning to suspect that even if the sofa pulled open, it wouldn't tonight. I moved forward, and when I was directly over her and beginning to lower myself, I reached out with my right arm to turn off the lamp behind her. The thing was ancient and actually had a pull cord, but it didn't take anywhere near the seven weeks it felt like to turn it off. There was another light on in the apartment, but it was a distance away, and dim enough that we were in a shadowy semi-darkness.

"Are you trying to hide your tattoo?" she asked, when our lips were about three inches apart and closing.

"No," I said. I didn't move.

"Let me see it."

I shifted a little and turned my arm so it was as visible as it was going to be without more light. She ran a hand over it and studied it for a minute, though how she could read it was beyond me.

"Your mother is dead?"

"Yeah. A couple of years."

"I'm sorry."

"Thank you." The record ended then and the apartment was absolutely quiet.

"Why didn't you say anything?" she asked.

"About what? My mother?"

"Yes. I asked you a few questions about your family. I would have thought something like this would come to mind."

I was much too close to her eyes to think about turning away.

"Does this have to do with your 'problem' about voluntarily giving out information?" she asked.

"Yeah," I said, "kind of. It's not something I like to talk about."

"You didn't want to talk about your friend who died, either."

"That's true, I didn't. And still don't." I moved a few inches away from her face so that I could get a better look at it and gauge the seriousness of her mood. I didn't much care for the direction this was taking.

"What else don't you like to talk about?"

"I don't know. A lot of things, I guess."

"Do you have a girlfriend?"

"No."

"Really?"

"Really. I was almost engaged, but we broke up a couple of months ago. Why? What's bothering you? Is it because I hid the tattoo?"

"No. I think the tattoo is interesting. I just don't like you not telling me about your mother when we were discussing families. It feels like you're not being up-front with me."

"I'm being completely up-front with you," I said. "Some things are just hard for me to talk about. I'm sure you don't bare your soul right off the bat with people."

"So this is about weakness—not appearing vulnerable?"

I felt trapped. I decided that all those times when I thought Kathy was out in space she was actually taking it all in, and hadn't missed a word I'd said or my inflection when I'd said it. She seemed angry, and I didn't have the slightest idea what to do.

"Do you have a boyfriend?" I asked, smiling.

"I'm seeing two men, but neither thinks it's exclusive."

I stopped smiling. "You're seeing two guys?"

"I'm seeing anyone I please. I go on dates. Right now there are two men I date more or less regularly."

I hated the word "men." Why couldn't she call them guys, boys, dudes, anything? Men sounded like Brooks Brothers trenchcoats, gray hair at the temples, attaché cases, and the *Wall Street Journal*. It sounded like money and power. It sounded like not me.

"Let me ask you something," I said. "If you were to become serious with one of these guys . . ."

"I don't plan to become serious with anyone."

"Nobody plans or doesn't plan to become serious. It happens."

"I plan. And I'm pretty accurate."

I sat up. "Why don't you want to get involved with anyone?"

She propped herself up on her elbows and kind of shrugged. "Many reasons. Exclusivity indicates ownership."

"Come on. That crap is right off the back cover of one of those books. You didn't even have to bend the spine."

"You don't agree? Do you think it's better to have a relationship where one partner thinks it's exclusive and the other one is deceptive and sees other people anyway?"

"I don't have a fucking girlfriend," I snapped.

"It was a hypothetical question," she said very softly.

I suddenly remembered the Sundance Kid telling Butch Cassidy to save the last bullet for himself.

What had gone wrong? I was still in the ballpark. Nothing really had to change. I could just pretend it was all right, like I did with the politics and the social shit, but I didn't want to. Besides, there was too much honesty floating around this room, and too much honesty was a very dangerous thing.

"I think I'm gonna go," I said. "I apologize for yelling."

Kathy looked quite surprised, but she didn't say anything. I put my shirt back on. She got up and went to the closet for my jacket.

"How much of this has been you tonight, and how much was an act?"

"All me," I said. "No act."

"I'll see you in school? I have notes for you."

School. Jesus. "Yeah, I'll see you in class. I want to get those notes xeroxed. Thanks."

"Okay." She was looking at me like she knew I was full of shit. I had to get out of there.

"Thanks for dinner, really," she said when I was at the door. "And don't fall off the planet like that again. Try talking to me. It isn't so bad."

"Yeah," I said as she closed the door, but I knew I wouldn't. It would be like learning a whole other language, and I was too old to try anything that new.

When I hit the street I felt safe again. It was like coming out of a coma. The air was cold and I could think straight. I almost turned around and went back, but the part of my brain that spends its life on hold kicked in and kept me moving toward the car. I'd had my ass kicked once already and discretion was, after all, the better part of valor. Besides, I was scared to death. Kathy seemed to live completely on the surface. I felt that there was nothing I couldn't ask her; she had no masks at all. I not only couldn't imagine living like that, I didn't even accept that anyone else could. It was unnatural. One of the earliest rules that my father taught me, long before I understood its meaning, was: Never volunteer information. He'd drilled it into me, buried in the midst of all the standard little kid teachings. Don't talk to strangers. Don't cross against the light. Never volunteer information. Chew your food well before you swallow it.

I had this image of me and Kathy at age four: her father telling her that the policeman is your friend, mine telling me not to let anyone know where I lived.

It wouldn't work out with Kathy, and that was a shame. I liked her, but to live like that would drive me nuts. Not to mention her seeing two guys. She had tossed that off like it was nothing. Still, spending time with her convinced me of two things I'd been leaning toward already. I didn't much want to work for Tony and I really didn't want to marry Gina. Not now anyway. Probably never. That realization made me feel pretty happy. I'd have to thank Kathy. Maybe there was something to all this openness. Apparently I'd been withholding information from myself.

Driving over the bridge, pieces of the Manhattan skyline lit up my rearview mirror. At that time of night I knew it was just under fourteen minutes from there to my door. Manhattan was supposed to be the center of the universe, but like most Brooklynites, my neighborhood, and then the borough, was my universe, and Manhattan was the playground out in the backyard. Close enough to go frolic whenever the mood struck; far enough away that you didn't hear the noise when you came home. And like an amusement park that never closed, the skyline seemed visible from everywhere. That view at night was one of the most impressive sights I'd ever seen. I'd watched its neon silhouette grow and change from my bedroom window all my life, and I never tired of it. But I did rather like keeping it where it was, out there in the backyard, and I always felt a certain relief when I was off the bridge and back on the streets, heading home.

Chapter 12

Tuesday was my first solo run, and before I left the apartment I was already thinking of when and how to tell Tony I was quitting. I had to make at least a few trips so it would seem like I'd really given it a shot, but I'd decided my father's suggestion of several months was excessive. If I split the difference—his wanting me to do it for two months or so and my wanting to quit the day I started—it left me with a month, which was probably about right. That would be eight or nine runs. I could pick up a fair amount of cash and leave without losing face. It was a good plan, but it didn't do as much as I'd hoped to make me feel better.

My father was up and dressed before I even hit the shower. He was always an early riser, no matter how late he'd stayed out the previous evening. When I was ready to go we left together, stopped at the candy store around the corner, and had egg sandwiches and coffee at the counter. While we were getting grease stains on the Post and making jokes about the most recent mayoral blunder, Little Joey walked in with a list of coffee orders from the car service. He came over and sat with us while his order was being filled. We hadn't spoken since the night Nicky died, but if anything was bothering him I couldn't see it. A chill passed over me and I thought for a moment that if it had been me instead of Shades who was killed that night, Joey would still be here getting coffee, somehow turning it into a win. Who would he care about? Lou? Tony? His brother or his father? Where would Joey draw the line? He'd spent more time with Shades than I had, but he seemed to blow it all off like it was nothing. I realized sickeningly that that had to be how a lot of people saw me. Suddenly that cold-blooded image lost all its appeal. I didn't want to be grouped with Joey.

"You don't come around no more," he said, as I finished my coffee. "You got a big-shot job an' now you're too good for the regular drivers, hah?" He winked at my father, who was doing a thorough job of pretending Joey wasn't there.

"I've been pretty busy," I said, "but I'm still around. I don't think I'm too good for anybody. In fact, I'll walk around to the store with you now. I have to see Lou. If you're nice to me maybe I'll let you kiss my pinkie ring."

"Kiss my prick."

"Buy me a drink first."

Joey paid for his coffees and our breakfast as well, and I left my father there and walked around with him. Lou had told me to see him for a set of car keys. I hoped the car he had in mind was halfway decent.

"Jesus Christ," Little Joey said, "will you look at that."

Diagonally across the street, emerging from the corner building that the red Buick had crashed into a few weeks back, was Nicky's girlfriend, Louise. The house was a six-family brick with four apartments upstairs over a doctor's office, which took the whole first floor. He was a doctor of obstetrics, and that was good because Louise looked as big as a barn. She had to be seven months gone if not more. I realized that Joey probably hadn't even known she was pregnant. I raised my arm to wave and started to call out to her, but he grabbed my hand and stopped me.

"Don't." He said. "Are you nuts? Don't. What if . . . you don't know."

Little Joey pulled me closer to the building line, out of her sight. He looked terrified, but not the way he had the night Shades was killed. For all his tough guy stance and his rapidly receding hairline, he looked like a very young child who had been caught doing something he knew was horribly wrong. I knew what he was concerned about and I guessed that if I'd given it any thought I wouldn't have tried to call out to Louise, but actually, the odds that she knew what had really happened were astronomically small. Nicky had been a doomed soul since he went back on junk and a dead man since he'd robbed the club, but I doubted if a dozen people on the street knew who'd aced him. Joey's sudden terror fascinated me and I stared into his face as we stood nearly hidden in a doorway. Louise lumbered awkwardly around the corner and out of sight.

"Are you okay now?" I asked when she was gone.

"What? Yeah, I'm fine. I just didn't want you to call the bitch over an' then we gotta listen to some sob story." His hands were still shaking a little and one of the coffees was leaking and had soaked the bottom of the bag.

"Oh," I said. "Yeah, that's what I figured."

We walked around to the store and when we hit the corner Joey looked warily down the street. Louise was almost a full block away by then and was completely indistinct. Her form and movement from that distance reminded me of the permanently mourning black-clad old ladies who prowled the churches, streets, and grocery stores of the neighborhood like some secret sect. Little Joey watched her for a moment, then relaxed, and we walked the other way.

The bottom half of the car service's storefront windows were painted green, and even on a sunny day they filtered the light so that the place always looked smoky and overcast. Days that weren't so sunny, it was already smoky and overcast in there, so the windows made it seem like the middle of the night. On the other hand, in the middle of the night it looked perfect.

It was a beautifully clear morning when Joey and I walked in, and squares of sunshine coming in through the top half of the windows hung like framed prints on the cheap paneling of the back wall, just too high to illuminate the card game or anything else. The guys sitting around Lou's desk greeted me, and the players in the game acknowledged no one, reaching blindly behind themselves for their containers of coffee.

"You're welcome," Joey snarled when Sal took his cup without looking up.

"Fuck you," Sal said absently, studying his cards.

I sat on a corner of Lou's desk and held up my end of a conversation, which swung from politics to sports to carburetors versus fuel injection. We were debating whether they put the dump on Staten

Island because that was where the most open land was, or because it was where white people with jobs lived, when Lou stood up and motioned me to follow him outside.

"Okay," he said, closing the door behind him as we stepped into the street. "This is probably what you're lookin' for." He tossed me a set of keys fastened to a ring with a ridiculously large letter R on it. I could barely get the damn thing in my pocket.

"I'm afraid to ask," I said.

"No," he said, "you didn't do bad today. Don't get spoiled though; it won't always be this good. It's the silver Cutlass down at the end a' the block. You can see it from here."

"What is it, new?"

"Last year's," he said, like that wasn't new to me.

"And when I'm done it goes . . ."

"Back there, or as close as you can get it. You remember the directions?"

"Yeah."

"An' the address?"

"Yeah."

"Good. Just take it easy. No speeding. There shouldn't be any traffic now. I'll see you when you get back." As I started to walk away he said, "Listen. Remember—you don't take any shit from that gorilla nigger."

"Take no shit," I repeated over my shoulder. I still wondered what his problem was with Todd. I walked down the block and let myself into the Cutlass. The alarm was easy enough to find and turn off, but there were two separate kill switches that were a little tricky. Of course I'd die before asking for help, so I spent about twenty minutes screwing around with it before I got underway.

The trip up was clear of traffic and the car rode beautifully. It had a tape deck, but I hadn't brought any tapes so I listened to the radio, switching back and forth between a classic rock station and one that played a lot of rap. I didn't know whose car it was, but I figured the owner was pretty young because the stations were programmed into the radio.

A part of me felt like I was on my way to a picnic, or to visit an old aunt in the country, even though I'd never done that before, and in fact as far as I knew, I had no old aunts in the country. Leaving the city—I supposed because I did it so rarely—tended to lull me into that sort of whitebread middle-American fantasy.

Several times early in the trip I was inexplicably overcome with a sense of dread. I couldn't figure it, but the feeling was real enough that I had to talk myself down from the edge of hysteria more than once. I was embarrassed by it, and got angry with myself, but that didn't fully put it to rest. The truth was that I was on a run—a job—and the little bit of my brain that wasn't reacting like I was on a weekend jaunt was saying that I had no business doing this. It was the feeling of being a child competing with adults. I'd had it before, plenty of times, but not this strongly.

The calming aspect was that my father knew what I was up to and would not have sanctioned anything he perceived to be dangerous. Whatever was going on here was small potatoes. Still, I wanted out as soon as reasonably possible.

Between my prozac-moment moodswings, I spent the ride up thinking about women. I found myself stupidly contrasting Gina and Kathy. The more thought I gave it, the more I realized that I'd never marry Gina and that I really needed to break up with her as soon as possible. On the other hand, if the rest of what was out there was like Kathy, maybe I shouldn't move too quickly. I was actually very fond of Kathy, and it was screwing everything up. Whenever I'd cheated on Gina in the past, I tried to pick girls who were attractive, but vacuous. I never really understood the concept of mistresses, or even a steady girlfriend on the side, though that was what most of the middle-aged guys in the neighborhood seemed to favor. I understood that it was less trouble finding someone when you wanted to go out, but if it came with all the emotional baggage of a relationship, why not just hang out with your wife? I had always looked for girls who could be led easily in conversation and into bed, but that you wouldn't want to see more than once or twice. They were mostly Brooklyn bimbos from other neighborhoods or Manhattan space cadets. Kathy had fooled me. I'd pegged her as a space cadet, and I didn't tip to how sharp she really was until the middle of our date, which was pretty goddamn slow for me. Still, I felt like I couldn't contend with her long term. If Kathy and Gina could be combined, you might get the perfect girl. Of course the perfect girl would tell me to fuck off, so there was no advantage in trying to mind-meld their brains in my basement laboratory.

As I played the Gina/Kathy tennis match in my head, I was interrupted by the image of Louise waddling around that corner, alone. I didn't think I felt quite as fucked-up about seeing her as Joey did, but I certainly didn't feel good. I tried not to think about it, and that worked for a while, but the picture kept coming back to me.

She'd obviously decided to have the kid. I suddenly wondered if her pregnancy could have been what tipped him back into dope. I'd probably never know, but I wanted to talk to her. As far as I knew, she had no family in this country, and I wanted to know how she was getting along and where she'd stay when the baby was born. I'd have to find out if she was still in their old apartment. That was the direction she'd walked in, but it didn't necessarily mean anything.

I felt like I had a sense of purpose then and I couldn't wait to get back so I could look her up. I got off the Thruway and onto Route 9 North, and a little while later I was weaving through the decidedly upscale neighborhood where I'd make my pickup.

When I pulled up in front of the house I stopped at the curb because Lou had, even though the driveway seemed like a quarter-mile hike, and there were no other cars on the block that were parked in the street. I didn't think I'd need the alarm or kill switches.

The doorbell didn't make any noise that I could hear, but about fifteen seconds after I pressed it a very short black guy in jeans and cowboy boots opened the door. He was wearing a corduroy sports jacket over a white shirt. He stared at me, said nothing, and didn't move a muscle.

"I'm here to see Todd," I said.

If he heard or understood me he was doing a great job of hiding it. I could have sworn he was looking right through me at something on the other side of the street.

"I'm supposed to pick up a package from Todd. Tony sent me."

Nothing.

"Todd. That's not his whole name. Tall. Skinny. Are you getting any of this? Is there anyone else I can talk to?"

The short guy closed the door in my face without ever having made eye contact with me. It was as though he'd heard the bell and answered it to find no one there. I stood for a moment trying to decide whether to ring the bell again or walk around to the back of the house, when the door swung back open and Todd was standing behind it.

"Michael, isn't it?" he said in impeccable English. "Please come in."

I stepped into the entryway and Todd closed the door. "I wasn't sure the little guy told you I was here," I said. "I didn't think he understood me."

"Little guy?"

"The guy who answered the door. I was about to start drawing pictures in the dirt with a stick for him."

"Dar speaks English fluently," Todd said, "but he did not tell you were here. I saw the car from the second-floor window and assumed it was you. People don't park on the street here." He smiled at me and I felt like he was being very condescending. Plus he was full of shit. I knew that cowboy midget had told him I was there. I got the impression Todd enjoyed playing games.

"If Dar speaks English fluently, then it must have been someone else who answered the door, because whoever answered it didn't seem to understand what I was saying."

"Everyone in this house speaks English, though they are sometimes very literal. Perhaps you weren't clear enough."

"Perhaps whoever answered the door is an idiot, or just wanted to fuck with me." I kept my voice extremely pleasant, and matched his smile. He looked at me like I'd pissed on the rug.

"You are almost as abrupt as your friend."

"I'm beginning to understand why he feels the way he does," I said.

"This is a changing world. Your boss sees it if his brother doesn't. You must adapt to ... different cultures."

"This is the suburbs of Tarrytown. The only culture is playing tennis badly and wife-swapping. How are you adjusting?"

"I do not play tennis." A swinging door opened from behind him at the end of the entrance hall, and Dar emerged, carrying the knapsack. He walked over to us silently and handed the package to Todd, who sort of hefted it once or twice, and then extended it to me. "Your package," he said.

"Thanks," I said, taking it from him, "but it's not mine any more than it's yours. I guess we're both just hired help."

"I suppose," he said, still smiling. He looked like he was going to say something else but changed his mind. He opened the door for me and extended his hand. I shook it and walked out, deliberately ignoring the driveway and cutting across the lawn back to the car. I hoped

Tim McLoughlin

I had pissed him off at least half as much as he'd gotten to me. Pompous fuck. No wonder Lou didn't like him. He probably cut Lou to shreds.

The exchange with Todd had left me in a foul mood and before I was back on Route 9, I was thinking of quitting again. I didn't want to do this, even for a month. I'd never had any illusions about being a mover and shaker. In fact I hated the idea, but I really felt like a piece-of-shit lackey all of a sudden. I wondered if my father ever got these feelings, and how he handled them if he did. I considered giving my notice after two weeks. That would be long enough to satisfy my old man. I was running down all the arguments I'd give him while I headed back. I just missed the light at the only intersection before the Thruway, and I played with the radio while waiting for it to change.

I heard a throbbing sort of rumble come up behind me. It sounded like a motorcycle, but when I glanced in the rearview mirror I saw it was a car—an old Lincoln. It was green and dated to the mid-'70s, when they made them like battleships. This one had seen better days, if that muffler was any indication.

It pulled up directly in back of me and came to a complete stop with its left directional on. I was in the left lane, but I was going straight ahead. It sat there for all of five seconds, then swung quickly out to the right, passed me, and turned in to the left again at a forty-five degree angle in front of my car.

This wasn't unusual behavior back in the neighborhood from impatient young Guidos in their Iroc-Z's or maybe even the Dadillac, but I was thinking that it was a fairly gutsy maneuver in a beat-up Town Car, when the rear doors swung open. Two black guys jumped out and ran to either side of my car. I threw it into reverse, but a string of other vehicles had now pulled up behind me. I didn't know what to do. Stupidly, I leaned on the horn and made a move to raise my window, but I wasn't all that used to the car and by the time I found the control they were there. The one on my side had a gun. He reached into the car and placed it against my stomach, below the level of the window. With his other hand he lifted mine from the horn. Then he used the control on my side to lower the passenger window. They were moving quickly, but smoothly, as though this was exactly what should occur and they'd rehearsed it a dozen times. The guy on the far side reached in for the knapsack. It was next to me and I put my right hand on top of it as he grabbed a corner. For a second or two we both kept our grip, and I turned my head a little to look at him. He didn't look angry. Behind me I heard car horns honking, distantly, and realized the light must have turned green.

"Let it go, brother."

It came from the one with the gun, and was barely more than a whisper. Then he reached across me with his free hand toward the gearshift. That was when I realized they were going to kill me. The Lincoln would be stolen and they wouldn't much care who got its description or plate number, but if they shot me while I was in drive I'd roll right into their getaway car.

Without looking at either one of them I nailed the accelerator. The car threw itself forward, and the second it moved the gun went off, sounding like a cannon in the confines of the car. I hit the Lincoln and stopped, but I pumped the gas on and off as if trying to rock out of a snowbank, and after ramming it five or six times I moved it enough to open a path. Then I was clear of the intersection and on the highway ramp. I kept the pedal down for as long as I could.

My right side felt numb and I knew I was in trouble, but I was afraid to look for a while. There was a loud rattle coming from the front of the Cutlass and I figured something was pushing against the fan. The right corner of the hood was pushed up a little. It didn't look like much from where I sat, but I was sure it looked like hell from the outside. It would be a beacon for cops and whoever had jumped me, but I slowed down anyway because the fan noise was getting louder and I wanted at least a chance of making it home. After a mile or so I realized I was still clutching the knapsack.

My hands were shaking so badly that I dropped my keys twice trying to open the street door to my building. When I stepped into the hallway I hesitated for a moment, then walked back along the corridor that ran beneath the stairwell. Though the foyer and stairs were well-lighted, the hallway leading back to the basement door had been in a perpetual twilight for as long as I could remember. I hadn't waited long enough for my eyes to adjust to the sudden dimness, so I hit the wall three or four times on the way back. The door to the basement was stuck, as always. Normally all it required was a healthy tug, but I found it nearly impossible now. I pulled as hard as I could, and my side burned as if I were being branded. When it finally swung open I was sure its trademark creak could be heard for miles. I stepped in and attempted to close it quietly behind me.

With the door closed I stood on the upper landing in absolute darkness. The pain in my side felt awful and I began to feel mildly dizzy. Crouching down and leaning my back against the cool, damp concrete wall seemed to help. I closed my eyes and, after a few minutes, the sharpness of the pain ebbed, until it became a vague throbbing over a large part of my upper body. The bleeding seemed to have stopped, but I hadn't been able to bring myself to look at the wound. I stood and walked gingerly down the wooden steps to the basement, pausing on about every other step for a few seconds to listen. The only identifiable sounds were typical old building noises, but that was little comfort in my state of mind. Every creak, or blast of hot air from the furnace, or muffled rush of water through the fossilized plumbing, had me jumping out of my skin. I was sure that either I'd been followed home, or that the people who had jumped me already knew where I lived.

Sunlight filtered in through the two small, dirty windows at street level, high up by the ceiling in the back. I made my way to the boiler, which took up a fair amount of space over in one corner, sitting almost flush against the staircase wall. Almost. As a very young kid I would hide behind it in warm weather, when the heat was off. It was my secret place: the entrance to the Hole in the Wall, where I'd stand shoulder to shoulder with Butch Cassidy and fight off lawmen, or an alley in a small French town from which to ambush Nazis. It was barely a foot wide. The furnace was running now, so just standing there was uncomfortable. I dropped the knapsack on the floor at the opening and pushed it as far as I could with my foot, until it was invisible in the darkness.

Next to the boiler two old army cots were folded up, leaning against the wall. We used to use them when my mother's family stayed with us overnight, but that hadn't happened since she died. They stank of mold and the canvas looked like it might tear under any weight, but the action was surprisingly smooth, and I was able to open one easily. I set it near the furnace, and sat down. The exertion caused another slight wave of dizziness. When it passed, I stretched out. I needed to figure out what to do next. I had to get in touch with my father, but I didn't want to go upstairs and risk being seen by anyone until I knew who had been after me and why. The heat from the furnace felt soothing along my side, but I had difficulty concentrating on what I should do next. Within a few minutes, I drifted off.

I found myself lying on a cold, hard floor. I was in a room too vast and dark to define. Though any dimensions were beyond guessing, I knew there were walls and a roof. I thought it might be the basement of an enormous warehouse, or maybe an old airplane hangar. I could move around, but sluggishly, with the dull ache of having fallen a great distance.

I stood up. As my eyes grew accustomed to the dim light, I could see that I was in a huge cavern. I was surrounded on three sides by walls reaching a hundred feet to a stalactite roof. In front of me the cavern narrowed into a tunnel too long and winding to figure out where it went.

I started walking slowly toward the tunnel, and discovered that the lighted area I'd been standing in traveled with me. I picked up my pace and soon I was jogging. After a few minutes I looked back, but I'd lost sight of the cave completely. The tunnel sloped gently upward and a cool breeze was getting stronger the farther along I moved. I picked up speed. The sound my feet made slapping the stone floor was shocking because I felt nothing. I was conscious of my movement, but I felt as though I wasn't expending any energy. The tunnel angled up more sharply, and again my speed increased. I noticed that the tunnel was getting smaller. I was really moving now; I felt like I was on a motorcycle with no helmet. It was a struggle to keep my head upright. I leaned into it. My arms and legs began pumping like a machine. The tunnel narrowed some more and up ahead I saw rock formations from roof to floor blocking the shrinking passage. I tried to veer around them, but discovered I couldn't steer any more than I could slow down. I hit the first one and it shattered with a sound like a seven-ten split. I didn't feel any pain, but I knew my body couldn't take that kind of a beating. The tunnel was tight—impossibly small now—maybe three feet square. The grade had become almost perfectly vertical. I could not be running. I couldn't even stand. I was flying. Flying face first toward a pinpoint of light directly above me. If I got out into the light before the tunnel closed I knew I would survive.

"You can do it." The voice belonged to Shades.

"Nicky," I screamed, but the rushing air pushed it back down my throat. The walls were so close that they were scraping both my shoulders, my arms were flat along my sides, hands gripping my thighs.

"You can do it."

I couldn't do it. There was one more outcropping of rock just before the opening. I was going too fast. I was a bullet. A stalactite jutted out from the rocks.

You can do it.

I was too close. Too fast. There was no way to dodge it. It was going to impale me. I closed my eyes. It tore into my left side. I screamed.

My father had his hand flat against my chest, holding me down on the cot. I screamed again.

"I know," he said gently, "I know. But he's gotta clean it."

I yelped a few more times before the business of cleaning me up was over, but not as loudly as when I was coming to. As my head cleared and I remembered my predicament, the cave and the stalactite-dodging didn't look half-bad. I recognized the thousand-year-old guy working on me as one of my father's customers, a drinker from Peggy's day shift.

"Dad," I said, "am I all right? How did . . ."

My old man stopped me with a wave of his hand. He shook his head slowly but emphatically and glanced at Methuselah's father, who was finishing taping my side. I shut up.

After I was scrubbed and bandaged, my father ran upstairs, and returned a few minutes later with clean clothes from my room. He helped me out of the mess I had on, and transferred all the shit in my pockets to the new jeans before giving them to me. Then he and the old guy walked me up the stairs and out the rear door of the building. Our super was sitting behind the wheel of his car in the alley. The three of us got in the backseat, me in the middle, and the super pulled away without uttering a word. We only went a couple of blocks and then he was pulling into another driveway, of what looked like a one-family house. As soon as we got out, the super took my rolled ball of bloodstained clothing and drove off. My father held my elbow and helped me up a short flight of stone steps and into a very dark front room.

"Jesus, Georgie," my father said, "turn on a goddamn light."

Georgie either didn't hear what my old man had said or chose to ignore it. He locked the door behind us and led the way through the house and down a flight of stairs. When he did turn on a lamp, we were in a small den in the finished part of the basement. There was a sofa and a chair, a small writing desk, and about a million dusty old books on shelves lining the walls and in piles on the floor. There were two closed doors, and I knew that one of them had to lead to the rest of the basement. My father helped me onto the couch and then sat down on the other end. The old guy went back upstairs, leaving us alone.

My father was very patient, an attitude he affected when I fucked up royally that has always been successful in terrorizing me. He explained that the super had been bringing the trash cans in when he saw blood on the hallway wall. He checked the basement and found me, then ran upstairs to get my father. My old man got hold of Georgie who—no big surprise—was at Peggy's, and they cleaned me up. The super brought his car down the alley, and they packed me off here until they could figure out what to do. That was his story. He smiled, then leaned back and lit a cigarette, waiting for mine.

I took a few shallow breaths, then tried a fairly deep one. I was conscious of the injury, but other than feeling sensitive and achy, the pain had pretty much subsided.

"How bad is this?" I asked.

"Nothing. You got lucky. I could see right away it didn't even go in. That's why I brought you straight to Georgie. Didn't even put a hole in you—just more than grazed you. Just enough to take a little piece outta your side and make you bleed like a stuck pig."

I felt confused. "I thought it was a lot worse than that."

"Cause you were so scared? I guess you're just a fag. You got shot an' it scared you." He took a long drag on his cigarette. "Well? From the top, huh?"

"Okay. From the top." This was the difficult part. Lying to my old man was an art I'd never mastered. He had a fine-tuned bullshit detector, and I was hoping bells wouldn't go off in the middle of my story.

But at some point on the way home, I'd decided to keep the bag. I felt like I'd earned it, almost been killed for it. I was also considering that maybe I'd been set up as a dupe by Tony. Not to be ambushed, necessarily, but he must have known there was something dangerous about the run. I knew my father would never buy that theory, and he'd insist on running straight to Tony with everything, so I made it up as I went along, keeping as close to the truth as possible.

"You know this was my first run alone," I said. "Lou showed me the route Tuesday. It was no problem; I knew where I had to go. I rode up and saw this guy Todd. He gave me the bag. We said a few words and I split. I took the road Lou had showed me back to Ninety-five, but just before the highway I get jumped. A bunch of blacks in an old green Lincoln cut me off at the last big intersection before the highway entrance. I couldn't say whether they'd been following me, I don't know. Tell you the truth, I wasn't paying attention." I stopped talking, surprised at how quickly I got winded.

"Take your time," my father said. "Catch your breath."

I nodded. "Anyway, the car noses me into the curb and two of 'em jump out. They were young. One comes to my side and one comes to the passenger side. They both have guns. The one on my side says something like 'give it up' and the other one reaches for the bag. I made a grab for it without thinking—you know, reflex—and the one on my side popped me—bang—just like that. I lost it. I just looked at my side and the blood. The other one grabbed the bag and they jumped back in their car. I just sat there for a minute, then I realized that they weren't pulling away. They were checking out whatever was in the bag while they were still parked, blocking me in. I got scared, Pop. What if it wasn't what they were expecting? What if they got what they wanted, but were gonna do me anyway?" I paused again, and realized that I *was* scared. My father held out a hand, palm down, and patted the air a few times. I took his cue and continued more slowly.

"I was bleeding all over the fucking place and I thought maybe I was gonna die. So I put it in drive and plowed into them. I hit the front driver's side around the wheel and the Town Car jumped pretty much right out of the way. Then I got on Ninety-five and came straight home. I was dizzy, it really hurt bad. I was afraid to try a hospital because I know what they do with gunshot cases.

"I can't believe they just grazed me. You know I held my side all the way back. I thought I was holding my intestines in, that if I let go they'd come out all over the car and I'd die. I had to get to you, but I didn't want to go upstairs until I knew there were no more surprises waiting for me. Pop, I don't get it. Who did this?"

He closed his eyes and said nothing for a minute. "You sure it was spades in the car?" he asked.

"Dad, what do you think, it was chinks and I got confused? They were spades. Four or five of them."

"There's no reason for it to be anyone on this end. Tony already has the run. This guy Todd is from Africa, right?" I nodded. "What was in the bag?"

I looked at him. "How the hell do I know what was in the bag? Tony told me it wasn't dope, but I figure the odds are decent he's lying."

My father looked surprised. "Why would Tony lie to you?"

"Why not? He saw that I didn't like the idea that it was dope, right after what happened to Nicky and all."

He rolled his eyes. "You're so fuckin' young," he sighed. "I wish I was that young again. Nobody lies to you unless you're worth lying to. Tony couldn't give a fuck you take this job or not. If he says it wasn't dope it's because it wasn't, and because he don't mind letting you know it wasn't. Try to think straight."

"What made you think I'd know what was in the bag?"

"I don't know," he said, shrugging. "Maybe Lou said something."

"He didn't."

"Okay."

Now he was lying. He knew damned well Lou never would have said a word. Which meant he was already thinking I'd looked.

"I better see some people," he said. "Talk this through, you know. I gotta see Tony, maybe even the Old Man. Have a sit down. I want you outta sight."

"I could go to Gina's."

"Brilliant. Everybody in creation knows you're with her. You wanna stay with your uncle in Red Hook?"

"I'd rather get shot again."

"Well, you think about it. Stay here for now; I'll be back in a coupla hours. Georgie will look in on you. What'd you do with the car?"

116

"It's in front of the house, at the pump."

"Gimme the keys."

"In my jacket."

He fished the keys from my jacket pocket and walked to the door. "Don't move around too much, and let Georgie take care of you till I come back. Make him give you soup or somethin'."

"Okay." He left.

It was cold in the den, so I slowly stood and carefully walked across the room to where my jacket was hanging on a hook, took it down, and on impulse checked the front flap pockets. Kathy Popovich's number. I had half-remembered it was there. I went to the phone and tried it. Busy. I got back on the couch, draped my jacket over me for a blanket, and let myself drift off to sleep.

I was awakened by a sound that I thought was running water. It turned out to be Georgie pissing in the toilet with the door open. I was trying to sit up when he emerged from the small bathroom off the den.

"What time is it?"

"Quarter to ten," he croaked. He looked shocked, like he wasn't used to the sound of his own voice.

I was stiff as hell. Sleeping on a Flintstone-era couch will do that, I guessed. My side hurt again. The dressing still looked clean so I figured I hadn't bled anymore.

"Quarter to ten at night?"

"Yeah."

There was a half-empty bottle of Fleischman's and an empty glass on the desk next to his chair, and a large paperback lay open, face down, by the phone. His eyes were a bit glassy, which was surprising. Georgie was one of those pensioners who virtually lived in the neighborhood bar, but he wasn't a big drinker. He'd nurse four or five small glasses of beer over an eight-hour day, and usually leave with the other old-timers in the early evening, when the younger crowd rolled in. He had hung around well into the night and gotten trashed on occasion, but probably not more than twice in the months since I'd begun frequenting Peggy's.

"Where's my father? Did he call?"

"No." Georgie shook his head emphatically. He seemed nervous as hell, and I wondered if that was the reason he was into the rye. He'd probably been rattled enough at having to accompany my father to get me, and I was sure that he wanted no part of babysitting me alone. I didn't blame him.

"What time did he leave?" I asked.

"About four."

"That's too long, Georgie. Where was he going? Did he say?"

"No, but he said he'd be back by dinner and to watch you. It's way past dinner and I been watchin'; but Mike, I haven't had a touch all day except for a drop or two here," he nodded at the bottle, "and I'm kind of parched. I don't like to drink at home. A man who drinks at home alone has a problem, you know." He nodded somberly.

I didn't think he needed to get to a bar all that badly. He was looking to distance himself from me, and was too decent or too scared to ask me to leave. Although I understood completely, it still made me feel like I had plague.

"Go on out, Georgie, I'm okay. I'll be fine. Does your front door lock without a key?"

"Yes."

"I'll pull it closed behind me. Where are we anyway?"

"Seventy-second and Tenth. You know—I could stay a little longer."

His eyes were begging me not to ask. "Go," I said. "I'll let myself out. But Georgie—one thing—you have no idea where I am."

He made a twisting gesture with his hand in front of his lips, then turned and hobbled out. I figured his vow was good for a few drinks, which, coupled with the walk to Peggy's—if he even went there—gave me about an hour to clear out of his place. I stood up quickly and a gentle internal tug at my side reminded me not to be stupid.

It dawned on me abruptly that the whole idea of my working for Tony had been insane. What the hell did I think I was doing? I'd been shot, and quite frankly I was still terrified. Then when I had the chance to tell my father about the bag, and turn it over to Tony, I decided to play games instead and dig myself in deeper. I was turning into Nicky, and I didn't even get to become a junkie first.

I tried Kathy Popovich's number again. It rang twice, someone picked up, and a guy's voice said hello. I slammed the receiver down so hard fire shot up my right side and tears welled in my eyes. What was wrong with me? I hardly knew this girl and I was furious with her for being with someone when I needed her. This was not good. I knew I didn't have the luxury of getting this fucked-up, so I tried to forget it and calm myself down.

I picked up Georgie's book from the desk and looked at it. It was called *Touch of the Poet,* but it wasn't poetry. It looked like a play, complete with stage directions. It was an old book, and well-thumbed through, with notes in pencil scribbled along the margins. I wondered if Georgie had done that, or if he'd bought the book used. I looked at a few of the other books on the shelves nearest the desk, and realized that they were all plays. There were some famous names that I knew, or titles that had been made into movies, but most of them I'd never heard of. There was also a stack of typing paper on the desk, but I didn't see a typewriter anywhere. Maybe Georgie was really Shakespeare. He was about the right age.

I put the book down, picked up the phone again, and called Gina. I didn't want to do it, but when I ran down my options it didn't take long for me to see that I had little choice. She gave me a song and dance about not hearing from me for so long, but I cut her short. I told her that something was up and I'd be coming by to stay for a while. She got all bubbly then, and started in with lots of playing-house scenarios. She said she'd fix a room for me upstairs. That apartment. That apartment was waiting for me. It gave me chills. I told her it would be fine. After we hung up, I stole a drink out of Georgie's bottle. It felt great going down, but it kind of exploded in my stomach and I got dizzy. I realized I hadn't eaten since early in the morning.

I was worried about my father. He should have been back by now. I didn't know if he'd gone straight to Lou or Tony, or even the Old Man, or if he'd had some other plan in mind. Whatever he was doing probably wasn't going well or he would have come back or called. He was right about everyone knowing about me and Gina, but I couldn't think of anything else, and besides, I wanted to be someplace where he could find me.

I turned out the light in the den and slowly pulled myself up the stairs with the help of Georgie's rickety handrail. I made my way through the musty house to the front door. When I opened it, Lou was coming up the steps.

Chapter 15

We both stopped and looked at each other. I couldn't begin to guess how he'd found out I was there. There certainly hadn't been enough time for Georgie to have spilled his guts. Looking at Lou then, I thought about the night with Shades. I knew Lou had only been doing what he thought he had to, but what was he thinking about tonight? Was I still an employee, or had I become another problem to be handled?

"Got Edward in the car?"

"Huh?"

"Nothing. What are you doing here, Lou?"

"I could ask you the same thing. You're a little late, Mikey."

"Yeah, well, shit happens. You left a few details out of the fucking job description."

"I heard. Get in the car."

"Not sure I should."

"What the hell does that mean?"

"It means I don't know who to trust anymore. Who are my friends? I'm a little edgy right now. Two days ago I couldn't believe you were handing me cash for a bullshit job like this. Now it kind of makes sense. Either the run is dangerous enough to warrant the pay, or I got set up for a fall. So tell me, Lou; who are my friends?"

"Don't be fuckin' stupid," Lou said. "How do you think I found you? Your father called Tony an' tole him where you were. Think about that. You're becoming goddamn paranoid."

I pulled the front door closed while I thought about it. It made sense, actually. Nobody knew I was there except Georgie, my father, and the super.

"Why'd my old man call Tony?" I asked, as Lou took my arm and helped me down the steps.

"Well, that's one a' the things we gotta talk about," he said, holding the car door open for me. I seemed to have gotten used to new cars; I didn't know if that was good or bad.

"What's up with my father? I know something's doing."

"He's in jail," Lou said. He started the Caddy.

"Jail?"

"Jail. You know. Cops, arrest, jail. Jail."

"Lou, tell me. Say words. What happened?"

"You had a car. The one I gave you the keys to this morning. The way that works is, there's some guys around. Guys that—you know—get behind a little. Not much; a nickel here, a dime there. But it all adds up. And when the shys can't collect, they come to us to, like, negotiate. So we work out deals, if the money ain't too much. Every now an' then we borrow a car, for some kinda run. If the run goes okay the car gets put back, an' it's no harm done. But if something gets fucked, then the guy calls the car in stolen an' everybody's off the hook."

"Except the driver," I said.

"What?"

"Except the driver. You're going to tell me somebody reported the gray Cutlass stolen, right?"

"We hadda go that way Mike, by four o'clock."

"Jesus Christ." I was practically screaming. "My old man climbs behind the wheel of a car for the first time in about four years and he gets locked up. What are you going to do? Can I see him? Is that where we're going?"

"No. Calm down. You can't see him till tomorrow. Arrest to arraignment is at least twenty-four hours. If we pull any strings, everybody ties him into some operation an' then they watch him afterwards for a million fuckin' years. If they think he's just some jerk off, no offense, we got a better chance a' gettin' him out right away an' everything dropped."

No offense. I'd been shot and my father was probably eating baloney-and-cheese sandwiches with a Jamaican crack posse. Plus, I still didn't know where Lou was taking me. "No offense," I said. "None at all. Where are we going?"

"We're gonna see Tony. He says he needs to talk to you."

"I'll talk to Tony when my father is out and standing next to me." I leaned back and closed my eyes.

"Hey, I like you Mike, an' I know you're ragged out cause a' what happened—but this is for real. You'll talk to Tony now. You're walking a line here. One side is you're calm, in control. You think on your feet. Tony seen that in you. He likes it. The other side is you're an arrogant little fuck. I see that in you an' I don't like it. You better grow out of it before Tony ever sees it in you. You'll do a lot better in the long run."

I didn't say anything, mostly because I didn't know what to say. I considered the possibility that maybe I was an arrogant little fuck. What if I was? It didn't change the fact that I'd been shot or that my father was in jail. Lou was right about one thing, though: I was walking a line here. I could be—had to be—pissed off with Tony, but—from the way Lou acted, anyway—refusing to talk to him at all until he got my father out would be an unacceptable way to behave. I glanced over at Lou. How did he know where that line fell? Was there a manual or something that everyone in the neighborhood except me had been issued? It often seemed that way. I wished to hell I could talk to my old man. He would know how to play this. He'd always told me to shut up and think before I opened my mouth, so I practiced for the rest of the ride to Tony's house in Mill Basin.

My father had been locked-up before, but not for a good many years. I remember my mother dressing me in my Easter suit when I was very young and dragging me down to criminal court so we could stand teary-eyed in the front row, while some judge who looked seven feet tall arraigned him ominously and then met my mother's gaze and "duly noted that the defendant's family is present in court." Then he cut my father loose and that was the end of it. I'm sure there was a fine or something, but I never did find out. My father hadn't been arrested since long before my mother died, and now it occurred to me again how truly alone he and I were without her.

His previous arrests had always been for gambling or fighting. This was the first time he'd been charged with stealing something, and I wasn't sure that they'd let him walk. Another thought came to me as the Caddy slid quietly along the Belt Parkway, past the skeleton of the parachute jump. I remembered the contempt my father had displayed for the other defendants, either in the pens or in open court. He spoke as though he had nothing to do with them, as though he were there for some reason other than having been arrested.

"They're fuckin' animals," he told me one night when he arrived home drunk from a matinee court appearance. "Strong young men, not a thing wrong with 'em, and they won't work. Every guy in that pen with me had a welfare card. Every fuckin' one. I was the only one in there with a job. They steal money from your taxes then pop an old lady for her social security. I don't want you thinking it's cause they're black or P.R.s," he said, pointing at me. "You got plenny a' guys like Chuckie out there that ain't afraid a' work. But these fuckin' bums, they make the rest of 'em look bad.

"When my father couldn't get work after the war—when we first got here—you know what he did? He shined goddamn shoes. He was in his thirties with a family an' he shined goddamn shoes cause he wouldn't go on home relief. He went everyday to Wall Street an' stayed there ten, eleven hours till he made enough he could go home. The only thing, he was embarrassed to walk through the neighborhood with the box. I'd haveta meet him by the Rex—I was maybe ten years old—an' carry the box the six or seven blocks home. In the morning I'd carry it back there an' that's where he'd take it from me. Do you understand that kind of pride? Of not takin' charity? Of knowing you're worth something?"

Yes, I'd said at the time. The story impressed me fiercely. I didn't get some of what he was telling me, but I never forgot how important it all seemed.

From the day that he faked his injury and got out on three-quarters disability, I felt that I needed to know how that was different from the defendants my father despised for ripping off society. I never asked. My old man could always explain everything he did, but in the back of my mind I suspected there was no acceptable explanation for this, and, more importantly, I was afraid that to even ask would put a wall between us where one had never existed.

"What'd you do, fall asleep?" Lou asked as we drove off the King's Plaza exit ramp.

"No. Just thinking. I hope my old man's okay."

"Your father's a fuckin' bull. Don't worry about anything."

We moved through a series of winding, quiet streets lined on both sides by impressive detached houses that would have seemed more appropriate someplace wealthy like Long Island or Connecticut. They might as well have been in Long Island or Connecticut, I figured, because it took almost as long to get around to Mill Basin, out on the ass-end of Brooklyn. Lou made a right down a deserted-looking block and stopped in front of a fieldstone house with the kind of elaborate wrought iron designs over the windows that are supposed to fool you into thinking they're decorative instead of protective. The place was set far back on the building lot. It looked more like a fort than a residence. Lou parked in the driveway and we got out. I looked as far as I could down the street in the dark.

"Dead end block?" I asked.

"Jesus, don't let Tony hear you say that. He almos' took my fuckin' head off once I called it that. He says it's a cul-de-sac."

"You serious?" I asked. Lou shrugged. "I'll try to remember."

We went to the door and Lou pressed a series of numbers on a keypad over the lock. When a beep sounded, he inserted a regular key and opened the door.

The entryway and foyer looked like a catering hall or a funeral home—glass and red drapes, dark wood, and marble. Lots of pieces of furniture that serve no purpose but to stand against a wall. All in all, about what I expected. I'd never met Tony's family. I knew he was married and had a couple of kids, but the house was as quiet as Saint Rosalie's used to be when I lit the candles before the seven a.m. mass back in my altarboy days. The silence of the church had terrified me back then, and I felt a similar panic growing now as we walked down the heavily carpeted stairs. Tony was behind the bar in a finished basement that would have made a very upscale after-hours. Besides the bar, which had a wet sink, there was a regulation-size pool table and an art deco–style jukebox in the corner. Tony came around the bar quickly with both hands extended and a serious look on his face. I put my right hand halfway out in front of me, not sure whether I'd be shaking his or defending myself. When he got near me I thought I was going to be hugged, but what he did was grab both my shoulders firmly and look directly into my eyes.

"Are you all right?" he asked. "How's your side?"

"Okay," I said. "A little raw. Doesn't feel like much anymore."

"Good. Very good. I was concerned."

"Thank you," I said, knowing that was an inappropriate response and wishing again for the neighborhood manual.

"Your old man, he's okay; I want you to know that. We got someone at central booking looking out for him."

"That's good to know. I was worried."

"Of course you were worried. He's your father. Tomorrow this time he'll be home. Around noon, he sees the judge and they should cut him loose then. The next day, the owner of the car goes to the D.A. and explains that he forgot he loaned it to your father. Charges dropped—case closed. But enough of that. I'm wondering what kind of scumbag you must think I am that I send you on a run where you get hijacked. Am I right?"

"No," I said instinctively. "I mean, I want to know what's going on and all, you know, but I don't think you pulled anything on me."

"Why? Why wouldn't I do it?"

"Why wouldn't you hijack your own stuff?" I was stalling.

"Why wouldn't I set you up?"

I did not know what answer he was looking for and I got the impression that this was somehow very important. I looked at Lou, but he was concentrating intensely on the pattern cut into his crystal whiskey glass.

"My father," I said.

Tony started to speak, then stopped, then began again. "You're a man. You and your father are two different people. You can't count on a thing like that."

"I can't count on fucking up and you covering it because of my father, but I can count on not being set up. Don't you believe I don't think you did it?"

"I know you don't think I did it. I just wanted to know why. At least you didn't feed me any bullshit about being too nice a guy to do something like that, which by the way, I am." Lou stopped studying his drink and rolled his eyes. "Cut it out," Tony said without turning toward him, and Lou stiffened behind the bar. "Make Mikey a drink."

"No drink," I said. "I'm starving, and I still don't feel a hundred percent."

"Okay. Lou'll get you something on the way home. You should be there tomorrow when they arraign your father. It looks better—in case the judge is a prick—that you got family there."

I was totally lost. It didn't seem possible to me that Tony wasn't going to ask me about the package, or at least about what had happened to me, yet it felt like he was concluding our meeting.

"I was going down there anyway, but thanks. Tony, don't you want to hear about this morning?"

"Did you set it up and steal the bag?"

"No!" I said quickly.

"Do you know what was in there?"

"No."

"All right. Go home. Your father gave enough on the phone. Whatever else we have to talk about can wait till he's with you."

"I want to know what's going to happen, and why things went down this way."

"So do I," he said tonelessly. "Good night, Mikey."

"Good night, Tony," I said.

He took a few steps toward the stairs, then turned, walked back over to me, and shook my hand. Then he went upstairs without saying good night, good-bye, or anything else to Lou.

"Let's hit the road," Lou said. He was scowling and looking up the empty stairwell. At times like that I felt really bad for Lou. He was like a large child, or a big friendly dog that keeps waiting for the pat on the head that never comes.

On the way home we stopped at Miller's Diner on New Utrecht, and Lou ran in and brought back two large bags of hot food. When he dropped me off, he said he was sorry about my father. He had the same look of embarrassment that he'd exhibited after Shades' death. I assumed it was because I'd just seen Tony snub him. I said good night and, balancing both bags on one arm, let myself in my building.

The apartment looked the same. I couldn't tell if someone had ransacked it or brought a maid in to clean it up. I unpacked the stuff from Miller's, and though it was standard diner fare, it tasted like the best food I'd ever had. I was ravenous, and by the time I finished I'd eaten almost everything Lou bought, which seemed to be two full meals. I called Gina then, though it was almost two in the morning, and told her I wouldn't be staying upstairs. She reacted with the calm, ladylike acceptance that I had expected. When I could make myself heard over the screaming I told her about my father being arrested, that we would have to go down there in the morning, and to dress appropriately. Then I hung up and went to bed, setting the alarm for ten o'clock so I wouldn't sleep for a week.

Chapter 16

I woke with a start at eight in the morning, my body clock touched off by the fear that I'd miss the arraignment. I called Gina and woke her up, then had some cereal and started to get ready. I showered, and even though I'd shaved two days before I did it again, wanting to appear as young and concerned as possible. Then I began to get dressed. As much as I'd always tormented Gina for taking three days to get ready to go out, I found that I absolutely couldn't figure out what to wear to court. I must have changed my clothes a dozen times. For work and school I dressed the same: jeans, sneakers, a t-shirt, or a work shirt. That was it, day-in–day-out, all year round, and it constituted ninety percent of my wardrobe. The rest of my stuff was more fancy, but it was evening wear—club clothes—and definitely not for standing in front of a judge.

I did a sort of mix-and-match, but that didn't work very well. I tried jeans with some of my nightclubbing shirts and jackets, but I looked like the drug dealer in a Queens disco. Dress slacks with a work shirt looked even worse. In desperation I tried my dress pants with some of my father's shirts. It made me look like him. He had half a room full of genuinely expensive clothing, and everything I put on made me look like I should be hanging out at the track. I finally decided on jeans, a plain white shirt, and my father's most conservative gray sports jacket. I checked myself out in the full-length mirror on the inside of his closet door. I looked like a car service driver trying to dress up.

I collected wallet and keys, money, and all my sundries, and went downstairs. My side was still sore, but considering the time frame, I felt surprisingly good. I'd showered around the bandage, which was holding nicely, and I seemed able to stretch a little more than the previous evening.

It took a few minutes for me to remember where I'd left the car, and when I got there and started it I found that I needed gas. I treated myself to the luxury of that endangered species, the full-service gas station. I didn't want to compound my bumpkin appearance by reeking of Texaco. My father and I used to try to guess what countries the gas jockeys came from, but times had changed. As I hovered over the guy who was filling my tank it occurred to me that I couldn't even place the continent anymore. I paid him and he grunted at me. I grunted back and he walked off, seemingly satisfied. I could never figure out whether I was being told to have a nice day, or to go fuck myself.

Leaving the gas station, I made good time up Sixty-fifth Street, and I was in front of Gina's house by ten-fifteen. I honked twice and a moment later she came to the window and waved, then disappeared. I waited fifteen minutes before storming up the stoop and ringing the bell. She answered the door in jeans under a robe, bare feet, and some sort of sack on her head that I assumed covered curlers.

"What?" she said. "I'm getting ready."

"Getting ready? I told you to be ready at ten. I didn't get here till a quarter after and now it's half-past. You look like you just woke up."

"I been getting ready since eight-thirty. You can ask my mother. You know it takes me a while, but you said to look good. Good takes time."

"We're going to court. I said to look appropriate."

"Appropriate means good. Come in. Have some coffee. I'll be ready in a couple of minutes."

"You'll be ready in a half hour, if I'm lucky. But I'm leaving then with or without you. I'll wait in the car."

"Didn't you ever have a hard time figuring out what to wear?" she asked.

"No. Never."

"Well," she shrugged, "it's different for guys. You sure you don't want to come in?"

"Your mother's home, right?"

"In the kitchen." She sighed.

"I'll wait in the car."

"Suit yourself."

She stood up on her toes and gave me a quick kiss. Then I told her again about the time and went to go sit in the car.

The entire debate about getting ready was theatre, and we both knew it. Lou had told me that my father would be arraigned between noon and one p.m. I told Gina to be ready by ten so that she would be ready by eleven-fifteen, and we could get downtown and park by eleven forty-five. This had gone on for years and only required occasional adjustment when Gina became used to the time frame and, of course, exceeded it. That hadn't happened in a while, and I was fairly confident I still had a decent cushion.

I sat for the half hour, and then ten minutes past the time I'd promised, and like clockwork, Gina emerged. Up to that point it hadn't occurred to me that there was any real possibility of us being late for court or of missing my father entirely. I hadn't counted on Gina's concept of appropriate.

Her outfit, from head to toe, was white. She wore jeans tight enough to guarantee that she would have to ride slouched at a forty-five-degree angle in the car. They tapered down to a pair of spiked heels which looked from that distance higher than her usual four inches. A leather cowboy jacket, complete with fringes, covered a cotton blouse with the top three buttons open. Her hair, which was light brown frosted to blonde at the edges, was done up like she played bass for Motley Crue. She had a white leather purse almost large enough to hold a stick of gum.

The thought occurred to me that I had an axe in the trunk and that she probably couldn't run very fast with those heels. It wasn't a productive thought, but it cheered me up.

The temptation to give in to my temper and go off was overwhelming, but I had my father and the larger picture to consider. The important thing was to keep my priorities straight for now. What goes around comes around, I reminded myself, and this scene could always be played out later at a higher volume, or saved until the next time I needed a moral ace in the hole. I got out of the car and walked over to the stoop while Gina was tottering down the steps.

"Listen to me," I said calmly. "Turn around and go back inside. Get rid of this costume and put on people clothes. Don't complain and don't argue because there isn't any time. You have ten minutes, for real. It would be better if you were with me, but if you aren't ready I'm going without you. No heels. Conservative. Ask your mother what it means."

I went back to the car, got in, and started the engine. Gina hobbled back up the steps slowly, pausing twice to give me her best wounded fawn look. If I missed seeing my father, I thought, that purse had better contain a subway token.

As I supposed was true of most relationships, Gina and I tested each other almost constantly to see where limits fell on a variety of subjects. I put up with the dressing ritual, the shopping pilgrimages, and having my balls broken about getting married. She put up with my mostly not wanting to be around. But her failure to see what was wrong with her outfit, while not necessarily her fault, was still her responsibility. She knew she'd hit a nerve, so—no big surprise—she managed to change and reappear in ten minutes, earth time.

Her mother came to the door with her, smiled, and waved to me. It was like she was showing off what she'd accomplished. I stared straight ahead and didn't acknowledge her. Gina was pouting. She kissed her mother, then actually looked both ways up and down the block before going quickly down the steps and practically sprinting to the car. She got in and closed the door. We drove off with her mother still standing on the stoop like an idiot, waving to us as if we were leaving for Europe.

"You look good," I said after a few minutes.

"I look like a fucking child," she said.

"Gina," I said in my most placating tone, "you're being silly." That was what I usually told her when she was upset about something and I couldn't rationally talk her out of it because she was right. I patted her leg and made whatever soothing noises came to mind. In fact, she looked quite adolescent. Her frame was tiny and her mother had done a good job of dressing her down and scrubbing the war paint off her face. Her hair was moussed or something so that it was flat enough to look normal, but when I touched it, the sensation was like she'd dipped her head in lucite.

Her motif was all blue now, except for the white capezios. She wore jeans and an aqua sweater under a navy blazer that must have belonged to her mother. I thought about us driving around—me in my father's jacket, her in her mother's—in my ancient car. It made me shudder.

"What's the matter?" Gina asked. "You cold?"

"No. Nothing. I'm not cold. Is that your mother's jacket?"

"Yeah. I look like I'm in Catholic school."

"Don't be stupid. You look good. The look is professional, businesslike." She looked like she was in Catholic school. Except for the fact that she had a really decent set of tits, Gina could have passed for fourteen. I remembered fourteen-year-olds with tits that big, but they were always the heavier, chunky girls with short hair; the ones you knew would develop into dykes or baby factories. When they turned about sixteen they tended to attract the attention of guys who drove tow trucks.

Gina looked different. She'd been slim since the day I met her. My father said her hips were too narrow. He told me she'd have trouble having kids, that she wasn't a breeder. He was at least half full of shit, because my mother was built the same way. A frame like a white woman, he called it. What the hell does a white woman know about breeding, he'd ask my mother. Just enough, she'd tell him, ruffling my hair. I was a little kid back then, six or maybe eight, and I didn't have the slightest idea what they were talking about. I knew it involved me, though, and that my mother was in some way proud. Just enough, I'd echo, stepping out from under her hand and strutting over to my father. The two of them would laugh like hell.

"Just enough," I said out loud.

"What?" Gina asked.

"Nothing."

I turned the radio on. CBS-FM, the oldies station, was playing *Love Potion #9* by the Clovers, and I sang along. It was one of my father's favorites. I hadn't given him much thought all morning, but I found myself worrying again as we drove downtown. Tony had assured me that he was being looked after and I had no reason to doubt that. Also, it wasn't like this was his first trip through the system. Still, he wasn't a kid anymore, except in his own mind, and that troubled me.

The Gowanus was under construction as it had been for most of every year since just after it was built in the '50s. Traffic looked a little too risky, even at that hour, so I decided to take the streets. Within fifteen or twenty blocks we'd moved out of the protective invisible dome that everyone mentally drops over their neighborhood, and into the real world. I stayed under the highway, and we slid quickly from Bay Ridge to Sunset Park to that nameless industrial area that none of the adjoining neighborhoods—especially Park Slope—was willing to claim.

We went around the bend where Third Avenue runs into Hamilton, and stopped for the light at the drawbridge on Ninth Street. I looked across into Red Hook and thought about my mother's family. I wondered if I should stop off and tell them my father had gotten locked up, but decided we couldn't spare the time.

"Can I change this?" Gina asked, turning the dial without waiting for a response. She passed static and classical music and stopped at rap. I made a right turn onto Clinton Street, and before the end of the song we were downtown.

I parked in a municipal lot on Atlantic Avenue and we walked the block and a half to the courthouse. Along the way I tried to coach Gina on the right facial expressions and gestures of concern.

"What's the big deal?" she asked. "He's been through this before."

"Yeah, but now they think he stole a car. I'm afraid it's more serious."

"He didn't steal anything. He doesn't even drive. What was he doing in the car?"

"Later. I'll give you the whole story later. Just try to look worried. And if the subject comes up, you're his daughter—my sister. Got it?"

"Why can't I be your wife if we're pretending?"

Because you look fifteen, I said to myself. "Because it looks more like he's needed if there are two kids," I said out loud.

When we turned the corner onto Schermerhorn Street I stopped dead and just stared. There was a line of at least two hundred people standing more or less single file, waiting to enter the building.

"Jesus." I looked at my watch. It was eleven-fifty. "I think we're in trouble here." I took Gina's arm and hurried to join the line ahead of a busload of people coming from the opposite corner.

Although it looked like a real nightmare, the line moved quickly. I was afraid it would be like the Department of Motor Vehicles, where you had to bring food and a change of clothes to get anything accomplished. Once we cleared the doorway it became obvious why the line was proceeding so rapidly. Inside the lobby it split into four lines created by police barricades. Each line fed a metal detector manned by two court officers who searched bags and packages, and apparently the contents of people's pockets. I did a quick mental inventory of my possessions and decided I'd be all right.

The lobby of the courthouse was huge, and impressive in that sad way that many government buildings are. It was easy to see that it had once been an elaborate, almost churchlike structure. Marble columns, dark wood, and thirty-foot-high ceilings all must have created the air of reverence that the architect had in mind for a court. Time and a downtown Brooklyn location could rob the air of reverence from the Sistine Chapel, and the courthouse hadn't fared any better. The marble columns were filthy above a height of ten feet, apparently the highest the janitors could reach. Parts of the mahogany woodwork had been painted over, almost randomly, in white and that horrible pale public-school green. There was graffiti on a wall under a plaque that read: No Writing Graffitties On This Wall. Graffitties? I wondered if they got inmates to make up the signs or if that was a joke.

Within ten minutes we were close enough to the front of the line that I could hear the bored litany of the officer working the metal detector. He slid an empty tray across the table next to the machine.

"Put all metal objects in the tray. Anything made of metal. Keys, coins, cigarette lighters. Anything made of metal."

Occasionally, the machine would beep as someone walked through. The guard would send them back out and have them remove more items. One guy had to take his belt off. We'd been channeled into the last line on the left. Behind the guy who was searching people, two other guards sat in chairs against the wall. One was casually watching the crowd. The other was hidden behind an open newspaper.

Between the four lines there must have been five hundred people in the lobby, and as far as I could tell the line out in the street was as long as it had been when we arrived. I couldn't imagine how this many people came here everyday and anything got done. In terms of numbers, it was worse than the DMV.

"Next. Let's go. Everything metal goes in the box. Coins, keys, change, lighters."

I stepped forward and started emptying my pockets into the tray. I left my wallet in my back pocket because there was nothing in it that should have set the unit off. When I had finished dumping the contents of both front pockets into the tray I took a step toward the machine.

"Hold it," the court officer said, a little more loudly than I thought necessary. I stopped. He reached into the tray and picked out the hundred or so dollars that I'd tossed in, folded in half, along with my keys and change.

"Is this metal?" he said. "This isn't metal. Put the paper away."

He handed me the money and I put it in my pocket. He waved me through the machine. I stepped in and stopped for a second, then stepped on through. The unit beeped.

"Back out. Step back out," the officer said, clearly annoyed. I did.

"Do you have anything else made of metal?"

"No," I said.

"Then step through again and don't stop this time. C'mon."

I stepped straight through the machine. It didn't beep.

"Take your stuff," the officer said, "and step out past the barricade."

More police barricades were set up behind the metal detectors, running between the marble columns. It gave the people searching a rectangle-shaped area of about fifty-by-a-hundred feet. There was an opening at the far right corner where people funneled out after being searched. Some walked away and some waited just on the other side of the barrier, presumably for people who were still on line.

I started taking my property from the tray, but very slowly, so that Gina would have time to get through the machine before I was finished.

"Hold it. Put your bag on the table and wait there, honey," the guard told Gina. I realized that I should have let her go through ahead of me.

"My bag? Why?"

"Because I gotta search it. Everybody gets—Hey!" He turned to me. "You didn't take your stuff yet? Let's go. Take it and get past the barricade."

"I'm waiting for her," I said, indicating Gina. "We're together. I'm looking for . . ."

"I don't care why you're here. Information is Room 502. Now step past the barricade."

"Yeah, all right," I said, getting annoyed myself now. I pocketed the rest of my change. "I'm just waiting for her."

"Wait over there."

"I want to wait here. We're together."

"Lou," he called, turning his back to me and taking Gina's bag off the table.

The officer who'd been watching the crowd stood and walked over to me. He was older than the one who was searching, and slimmer. Their dispositions, however, were consistent.

"You have your stuff?" he asked.

"Yeah."

"Then step out. Now."

"I'm waiting for her," I said. The guy at the machine was going through Gina's bag, and she was still standing on the other side of the unit.

"Oh, I see. I didn't understand," he said very loudly. "You're waiting for her. Hey Vinny," he called to the guy reading the paper. "He's waiting for the girl. That's why he can stand anywhere he wants and he don't have to listen to us."

"Makes sense to me," the guy in the chair said. The newspaper never moved.

"Listen Mario," the one in front of me said, lowering his voice to a whisper. "Take a good look around you."

He was holding a small handscanner that looked like a metal coat hanger with a plastic base. He ran it over me as he spoke.

"Take a look at the lines. Look at the complexion of the crowd."

The scanner issued a shrill beep as it passed over my belt buckle.

"You're the only white guy here," he continued. "That means you're the only guy I can fuck up and nobody in this city will give a shit. And you're gonna be the one who breaks my balls?"

He jabbed me suddenly—sharply—right in the gut with the edge of the device, and just as quickly went back to scanning it over me. I leaned forward a few inches, but made a serious effort not to double over. No one, it seemed, not even Gina, had seen anything. I looked at the crowd and realized that Gina and I were in fact almost the only white people in the mobbed lobby. I looked back at the guard. His eyes had a glint to them that I'd seen before. It was the look of kids sitting on the stoop all summer, with too many ninety-degree days in a row. The look just before they went to break some car windows or pitch a cat off a roof.

I sucked a little air back into my lungs. "I'll wait past the barricades," I said.

"Good," he said, though he looked a little disappointed.

"He gone?" the one searching called over his shoulder, still not waving Gina through the machine.

"Yeah Tim," the one who'd jabbed me said as I walked off. "Got another convert."

What a miserable fucking way to make a living, I thought, rubbing my stomach. I leaned against the barricade and Gina came out in a minute or so.

"What were you talking to the guards about?" she asked.

"Sports. They wanted to know how the Giants did the other day."

"Oh."

After asking six people and getting six different answers, the blind guy who worked the newsstand finally told me which courtroom arraignments were being held in.

I hadn't been down there in years, but my memories of the place were vivid, and they hung in my mind in sharp contrast to the scenes around me. Everything had always seemed quiet and somber, with small groups of people in cavernous chambers.

The arraignment courtroom we walked into looked like a subway platform at rush hour. There were no seats available on the long wooden pews, and a couple-of-dozen people stood against the wall in the back and down both sides of the room. The flurry of activity surrounding the judge's bench was nonstop. Court officers, police, and lawyer-types dashed around the area in front of the rail like it was a giant ant farm. The officer standing in front of the bench called names in a loud, clear voice, but as soon as the prisoner walked out everything was done so quickly and quietly that I couldn't hear a word of what was going on. The judge was a small, uncomfortable-looking bald man in a light blue suit who seemed to be trying to take directions from everyone at the same time. The only voice I could make out above the others was that of one lawyer who kept whining, "But judge, but judge." I hoped that wouldn't be my father's attorney.

Gina and I stood in the back of the room for about five minutes. During that time I counted ten prisoners brought out and arraigned. Not once did I hear anyone ask if family was present, and I didn't see any family rush up for anyone. None of this seemed to matter, because out of the ten that we watched, nine were released on the spot and walked out of the courtroom. With those sort of odds I didn't think it could look too bad for my old man.

Heart of the Old Country

A tiny Spanish guy, no more than five feet tall, was brought out with no shoes on. I figured that meant that he'd been arrested at home. Two young women, one in the second row and one in the middle of the room, stood and walked to the rail. When they saw each other they started screaming and swinging wildly, slapping and scratching. The cops and court officers were on them in a second, and had them separated and out the door in about a minute. I took Gina's arm and led her up front to the seat vacated by the woman closest to the rail. In spite of some dirty looks we both managed to fit into the spot. From there I could hear some of the proceedings.

The lawyer for the little guy was telling the judge that one of the women was the man's wife and the other was his girlfriend. They lived in the same apartment house, and whenever they saw each other there was an immediate and furious fight. Someone always calls the police, the lawyer said, and poor Mr. Martinez winds up getting arrested. He also said that his client had had his shoes stolen while in the holding pen. The judge paroled him and the lawyer told him to wait in the front row for something. He walked past the rail and into the courtroom in his socks and sat directly in front of me. At least he was short.

The officer in front of the bench called two defendants with the same last name, and a pair of blacks who looked like bookends emerged from the steel door of the holding pens. Before the door swung closed behind them, I had a couple-of-seconds–worth of view into the pen area. That was when I saw my father. He was leaning against something, practically in the doorway, which must have meant that he was next. He was smoking a cigarette, and no one had stolen his shoes. I'd been walking around with a knot in my stomach and a tightness in my chest, and I hadn't known it until I saw him and felt the ache of the muscles relaxing. Our eyes met for a second, and he smiled and nodded once. He gestured with his cigarette that he needed more smokes. Then the door closed.

I gave Gina some money and sent her out to the newsstand for the cigarettes. He'd want them the minute he was out, but I didn't want to risk missing him. My adrenaline was pumping, and I felt happy and nervous. There was still an extraordinary mess to be cleaned up, but my father would provide the right questions and answers to walk me through it. I leaned back on the bench and closed my eyes. It was the questions he would have for me that had me worried.

Chapter 17

As it turned out, my father wasn't called next, or even the case after. He disappeared from view as the next two cases were called, and I was just starting to settle in when I heard his name announced.

He walked out quickly, and unlike every other defendant I'd seen, no one had to tell him where to stand or to keep his hands out of his pockets. The lawyers must have changed shifts or something while he was coming out, because the guy who'd represented the last three or four people was gone. Instead, there was a young woman standing next to my father. She looked like an anemic version of someone who does Ivory commercials.

The officer in front of the judge's bench called out the charges, which seemed to be grand larceny and driving without a license.

"How does the defendant plead?" the judge asked, sounding very tired.

"Not guilty, your honor," my old man's lawyer answered, with an accent that was straight off Walton's mountain.

"Facts of the case?" the judge asked.

"Your honor," a fat black guy in a bright blue suit, standing to my father's left, piped up, "in this case the defendant was stopped for driving erratically on Ocean Parkway. A plate check turned up that the vehicle was reported stolen. The defendant has no license. And," he paused dramatically, then added, "the arresting officers noted a substantial amount of blood on the front seats and recent body damage to the car."

If he was waiting for a collective gasp or for someone to yell stop the presses, I'm pretty sure he was disappointed. The judge said "Uh-huh," yawned without covering his mouth, then looked at my father's lawyer. "Ms. Beckett?" he said.

The little birdlike woman launched into an impressively passionate defense that had something to do with returning from rushing an injured dog to a vet. Her voice sounded strange to me, the occasional bits of legal jargon coming out in this Beverly Hillbillies accent. She moved her hands around as she spoke, resting one on my father's back and rubbing it as she talked about his disability and the tragic death of his wife. She seemed genuinely upset, and I wondered if my father had made up the dog story overnight and played it out to her that emotionally. When she finished talking she abruptly stopped moving, one hand still on my father's back. Her thin blonde hair took a moment to settle flat again, like a puddle of water when you throw in a small stone.

"Bail?" the judge said, as if he'd heard nothing.

"Your honor," my father's lawyer chirped, "the defendant has had no contact with the criminal justice system in the last ten years. He's never before been charged with a felony. He's lived at the same address for the past twenty-two years. He's not going anywhere."

Cruel but true, I thought, then realized the same argument could be made for me.

"People?" the judge said.

The fat guy in blue said, "The people consent to releasing the defendant on his own recognizance."

"R.O.R." the judge said.

My father's lawyer whispered something to him and then he turned and walked past the cop at the rail and into the audience. He sat in the first row next to the midget Don Juan, looked over his left shoulder at me, and winked.

"The girl says I gotta wait for some kind of paper," he whispered. I nodded, and he turned back toward the front of the room.

The next case was called and a Middle Eastern–looking guy walked out. Before the charges were read, the lawyer said they needed an interpreter.

"Five minute recess," the judge said, and they hustled the guy back into the pens. The judge left the bench and people began speaking freely and walking around the room. Gina hadn't returned with my father's cigarettes yet, and while that wasn't shocking, I knew he'd be asking for them. The newsstand in the lobby was only about the size of two phone booths, and I'd told her specifically what brand to get, but Gina would window-shop if she were buying insulin, and it was my own fault for not picking up smokes on the way down.

My father stood and stretched. I got up when I saw him stand. He turned to me and we hugged, a little awkwardly, over the back of the wooden bench. We were hovering over the little Spanish guy, and I saw him cringe, but he didn't look up or say anything to us.

"How are you?" my father asked. "How's the side?"

"Pretty good. I don't much feel it unless I move the wrong way. How are you?"

"Tired. Otherwise, fine."

"You didn't sleep?"

"Sleep," he snorted. "In with these fuckin' animals? You'll wake up an' find one of 'em spreadin' mayonnaise on your leg an' putting it between two pieces a' bread."

"Did you eat?"

"Yeah. Food sucks, but it was food. I ate enough." He smiled. "Where's the little woman?"

"Knock it off. She's getting your cigarettes."

"Great. I should have them by the weekend."

"If you're lucky. What are we waiting for?"

"I don't know," he said. "Let me go see if I can talk to Minnie Pearl."

The lawyer who had spoken for my father was shuffling a huge stack of folders and separating them into two piles. My father walked past the rail and over to her table. If any of the cops hanging around noticed this, they did an excellent job of keeping it to themselves. The woman spoke to my father, then began writing something out for him. Just as she handed him the paper, the door opposite the pen area opened. The judge rushed out, sprinted up the two steps to the bench, and sat down quickly, like someone with a real job might.

"Anything ready?" he asked loudly. The officer calling the names spoke to him quietly as my father made his way back over to me.

"No interpreter? No interpreter?" The judge was yelling. "Next ready case."

Jesus. I was glad they'd arraigned my father before the Jeckyll/Hyde thing kicked in. Maybe the guy smoked crack in his chambers.

My father stopped in the aisle in front of my row and gestured for me to follow him. Up front, the officer called out a French-sounding name with the word "saint" in it, and the most bedraggled-looking Rasta I'd ever seen stumbled out from the pens, looking blinded by the fluorescent lighting. He had a thick, seemingly solid mass of dreads to his shoulders, then five or six vinelike strands for a foot or so, then another thick clot of hair around waist level. A cop steered him over to the defense table.

I joined my father after climbing over a half-dozen people, and we started walking out. "You have everything you need?" I whispered.

"Yeah," he said. "Just the adjourn date an' her office number—you know—in case I want to discuss this crime a' the century."

"You have some imagination. Thank God nobody asked how the dog was doing."

"Wasn't my idea," he said. "I was shocked to shit when she came out with that."

We were at the back of the courtroom, right at the door to the main hall off the lobby. My father opened it and stepped out, holding it for me. I stood in the doorway and looked up to the front of the room. My father's lawyer was speaking for the Rasta. From that distance I couldn't hear any of her defense, but I saw her blonde hair dancing and her right hand gesturing frantically as she spoke. Her left hand was on the Rasta's back, under the patchy strands of dreads, rubbing back and forth.

When we got to the lobby, Gina was just returning from the newsstand and almost walked right into us. She had two packs of my father's cigarettes in one hand, and a pack of Virginia Slims and Juicy Fruit gum in the other, which she immediately snaked into a pocket of her blazer before giving my father a hug and kissing him on the cheek. It would almost be a shame to break up with her, I thought. Between her wardrobe choice and this, I was stocking up on ammunition that would last for months.

We went straight out of the building, past a line as long as when we'd arrived. Gina asked my father a lot of questions about how he was feeling and if he'd been treated well, and he answered them

Tim McLoughlin

politely. Her upbringing had been old-world enough that she would never ask about what had happened or why. She might bring it up with me at a future date, or not, but it would just be formality, really. She'd accept whatever I told her as long as I didn't insult her by trying to pass off something like the injured dog story. That idea amused the hell out of me, and I almost laughed out loud.

Gina insisted on letting my father ride in the front seat, and frankly, she didn't have to insist very hard. My old man had seemed up, even spirited, on the walk back to the car, but as soon as he sat down and we started rolling, he looked exhausted. I put the oldies station back on, and lowered the volume considerably. By the time we'd gone ten blocks, my father had dropped off to sleep. I didn't notice at first, until Gina tapped my shoulder and gestured toward him. She smiled and pointed to the radio. I lowered the volume again, until it was barely audible.

We took the streets back, and although there was never a time anymore when Fourth Avenue was free of traffic, it wasn't terrible and it moved. I avoided highways when I had the luxury of driving on the street. The Gowanus was an elevated roadbed, cutting across South Brooklyn about thirty feet above Third Avenue, and though I would have been embarrassed to admit it, riding along it always made me feel like a traitor. It was as if the act of physically leaving pavement level meant that I was abandoning the neighborhoods I passed over— seeing their rooftops instead of their people. More importantly, I'd miss any changes taking place down there, and I couldn't tolerate the idea of being out-of-touch.

Whenever we stopped for a light I looked over to see if my father had come around, but he slept for the entire ride back to Gina's, head bowed straight, chin resting on his chest. He'd been in custody long enough to need a shave, and I knew that must have been killing him. I'd seen him haul around some of the worst hangovers the gods had visited upon this planet, but I couldn't recall the last time I'd seen him with stubble. I knew that he used to keep a shaving kit at work when he was with Sanitation, but I didn't know how he managed to clean up on his all-nighters.

His beard was coming in white, and that unnerved me. I found myself glancing over at it even between lights. His hair had been gradually shifting from black to a kind of steel gray for some time, but it wasn't very radical. Also, his hairline hadn't headed south much. But white? It was a startling contrast to his face and hair, and combined with the hoboish look of stubble in general, it really aged him. Being asleep in the car didn't make him look any better. I drove a little more quickly.

When we stopped at Gina's, my father woke up. He looked disoriented for a second, then embarrassed.

"Great," he said. "Out the whole time. Maybe you could just drop me at the Medicaid office."

"You need about three hours sleep," Gina said, "an' a hot meal. Then you'll be fueled up for another six months of trouble." She leaned over the front seat and kissed him.

"I'm an old fart," he said, smiling. "I can only go three months at a clip."

"Hey," she said, shrugging, "there's guys I worked with where I temped who only go out on weekends."

"I've heard about that," my father said. "Be good, honey."

"You too," she said, then turned my way. "Call me when you get home?"

I said I would. I sat there until Gina was up the steps and inside her house, then we pulled away.

"So," I said after a block or two, "you want a hot meal? Cause I'm pretty sure Gina's mother could whip something up for you."

My father had leaned his head back and closed his eyes again. He started laughing without opening them. "Eye of newt, maybe?" he said.

"We had that yesterday."

We parked two doors from the house and went up to the apartment. As we passed through the hallway I glanced at the basement door, and my stomach muscles constricted. Going up the stairs cramped that way made me feel a little nauseated. I couldn't unclench, and I was glad that my father was ahead of me so he didn't see me grab the rail and pull myself along to keep up with him.

Now that my old man was out and all right, the fear I'd been able to keep on the back burner was returning in a rush. While my father was locked up I'd had this abstract notion that, like most of life's problems, he'd just take care of this. I'd been far too idealistic in thinking that something like this could be resolved as easily as a schoolyard fight or an argument with Gina.

As we reached our floor, and my father fished for his keys, I suddenly thought about my mother's last few days, when she finally gave up fighting; when I could no longer deny it was going to happen.

While she was in the hospital, my father would lug huge pastel-colored octagonal wig boxes back and forth every day, and he couldn't have looked more ridiculous if he'd been walking a little pink poodle with matching leash. My mother had had a head of stunning fiery red hair that she primped and tended with the pride of an award-winning rose gardener. One of the endless series of chemo treatments she'd received had caused all of it to fall out.

My father spent a small fortune on three wigs of human hair. Two of them looked exactly like my mother's; the third was pretty close, but a shade too light. No visitors—including me—were allowed into her room until he'd brought a wig in and helped her put it on and adjust it.

When we'd leave, he'd take the wig from the previous day and drop it off at the house of the girl who always did my mother's hair. She'd bring it to work with her in the morning and have it ready for us by visiting hours. The third wig, with the color a little off, was left at the hospital as an emergency measure; in case we were late one day, or if something happened to one of the others. I don't think she ever had to wear it.

Once, when her whole family descended on us and then left, we had an exceptional amount of get-well crap and little trinkets to gather before leaving my mother's room. My father was loaded down with shit and asked me to grab the wig box. It was the silliest looking carton of the three: blue-green with wide purple stripes running diagonally along it. The handle was a gold-colored metal chain. I told my father that I didn't want to carry it; that I was embarrassed. He looked at me for a second, then put down half the stuff in his arms. He scooped up the box on his way out the door.

He didn't talk to me for the rest of that day and all of the next, until we were back at the hospital. Then he acted as though nothing had happened. He never mentioned it after that, and never asked me to carry any of the wig boxes again. I was mad at him for a while, for being such a hardass and not even trying to understand how I felt. Now I was ashamed of myself whenever I thought about it. The irrational anger I'd felt had come embarrassingly late in life—at sixteen—with the realization that there were, in fact, things my father couldn't fix.

I'd always meant to talk to him about it one day, but it hadn't happened. I knew that he'd felt my resentment, and I knew that it wasn't right. He carried all the weight of guilt that came with being the one who'd be left alive. He'd get drunk when we'd come home from the hospital and tell me how unfair it all was. How he was the one who smoked like a chimney and drank like a fish. I never said a word one way or the other, and unquestionably made things harder for him.

As I watched my father fumble in the shadows for the pullcord to the overhead light in the foyer, I felt a hint of that childish rage, but I fought it down. I would take all the help I could get, I told myself, but miracles were few and far between; besides, I might already be over my quota.

I ran out to pick up a late lunch and brought back some Chinese food and beer. My father was going to call Joey to set up a meeting for the next day, but I convinced him to let me do it. He was surprised, but didn't argue. I figured that if I was going to do something as stupid as become responsible for my own actions, there was no time like the present. After a little pepper steak and a couple of cans of Bud, he turned in.

As soon as he went to lie down I called the number he'd given me for Tony. A woman whose voice I'd never heard before answered on the second ring. She asked my name and number before I'd said a word, and when I gave her that she said thank you and hung up. Five minutes later Tony called back. I told him how things had gone, that my father was fine, and that I was home.

"I wanted to talk to you about setting up the meeting," I said, trying to keep my voice even. I was sure he could sense my nervousness.

"I thought your father would call," he said, which didn't help me maintain composure.

"I told him I'd do it. He went in to lie down."

"He's all right, isn't he?" Tony asked, though I'd just told him that he was.

"He's fine," I said again. "You know, a little tired. I don't think he slept much inside."

"He could of slept," Tony said. "He didn't have to worry. There was always somebody watching."

"I know, Tony. I'm sure he knew too. He was probably just a little uncomfortable."

"Yeah, sure, I don't blame him. But he's okay, right? I mean, nothing's wrong?"

"Everything's fine," I said for the third time. I was starting to feel like I was talking to a great aunt with Alzheimer's. Tony sounded as jumpy as I felt, and I didn't understand why. "How do you want to handle the meeting?" I tried.

"The meeting? The meeting's set. You're good to go tomorrow," he said. "I'll call in the morning with the when and where."

"Oh," I said. "All right. I didn't realize it was set already. Okay, I guess I'll see you tomorrow."

"Me? Yeah, I guess. Yeah, tomorrow." He sounded either distracted or scared.

I wondered if he was watching television. There might have been a game on somewhere, and I knew he had a satellite dish. "Good," I said. "I'll talk to you later."

"Yeah. Uh, tomorrow. Good."

He hung up. It occurred to me a few minutes later that maybe he didn't like talking on the phone. He couldn't shake hands that way.

Although he'd taken me seriously enough, Tony's disconnected demeanor left me more shaken than before. Almost any other response would have been preferable. Even anger or suspicion would have at least made sense to me.

Who the hell was in charge of the planet anyway?

First my father, then Tony: human frailty was everywhere. Who'd bail out on me next, the pope? Maybe I was being overly sensitive, but none of this was doing my confidence any good. I felt like a six-year-old next to a grown-up, pretending to shave or drive the family car. The stakes were a little higher here, though. I was more like a six-year-old playing with the switches in a sawmill.

The knapsack down in the basement wasn't helping either. Now that my father was sleeping and the call to Tony had been made, there was nothing for me to do but worry. I felt the pressure of having Tony's property in the house. It seemed to seep up through the floors as though the thing was radioactive. It might have been, for all I knew.

Maybe Tony was dealing in black market plutonium. I fidgeted around for an hour or so and killed the rest of the beer. I leafed through my father's copies of *Playboy* and *GQ,* turned the television on and then off, did the same with my radio, and finally gave up. I checked on my father, who was snoring up a small opera, and quietly left the apartment.

The basement door was less vocal now that I had the strength and patience to inch it open, but it still made enough noise to keep me looking over my shoulder. When I got down the steps, I felt like it had been months since I'd last been there. The super or my father had folded up the cot and put it away, and I didn't see any signs of blood. I walked to the boiler and looked along the wall, but I couldn't see a thing. The heat was too intense to get very close, so I couldn't reach back any appreciable distance. I nosed around the basement for a few minutes, and up against a wall next to my old train set and C.H.I.P.S. bicycle, I found a whiffle-ball bat and a petrified string-mop. The bat turned out to be useless, but the mop handle was long enough to make contact, and I used it to slide the knapsack out into view. Until that moment, when I saw the bag again, I'd almost convinced myself that it wouldn't be there. I wanted to believe that they'd gotten the bag. Even if someone had removed it from behind the boiler, I could at least stand in front of Tony again and tell him I didn't have it without worrying that my voice would crack.

I picked it up. It was very warm—almost hot—but nothing like I thought it would be considering where it had been. I turned it over and looked at it carefully for the first time. The pack was made out of some kind of flat black textured fabric that felt more like nylon than canvas. The buckles on the front were black plastic, but the thing didn't look cheap. I turned it over again. No markings, no brand name. The bottom half of the back had a stain of dried blood about the size of a quarter. I tried scraping it off with my thumbnail, and only ground it in deeper. I scraped harder, but it got worse. I scratched furiously, digging into the bag until my thumbnail bent back halfway down, tearing away from the skin. I howled, dropped the bag, and kicked it against the stairs. I just stood there for a moment then, and tried to compose myself. I had my thumb in my mouth, and I glared at the knapsack as though I could will it to vanish.

When I calmed down, I walked over to the stairs and sat, the bag at my feet. I looked at my thumb. The nail was back in the right position, but it had a white line across the middle and the finger was bleeding underneath. I put it back in my mouth. It hurt like a motherfucker. Since I was alone, I didn't bother to fight the tears that welled up until they ran down my face and embarrassed me. Then I laughed. Shoot him and he's okay, but if he breaks a nail, watch out.

I wiped my thumb on my pants and picked up the knapsack again, keeping the side with the spot of blood away from me. I brushed my dusty footprint off the front. If they were smuggling Italian crystal I was fucked.

The bag was still warm. I remembered hearing somewhere that heat was no good for coke. I'd never had any coke long enough to know if that was true. Whatever was on hand—a half-gram or a half-ounce—was always a one-day supply. I shook the bag. No unusual sounds. My father had said it wouldn't be drugs. I unfastened one of the plastic clasps, then closed it almost as quickly. My palms were wet and I wiped them down my pants. I turned the buckle around to see if I'd broken any kind of seal, but if I had I couldn't tell.

I couldn't open it. I was definitely concerned that there was some non-reversible means of determining if it had been touched, but it was more than that. I didn't want to open it. If I didn't know what was in there, then I wasn't really guilty of anything. I hadn't stolen from Tony, I hadn't fucked everything up. As long as I didn't look.

I stashed the bag again, back where it had been. I couldn't think of anyplace else. I went upstairs, and even though it was barely evening, I decided to shower and go to bed. I felt like I'd spent the day unloading trucks. When I removed the bandage, my side looked surprisingly good. It was dry, and starting to scab. I dressed it less elaborately. As I climbed into bed I remembered that I'd told Gina I would call. I took the receiver off the hook and put it in my night table drawer. Then I stretched out and watched the ceiling, and wondered what would happen at Tony's meeting.

From outside I heard people on the street talking, sometimes guys shouting, and I recognized most of the voices. They were kids from the block, a couple of years younger than me, throwing a football around— just raising hell. They'd knock off soon and drift up to the corner in a huddle to curse out teachers or bosses; and later, when the girls came out, they'd strut and pose and try to get laid.

Chapter 18

Breakfast had never been a real big deal in our house, even when my mother was with us. She'd eat with me or my father, whoever was around, but it was pretty rare for the three of us to sit down together. The morning of our scheduled meeting with Tony, my father poured cold cereal in bowls for both of us, then came into my room and woke me up. Instinctively, I assumed he was just coming home, still drunk, until I remembered that I'd seen him off to bed the night before.

After we ate, he left to make his rounds. I rambled around the empty apartment, bored and edgy, until he returned. Neither of us had ever hung a picture, painted anything, or picked out wallpaper as far as I could recall. It was as though time had stopped when my mother died. Any decorating or renovating projects had been hers. I knew that my father dusted and cleaned in the most general sense, even though I'd never seen him do it, because the place looked pretty well-cared for. But there were telltale signs that it had been too long since a woman had exerted any influence. The ceiling in the kitchen was peeling badly and there was a water stain between the windows in the living room. I knew that the Russian who'd bought the building a few years ago was decent about repairs, so this stuff was only a matter of nobody bringing it to his attention.

As I thought about it, I realized that no one but my father and I had been in our apartment since my mother passed away. It wasn't like we'd been social butterflies to begin with, but at least the occasional friend or relative used to pop by. I couldn't remember the last time we'd had a visitor up. Most people in the neighborhood returned to the family's house after a funeral, usually with tons of food. After my mother's service everybody went to New Corners, on Seventy-second Street. My father had rented out the back room, and had it prepared with a buffet lunch. We ate and drank quietly at festively covered tables in the brightly lit restaurant, subdued Muzak coming in through the old speakers on the walls. It was like a wedding where all the guests know it won't last.

When my father came back in he had sandwiches and coffee, so we ate on folding trays in the living room, with the TV on.

"Two meals so far today, and it's not even dark out yet," I said. "Is there something I should know? Is this like, the condemned man's feast? Because meatloaf on rye doesn't quite cut it." I lifted up one of my slices of bread and looked underneath. "Especially with no gravy." I was smiling when I said it, but my father's look was serious.

"Don't joke like that," he said. "Not now. I'm not in the mood."

I'd been counting on him to help me remain calm, to convince me that this would all be fairly straightforward. But he looked preoccupied and grim. I wished again that they had gotten the package when they jumped me, or if they hadn't, that I'd immediately returned it to Tony. We were beyond any of that now, and I felt that at this late date I couldn't even tell my old man what was really going on. To begin with, it would upset him too much, and it would probably shake the righteousness out of whatever he'd say at the meeting.

"Is there anything we should talk about?" he asked, like he'd been reading my mind.

"No," I said, regretting it almost instantly. "Nothing that matters."

He shrugged.

We spent the rest of the early afternoon making small talk and watching TV. The daytime talk shows had the usual freak-fest. One of them featured a woman who had been disfigured and partially blinded by a man who threw acid in her face because she wouldn't go out with him. When he was released from prison three years later they got married, and now they sat on the stage on national television, holding hands. My father seemed to watch this with an intensity that I knew wasn't typical of him, and I doubted was healthy for anyone.

There were four calls that afternoon before Tony's, and with each one I tried to disguise the fact that I was jumping out of my skin. Three were people putting bets in with my father. The fourth was Gina. He said hello to her by name, loudly and with gusto, so I'd know and tell him what to do. I just shook my head, and he told her I'd gone out before he got in and that he'd tell me she called.

When Tony did call I knew it was him immediately. My father's tone shifted and he lowered his voice so much that I couldn't make out any of the conversation. They didn't talk long, and when he hung up he turned to me and said, "Okay, let's roll."

"Where are we rolling?" I asked. "The club?"

"No," he said with his back to me, putting his jacket on. "The Parlor Car."

"Up on New Utrecht?"

"Yeah," he said casually. "I haven't been up there in years. You ever been there?"

"No," I said. "Why the Parlor Car?"

"I got no idea. That's what Tony said. What's bugging you?"

"Nothing, I guess." I put my coat on and we left.

The Parlor Car was at the corner of Seventy-first and New Utrecht, under the El tracks right at the foot of the stairs leading down from the Bay Ridge Avenue station. It was about six blocks from the apartment, and without discussing it we went past my car and headed up there on foot. What was bugging me was that I had assumed we would be meeting in Tony's club, and if we weren't, I wanted to know why. Also, this place was along the strip where Nicky had been killed, and I'd avoided New Utrecht Avenue—and anyplace else that had elevated tracks—ever since.

It was cold out but there wasn't much wind, and the brisk walk would have been almost pleasant if I'd been going somewhere else. We hit New Utrecht at Sixty-ninth and turned right, approaching the bar from along the avenue. It was a little hole-in-the-wall place that had probably started as a quick shot-and-a-beer stop for the rush hour crowd coming off the B. I didn't think people stopped off that way very much anymore. It looked from the outside like every other sad old man's bar in the neighborhood. It was surprising that I hadn't been in there before.

I began to shift from nervous to outright panicky as we neared the door. Zak stood in front, leaning against the cream-colored stucco, under the fake wood calligraphy that spelled the bar's name. He smiled when he saw us, and his look had a mean kind of amusement that made me queasy. If it bothered my father he hid it well. Zak opened the door with a flourish and gestured broadly with his other arm for us to enter. He was really enjoying himself. I went in first, and as my father followed me he took a dollar bill and stuck it in the pocket of Philly's overcoat.

"Thanks," he said. "On the way out you can hail us a cab."

"Don't ever touch me, you fuck! Don't you ever touch me!" he yelled at our backs, but he wouldn't cross the doorway. It was like he was on a short leash tied to a meter at the curb. "You touch me again you leave here in a box." Then, the show over, he stepped back out and closed the door.

We stopped about ten feet into the place, at the end of the bar, to let our eyes adjust to the sudden dimness. The lighting was provided by three low-wattage hanging lamps suspended from the ceiling over the bar area, and a small hooded fixture attached to the top of the cash register. It wouldn't have been enough light for any room, and to compound the problem, the place was laid like a cave. The wood-grain formica of the bar was almost black, the surface hammered copper. The floor had a maroon carpet with black octagonal designs that made it look like tile if you couldn't feel it under your feet. Red shag carpeting ran up the walls, criss-crossed by fake wood beams as dark as the stuff covering the bar.

I was feeling a little better. Zak's theatrics had had a calming effect on me. He'd never be a threat to us, and seeing my father flake off his smug veneer so easily was a bit of a confidence booster. Down at the far end of the narrow saloon, where the bar wrapped back around to the wall, were the only two people in the place besides us. They sat quietly, just outside the perimeter of light from the farthest hanging lamp. As soon as I took a step or two in their direction, I saw that one of them was black. I stopped moving forward when I recognized him as Todd; and an instant later when I saw that the other one was Edward, I began to back up until I bumped into my father. I allowed myself to lean into him for a second then. He was as good as a wall at my back.

I closed my eyes, realizing that this was the second time I'd found myself under the El tracks in Edward's presence, and for the second time, I wanted to make myself disappear. My father put his hand on my shoulder and squeezed, then left it there and propelled me forward toward Edward and Todd. It was a gesture designed to look casual and friendly to an observer, and feel reassuring to me. I suspected that it accomplished neither. I let myself be moved to just beyond Edward's reach, then stopped. This time my father bumped into me and took a step backwards. If either Edward or Todd noticed our Laurel and Hardy act, they didn't acknowledge it. I had to suppress a giggle, and realized that I was feeling a little hysterical. I had the urge to laugh or cry or scream, and hoped that if I gave in to any of them I could try to make it come off as rage, or something equally acceptable.

"You must be Todd," my father said, and extended his hand past me and Edward. Todd was against the wall, and he almost blended in with the background in the darkness. I remembered the punchline of an old ethnic joke. Teeth and eyeballs. Todd wasn't smiling. He took my father's hand.

"Todd will do," he said. "Have we met?"

"No. My son described you."

"It must have been a very good description," Todd said, and I got that same sense of his fucking around that I'd had in Tarrytown. It had made me furious then, but now I welcomed it, looking for anything that would lighten the mood.

"It was a wonderful description," my father said. "Between the two of you," he nodded to Edward, "I knew right away who was Todd."

Todd flashed a brief grin and released my father's hand. Edward hadn't made eye contact with my old man since we'd walked in, but he'd been watching me intently. Even at that short distance—four feet or so—he seemed to be studying me. I felt like I was a bug in a jar and he was trying to decide whether to punch airholes in the lid. As soon as the image came to me I felt my throat close again, the way it had in the car the night they killed Shades. I couldn't have spoken just then if I had to. I coughed to shake it, not wanting to embarrass my father.

"I didn't know that you would be here," Todd said. "I thought our meeting was just with Michael."

"Really. I thought it was me an' Mike meeting alone with Tony. Is he here?"

"No," Edward said. He swung his head around slowly to face my father for the first time. "No one else is here," he said quietly. "Just us chickens."

My father nodded. "Well," he said, "I'm used to being bullshitted. I don't know about you, but I don't take it so personal."

"No reason to," Todd said. "We all are, as your son was kind enough to point out to me, hired help."

"What is it you've been hired to help out with today?" I asked. My father shot me a look that said shut up. I knew this was some kind of a dance, and I knew it was necessary, but the tension was killing me. We were still standing at the bend in the bar, and I was arching my upper body as far from Edward as possible. My back was throbbing along the spine. I pulled out a stool from the long side of the bar and sat. My father remained standing behind me.

"You are anxious to get down to business," Todd said. "That's good."

"I'm not gonna do anything," Edward said to my father, as though they were alone and he was finishing a conversation he'd started in his head.

"I didn't say you were," my father said.

"I just wanted to tell you. You can sit."

"I'm fine. Thanks."

I noticed that my father had one hand inside his jacket. It certainly looked like it might be resting on a gun. I'd never seen my old man with a gun in my entire life, but I was pretty sure he wasn't stupid enough to try to bluff someone like Edward.

I hadn't caught it before, but Edward had some kind of an accent. He spoke quietly, and the night of Shades' murder he hadn't said enough for me to pick up on it, but I heard it now. It was either the last remnants of a foreign language, or a really pronounced regional dialect.

"Would you like to talk about the bag?" Todd asked me.

I'd gotten my breathing under control, and I was pretty sure that my throat wasn't going to close up again, but when Todd mentioned the bag out loud I came close to pissing myself.

"Good," my father said. "What about the bag?"

"We would like it," Todd said.

"Sure," my father said easily. "Us too. I'm sure it's worth a fortune. Tony can't let something like that go. We'll help any way we can."

Todd wasn't paying any attention to my father. He was looking at me. "You will help any way you can? Is that correct, Michael?" he said. He came off his stool smoothly and stepped around Edward. He paused in front of me, then walked the length of the place and went around behind the bar.

"Any way I can," I said. I looked over at my father. He and Edward were watching each other like stray dogs over food. Todd came down behind the bar until he was opposite us. He turned to the bottles and studied them for a minute.

"There isn't much of a selection," he said. "What would you care for?"

"Nothing."

"Please," he said. "Join me." He filled four glasses with ice and set them on the bar, then picked up a bottle of Chivas. "I suppose this will be all right."

"Anything Irish?" Edward asked.

Todd turned back to the bar. "No. Wait, yes. Paddy's."

Edward shook his head. "The scotch," he said.

Todd poured for all of us. He bent down and stowed the bottle under the bar. "We would like your help in recovering the bag," he said to me as he straightened up.

"What do you want me to do?"

"We want you to tell us where it is," Edward said.

My father picked up his drink and sipped a little, then placed it gently back on the bar. "You want to find the bag," he said, "find the guys that took it."

"I'm attempting to do that," Todd said.

"Why isn't Tony here?" I asked.

"Tony has removed himself from this. If the property cannot be located, his people will take the loss."

"You should be looking for whoever jumped me," I said.

"We did look," Edward said. "We found them. And we know what happened."

I didn't dare pick up my drink. I knew my hand wouldn't be steady enough. I wanted to look over toward my father—see his reaction—but I didn't move.

"We didn't believe you were really attacked," Todd said. "Even after we found your assailants. The whole event was so amateurish, so poorly done, we were sure you set it up yourself. We owe you an apology. You had nothing at all to do with it."

"If you caught the guys who jumped him," my father said, "then you know who set it up."

"We know all that we need to know."

"Yeah, great," he said. "I want to know."

"You do not need to know anything," Todd said.

"You want our help with the fucking bag?" he snapped. "You want my help then tell me who shot my son." My father's hand had been resting on my shoulder and his grip now became painfully tight.

Todd and Edward glanced at each other, then Todd turned back to me. "You were attacked on your first journey alone?" he said.

"Yeah."

"There had been no prior incidents?"

"Not that I know of," I said.

"Your friend was never approached before, during the run. And you were not approached in his company. Very few people knew the exact nature of your business."

"Lou," my father said quietly.

Todd said nothing. Edward swirled the liquor slowly in his glass and focused on the receding amber film as though it were a science project.

"It's not Lou," I said. "Lou?"

"Tony does sort of treat him like shit," my father said, more thinking out loud than to anyone in particular.

"But it was me," I said to my father. "I was driving the motherfucking car. Lou set me up?"

"Maybe he told them not to shoot," my father said evenly, still just trying the theory out. "Maybe it was supposed to be cake but something got fucked."

"Maybe he did not think you would resist," Todd added.

"So you're saying it was him," I said to Todd.

"I've said nothing. We are all speculating."

"You could be blaming him," I said. "You know he doesn't like you."

Todd sighed. "The act, the organization, and the execution of the feeble plan was the work of someone quite, ah, limited. I leave the rest to you."

"What did Tony say?" my father asked.

"He's more afraid of the truth than the kid is," Edward said, looking at me over the rim of his glass. "If he sees it, he's got to do something about it. Closing the book early on this is costing him."

I thought of how Tony had sounded on the phone. Had he already gotten the news then? Was he trying to cope? I wondered what he was doing right now.

My father looked surprised. "Tony's gonna eat it himself?"

"He is," Todd said, "but the cost has gone more to his character than his pocketbook."

"Then the Old Man knows he called it off. How did that happen?" My father's tone had become vaguely accusatory.

"This is not a schoolyard game," Todd said roughly. "Your employer is a player. He has made decisions that have taken him out of the play. He will finish his days as you will, maneuvering in narrow corridors of power and shuffling small amounts of wealth generated by horses and whores from one broker to another."

"And how will you end your days?" my father asked. "In bed when you're an old man, your heart givin' out while you're in the saddle with a pretty little white girl? Or maybe burning in an alley with your fuckin' eyeballs gone cause you aren't always as smart as you think."

No one said anything for a very long time, and I thought that my father had pushed too far. When Todd finally responded, he spoke very quietly.

"How I end my days," he said, "is of no concern to you. I cannot make this more clear. I want the bag."

"Okay," my father said, "you want the bag. We all want the bag. The question is, why are we here?"

"You are here because, although he had no part in the planning, your son decided to capitalize on the situation."

"I can't believe that if Tony thought Mike had the bag, he would have 'removed' himself so quickly."

"No one has made any representations about what Tony thinks," Todd said.

"Then *you've* decided to capitalize on the situation," my father said. "You aren't recovering the bag for Tony."

Edward shrugged. "You keep mentioning Tony. All's we said is that we want the bag."

"How did you get the meeting set up if it's over?"

"Your son is being debriefed," Todd said. "Like an astronaut."

I felt my father shift his weight from one foot to the other behind me. "What did you tell him?" he said. "He would have wanted to believe anything. Did you tell him it fell down the sewer?"

Edward smiled. "Smuggled out of the country."

"By the assholes you found?"

"No." Edward glanced over at Todd. "He put it on two of his people."

"You set up your own people?" I said.

"You didn't seem terribly fond of Dar," Todd said. "The point is, Tony already considers the package a loss, as does my employer, who is being compensated. So no one is looking for it."

"No one but you," my father said.

Edward finished his drink. "Nobody but us chickens," he said.

"You have the bag," Todd said to me. "It can't be any other way."

"Is that what the guys who jumped me said?"

"Yes."

"You believe them?"

"Oh yes," Edward said.

"Are they dead?" I asked. No one answered me. "Is Dar dead?"

"We would like the bag, Michael."

"I don't have the fucking bag."

"What's the deal?" my father asked. "What are you offering?"

"To make everything all right," Todd said. "We leave you alone."

"Proof?"

"It's in our best interest," Edward said.

"If we harm you," Todd added, "it gives lie to the tale we've told. And you can't go to Tony about us without confessing to stealing it yourself. We're bound to each other's deceit."

My father pulled a stool out next to me and sat. He was quiet for about a minute. He finished his drink, then reached over and took mine. I hadn't touched it. "All right," he said finally. He turned to me. "Get the bag."

"What?"

"This is as good as it's gonna get. Probably better than if Tony did show up. Go get the bag."

I didn't know what he wanted me to do. It sounded like he knew I had it, but it also sounded like he was in on the whole thing. I couldn't tell if he was serious or if it was just a trick to get me out of there.

"You get the bag," Edward said to my father. "We'll all have another drink."

My father rapped the bar a couple of times with his knuckles, then looked over at Todd. "Let me talk to my son," he said.

We went down to the front of the bar and stopped by the small window. I looked outside for Zak. I didn't see him, but that didn't mean he wasn't out there. "Dad, listen," I said.

"Not now," he said quietly. "I'm not crazy about leavin' you here, but we ain't in any position to bargain. I think they're for real. It is a stalemate over the bag. They won't do anything while they're waiting for it, anyway. You have to tell me where it is."

"How did you know?"

He shrugged. "You were lyin' about something," he said. "Where's the bag?"

I told him.

I stayed seated where I was, at the end of the bar. My father went over to Edward and Todd, spoke briefly, then came back to me.

"I won't be long," he said. "You okay?"

"Yeah," I said, though in fact I was feeling very shaky. "Ah . . . I'm sorry about all this."

"Stop it," he said. "Give them nothing." I nodded.

When he left, I stood at the window and watched until he was out of sight, then felt embarrassed, like a puppy with its nose pressed to the glass in a pet store window. I decided to remain where I was, seeing no reason to join Todd and Edward. What would we do, I asked myself: talk about politics, the environment, how you could never really hope to understand women? We were already engaged in a fairly high stakes round of liar's poker. Truth was, I was so scared that I didn't know if I could hold it together in their company without my father.

It was a ten-minute walk from the bar back to our apartment, so I figured it would be about a half hour before my old man returned. He'd been gone almost a full minute, and I was making a conscious effort not to look at my watch.

I stared out the window at the street. It was pretty much deserted that time of day. A couple of old ladies and young mothers with infants. A kid skipping school. Every so often the sound of the B pulling in above, and a moment or two later a small group of foreigners coming off whatever third-world swing shift would have them getting home now. They would barely hit the sidewalk before scattering in all directions and disappearing.

It was mostly Russians and Chinese, the wave of immigrants du jour in the neighborhood. When I was about ten it was Greeks. My father said that when he was a kid it was Jews from eastern Europe. Of course whenever more than twenty people from the same country wound up in the area everybody would scream that the place was shot to shit, and half of them would run over the Verrazano to Staten Island. But the funny thing was that most of the foreigners only stayed for ten years or so before they made the jump to the suburbs. When I was thirteen, it seemed like half the stores in the area had been bought by Greeks, but six years later I doubted if you could find more than two or three. And the ones who did hang around, their kids grew up—whether they were Greek or Chinese or whatever—acting as Italian as everybody else. All my life I'd been hearing that the neighborhood was changing, but it was still as guinea as the day I was born.

I thought about Lou. It didn't seem possible that he would have set me up this way, but Todd and Edward had no reason that I could see to lie about it. It was virtually the only explanation for Tony backing out, and besides, my father appeared to have accepted it.

I didn't know that I would have called Lou a friend, but I might have. We'd hung together more than a few times, gotten drunk, gone to the track, that sort of thing. It had always been with a group, but what difference did that make? I wondered who I could really trust. Who among my friends would go to the wall for me? I wasn't sure, and felt like that had to say a lot more about me than it did about any of them.

Edward struck a match down at his end of the bar. He lit a cigarette and coughed softly. Todd muttered something, and they both laughed. I was getting more uncomfortable by the second. I didn't want them to start talking to me, or worse, move down to where I was sitting. I made myself face front at first, keeping my back to them, but it wasn't working. I felt too vulnerable. I swiveled the stool until it was at an angle where I looked out the window and at the door, but could keep them peripherally in sight.

The next few minutes ticked off in that same tense sort of stasis; me not saying anything, and only low murmurs from the other end of the bar. I forced myself to try to remain rational, if not calm. I knew for a fact that my father would take a bullet for me without blinking, but it did little to stem my paranoid fantasies of him boarding a plane to some South Seas isle with whatever valuable cargo was in the bag. I thought about what Edward would do to me if he didn't return. Even if it wasn't his fault. What if he got sick or had an accident or if the bag wasn't there because someone else had found it? Then my father wouldn't return right away, because he couldn't come back empty-handed. He'd have to figure some contingency plan, and that would take time. I thought about the crew that jumped me and what had probably happened to them. It was doubtful that any of them were alive. And Dar, one of Todd's own people.

The gentle pop of cracking ice broke the silence when Edward refilled his drink. I dug little canals out of the grime in the copper bar with the fingernails of my left hand as I tried not to scream. This was crazy. There was no reason to believe that they'd let us off even if we delivered the package. In fact, producing it was nothing but an admission of guilt. My father surely would have seen that if he'd had enough time to dope out the situation. If I'd told him the truth. If I hadn't fucked up. I slid off the barstool, slowly, inching forward. I risked a sidelong glance down the bar and saw Edward already moving toward me. That sent me into full panic, and I threw myself at the door. I wrenched it open with Edward at my heels and was confronted by my father's frame blocking the doorway.

He'd changed into a long winter coat, and he was carrying a duffel bag that I assumed contained the knapsack. His hair was uncharacteristically mussed up by the wind, and his expression was that of someone just discovering their hood ornament has been stolen.

"The fuck is going on?" he said, looking at me and Edward in the doorway. "Ringalevio? Hide-an'-seek?" He glanced at Edward's hand, flat against the inside of the door. "Some service. I expected more of you. You takin' lessons from that asshole outside?" He walked in.

Edward closed the door. I followed my father back along the bar toward Todd, Edward trailing the two of us. I hadn't said anything and neither had Edward, but I was feeling like I'd really fucked up. Our chances of this working out seemed slim, and I had punted whatever guise of professional demeanor my father had managed to put on. His stance seemed to have changed, though. Before he left, he'd watched Edward like a hawk. Now, he seemed to be ignoring him entirely. He walked straight to Todd, and laid the duffel across the barstool in front of him.

"Shall we conduct a little business?" he said.

"By all means," Todd replied. "Another cocktail?"

"Please." My father's grin was so wide that it gave his features an almost Oriental cast. I knew that look. It wasn't really pleasure. It was the intensity of the play. I'd seen it at the track half a hundred times. I'd seen it at the crap games in the back of the candy store, and I'd seen it when he played poker at Tony's club. It was the look that said the stakes were going up, things were getting serious.

Todd moved back around the bar and got four fresh glasses out. He added ice and poured Chivas in all of them. Edward had moved to Todd's barstool, across from my father. The bag sat on the empty stool between them. Todd remained behind the bar. I stood as close to my old man as I could without actually hiding under his coat. He picked up his glass, nodded to Todd, and drained about half of it. Edward was covering my father as intensely as before. If being ignored bothered Edward, he didn't show it. I wondered if he ever displayed any emotions. If he had any.

My father put his glass down and leaned over the bag. He pulled the top open and removed the black knapsack, setting it down on the bar next to his drink.

"Who wants the honor?"

"You've brought it this far," Edward said. "Open it."

My father looked over at him for a second, then back to Todd. "Your call," he said.

"Open it," Todd echoed. There was no fucking around in his voice now, no fake aristocracy. He sounded more tired than annoyed.

My father turned it around there on the bar once or twice, then opened the clasps that had nearly caused me a breakdown. I held my breath, half-expecting an explosion. He threw the flap open and looked inside.

"It's empty," he said flatly, staring into the bag. No one moved. Todd and Edward and I continued staring at the knapsack. "Kidding," he said. "Just kidding."

I started to shudder, and looked over at Edward, afraid he'd attack my father. It was what I would have done in his position. I felt like doing it anyway. As smart as he was, even I knew his timing was off now. I wondered just how nervous he might be.

He reached into the knapsack and removed a blue canvas draw-string bag pulled closed and sealed with a small padlock. It was about the size of a football. He laid it on the bar and sat back.

"Well," he said. "Who wants to try on the glass slipper?"

"Have you opened it?" Todd asked.

"I didn't know for sure I had it until about twenty minutes ago. No, I didn't open it."

Todd looked at Edward, who shrugged. He stood and reached under his coat, into his pants pocket, coming out with something that looked like a Swiss Army knife. He looked ridiculous holding the small tool, like a yeti with a salad fork. He cut the bag open across the top, clean, about an inch below the lock. He was slow and precise, and when he finished he gently laid the fabric on the bar. Then he pulled the bag open, blew into it, and turned it upside down. After shaking it carefully, a pile of what seemed to be straw spilled onto the copper surface. A small rock rolled free of the mess and came to rest in front of me. I picked it up and placed it on top of the pile. It looked like a tiny egg in a nest. I had always suspected that it was drugs, my father's opinion notwithstanding. I figured there was a small brick of coke, or a bag of heroin in the middle of the hay.

Todd leaned forward and picked up the stone I had set down. He placed it back on the bar. Then he began probing the straw with his incredibly long fingers, pulling it apart and gracefully plucking out more rocks and putting them near the first. This went on in silence for about ten minutes, until the straw was reduced to a long thin mat, and there were about twenty small stones in a pile, ranging in size from a pea to a cat's-eye shooter.

"My, my," Todd said finally.

I couldn't have put a finger on the moment it happened, but it seemed that the tension in the room had broken. Todd and my father looked relaxed, even Edward appeared almost human. He had picked up his glass and was sipping his drink. Idiot that I was, I was scanning the flattened straw for a sign of drugs.

My father picked up a stone, held it close in front of his face, and replaced it. "Uncut they really look like shit, don't they?"

"That is why we deal with our Hebrew friends," Todd replied. "It's like spinning straw into gold."

I looked at the pile of stones. Most were just gray rocks, smoother and rounder than gravel. The kind you'd find at the beach. One or two might have been just slightly opaque in spots, like ice cubes made with dirty water. "They're diamonds?" I asked.

My father looked at me like I'd farted.

"Very good," Edward said. "You get Rookie-of-the-Year."

I started to reach for one, but stopped. There was something about them that made them seem dangerous in and of themselves. It felt like opening the knapsack. I was afraid they'd burn through my hands.

The deal was done, I realized. We'd find out if we could walk away.

"What's it all worth?" my father asked.

"I couldn't say," Todd replied. "It depends on how they are cut."

"It looks like a helluva lot of money."

"I'm sure it is."

My father picked up two of the stones. "I think we should get a little something for our trouble," he said. "I'm not talking greed, just basic compensation. A souvenir." He hefted the diamonds in his open palm, as though their weight would tell him something.

"No," Todd said.

"That doesn't seem quite fair." My father closed his hand around the stones.

"For your trouble, as you put it, you get your life. You will not profit from your son's impetuosity and disloyalty."

"Let's call a spade a spade then," my father said, staring at Todd with his gambler's grin. "We get our lives because our deaths would raise too many questions. My son's impetuosity is making you two wealthy. And as for disloyalty, I'd ask the guys you set up to get this far."

"All true. Now return them."

"I think there's some room for negotiation here."

"You are a fool. I've already treated you with more respect than you deserve. Your position is untenable. This has little to do with money. You are a man whose existence is defined by an area no more than five hundred meters square from where we stand. I would be more stupid than you to permit you to leave here with them."Todd's voice had risen with impatience. I wished my old man would back down. "These things are virtually useless to you anyway," he continued. "The only avenue of commerce available to you is the source from which they've been stolen. Sooner or later you would approach his confederates or his enemies. Either way he would find out. Or you will simply get drunk and attempt to use them to purchase a hamburger," he sneered.

"Well," my father leaned a little forward as he spoke. "If you . . ."

Edward backhanded him so fast that I didn't really see it. His left arm became a blur below the shoulder, and my father went off his barstool as though he were made of styrofoam. The stool hit the floor, and my father came down on a formica-topped table that gave way under his weight and landed between the two red vinyl benches of the last booth. The stones he'd been holding flew across the room and landed somewhere beyond the area lighted by the bar lamps. Edward looked like he'd never moved.

I got to his side almost instantly, but my father was already trying to push himself up. I hooked my elbow around his, and managed to hoist him onto the seat of a booth so criss-crossed with gray electrical tape that it resembled the union jack. He stared at Edward as though he'd seen him spit fire. I didn't sense fear, more a look of absolute disbelief. "You fuck," he said slowly.

"It is time for you to leave," Todd said. "The meeting is over."

"Let's get the fuck out of here," I said, not quite whispering, but low, and only to him. Edward's shot had been so sudden and unexpected that I hadn't reacted to it for what it was at first. I went to my father's aid as if he'd been hit by lightning, or, more to the point, a truck. The casual savagery of it settled on me as I watched my old man trying to focus, shaking his head sporadically, like a wet dog. I remembered the businesslike calm Edward displayed when he torched Nicky, and I began to get claustrophobic in the dark, narrow bar. My father was still sitting, and I didn't like being so much taller. It made me feel like I was in charge.

"Take him and go," Todd said to me. He and Edward were staring at us as if we were tropical fish.

As soon as they had what they wanted their interest in us had seemed to evaporate. Even I had figured that was the best we could hope for. I didn't know what angle my father thought he was playing, but it looked like a miscalculation. I felt like we had to get away from there that minute. If we didn't, they would change their minds and kill us, either because it made more sense, or because they were bored. I pulled at my father's arm, gently but firmly, until he got to his feet. He took a step back toward Edward then stopped.

"You throw one hell of a party," he said. "I hope one day to return the favor."

Edward didn't acknowledge him. I tugged at his arm, feeling like a little kid dragging a grown-up over to see something of great importance, like a turtle or a go-cart. I knew it looked at least that bad, but I was afraid past the point of humiliation. Nobody tried to stop us, and my father let me more or less lead him out.

"And *you*," Edward said to my father's back as we reached the door, "expected more of *me.*"

Twice I tried to say something during the walk home, but both times my father waved me off. He was moving slowly, and he wouldn't let me help him. A block away from the bar he leaned over the trunk of a parked car and spat some blood into the gutter. The left side of his face was starting to puff out. I tried again as we were turning onto our street.

"I'm sorry," I said. "I'm really sorry. I know you don't want to talk about it right now, but I just want to tell you that much."

"Nothing to be sorry about," he said.

"This whole mess. What they did to you. I'm sorry I put you in that spot."

"What? I never got hit before? I never fell down?"

"You never had to take a shot like that. You never had to back off that way." We climbed the stoop and I opened the inside hall door.

"How the hell do you know so much about what I didn't have to do?"

"I never heard about it."

"Oh yeah," he said as we entered the apartment. "That would be the shit that you'd hear about. I talk about that all the time. What do you think, I brag about the fights I lost, or the times I been embarrassed? That's right, I tell you everything. Just like you tell me." He turned down the hall. "I'm tired," he said. "I think I'm gonna lie down a while."

"You want some ice for that?" I asked. If he heard me, he didn't answer.

Chapter 20

I slept terribly that night, fitfully—little forty-minute naps filled with troubling dreams that had me coming to in a sweat in my over-heated bedroom. At three a.m., after my fourth time waking up, I got out of bed and opened the window. It was only a couple of weeks until Christmas, but even at that time of night it felt like fifty degrees out.

When our Russian landlord bought the building about five years ago, he moved into a first-floor apartment and was his own super. Heat and hot water were always adequate, and he was a pleasant-enough guy, even though he spoke virtually no English and when his wife made Sunday dinner it smelled like they were stewing their garbage. Last year they had a kid and bought a house on Long Island. He hired a super, and now we only saw him every couple of months when he came to check on the building. The new guy was a retired longshoreman from the neighborhood, whom my father had known for years. He was the nicest guy in the world, but Christ, did he cook us all winter. He must have loaded ships in the Sahara. On a night like this, when he really could have shut the furnace down altogether, it must have been eighty-five in my room. Opening my window did little good without cross-ventilation, so I went through the apartment and hit the kitchen window too, then left my bedroom door open. It gave me the slightest breeze.

I lay back down, and though I didn't feel like sleeping, I dropped right off again. Although I'd gone to bed worried about my father, and was still feeling guilty and frightened, I didn't dream about any of it. I'd half expected nightmares of Edward coming through my window like Leatherface or Jason.

What I dreamed about was my mother. She was sick, like she'd been in the hospital, but she was at home with us. She lay in the mechanical bed, with the monitors all around and tubes hooked up to her arms and nose, and two that snaked under her sheets that I'd never asked about. The hospital room was our living room. I was in my bedroom. She was calling for my father. I went to the doorway and looked at her. The machines were shutting down, and all the fluid in the tubes was backing up and choking her. Her wrists were tied down to the rails at the side of the bed, so she wouldn't rip anything out when the morphine made her delirious. She struggled, but couldn't move. The fluid was overflowing now, spilling on the sheets and running off the bed onto the floor. She kept calling to my father, then started choking and gurgling. I didn't know where he was, if he was in his room, if he was home. I was afraid to go to her. I couldn't cross the living room because she would see me. There wasn't anything I could do to help. I stood in the doorway and watched her flail and choke. I started to tremble. I was still shaking when I woke up.

I didn't want to look out past my room, but my bladder wrestled with my neuroses, and as with all such battles, the body can up the ante until it isn't much of a contest. When I went to piss, the living room looked reassuringly faded and depressing. I knew I was done sleeping for the night. I showered and dressed, and looked in on my father. He was out like a light, and my moving about had not disturbed him. Once he settled in, Christ himself would have been hard-pressed to wake my old man before his internal alarm popped him up in the morning.

I went out, got in my car, and drove down to Shore Road. I stopped at a 24-hour deli on Colonial Road and bought a buttered roll and coffee. When I ordered, the Arab behind the counter looked at me like I'd asked to have sex with his sister. I wanted to watch the sun come up over the Narrows, but I was a little too early and a lot too hyper to sit still for long. The sky was just beginning to lighten when I got back in the car.

Tim McLoughlin

I drove along the shore until the street turned inland by the border of Sunset Park, then continued down through the desolate industrial stretch of Second Avenue where, a few hours earlier, Italians from North Williamsburgh and Bensonhurst, and local Dominicans and Puerto Ricans, got together for their only social interaction besides drug-dealing: the nightly drag races. There was no sign of any action by twilight, but the piles of beer cans and other debris along the curb made the place look like some weird urban Woodstock.

At Hamilton Avenue I turned right and followed Third to Atlantic, through the Wycoff and Gowanus projects, and took the streets onto the bridge. It was a little past peak sunrise, but the view going over the Brooklyn Bridge was spectacular, and I didn't feel bad about not being able to sit still at the shore.

I came off the bridge directly onto the FDR Drive and exited at Houston Street. I was in the East Village in five minutes and parked across from Kathy Popovich's house about ninety seconds later. I must have known I was heading there, but I hadn't really let myself think about it. I realized that it was the second time that I'd gone to see her when I was feeling restless, uncomfortable with myself. Was this a natural instinct, to seek out someone smart, interesting, and understanding, or was I running away, looking to escape? A good argument could be made either way. I locked up the car and walked a block west to First Avenue for another cup of coffee. It was barely seven o'clock, and I figured I couldn't try to roust her for at least an hour. I knew she had classes later, but I didn't know if she had a job or if she'd been out on a date. I didn't want to consider that there might be someone up there with her.

I'd bought a newspaper to look at while I had my coffee, but as was often the case, I could summon absolutely no interest in the vast majority of the stories. If there was a lurid murder, or a little girl kidnapped, or an especially spectacular robbery had been pulled off somewhere, I'd be intrigued. But the notion that anyone could get excited about the economy of Mexico, or North Korean students rioting, was pretty much beyond me. In fact, I frequently thought that interest in world news was like listening to modern jazz—an Emperor's new clothes thing, where everyone pretends to understand and no one has the balls to say it's just noise.

I thought about the last time I'd seen Kathy, and how I figured that

171

would be the end of it. I still couldn't see it going anywhere, but there was little point in denying that I was at least a bit hung-up on her. That may have been exacerbated by how fucked-up the rest of my life had been lately, but I didn't think so. I would have been drawn to her even under comparatively normal circumstances. I'd known girls like her in the past, but there hadn't been any substance behind their screwball artist facades. I almost got the impression that Kathy played down her intelligence.

At eight o'clock I decided to stop writing her resume in my head before I intimidated myself right back over the bridge. I'd have the rest of my life to hide under the covers, and probably would. Now was the time to be charming.

I started to head for her building, but thought better of it and walked back to a phone booth on First. She picked up on the fourth ring, sounding like I'd awakened her. I wasn't off to a sterling start. I had to give her my name twice before it registered.

"Mike," she said, "Jesus Christ. What time is it?"

"Eight o'clock. Did I call too early?"

"Too early for what? Are you all right? You're never at school any-more, and I haven't heard from you since you practically ran out of here last week. Now you call in the middle of the night."

This wasn't good. I found myself backpedaling from jump. Thank God I hadn't just rung the bell. "I'm sorry I'm disturbing you so early," I said. "I forget that everyone doesn't keep to the same schedule as me. I'll call you at a more reasonable hour."

She started to agree, then hesitated. "Wait," she said. "Wait a minute. It doesn't matter. I'm awake now anyway. I'm not going back to sleep. What's up?"

"Well . . ." I suddenly wished she'd let me get off the phone and call her back some other time. I felt like I was under pressure to make this compelling. "Nothing's up, really. I just wanted to talk to you. You told me to keep in touch."

"Uh-huh. Great sense of timing. Are you on a pay phone?"

"Yes."

"And you're sure that nothing's wrong?"

"Yeah," I said, "I'm fine. Look, I'm sorry about the hour. Sometimes I act first and think later. I can let you rest and call later."

"Mike, I doubt that you ever act without thinking first. Where are you?"

"I'm in Manhattan. I had an early run at work, and I figured I'd call you before I headed back."

"Are you near here?" she asked.

"On your corner."

"Really. That's wonderful. I haven't actually been stalked since I moved to New York, and I was starting to think there was something wrong with me."

"Yeah, well, I've been busy or I would have been here sooner, but it's going to be a very passive stalking. I'll be polite when I jump out from between parked cars."

"I'm sure. If you want to come up, ring the bell and I'll buzz you in. We'll have some coffee. But I warn you—you're about to see me first thing in the morning. It will be the scariest moment of your life." She laughed and hung up.

"If only you knew," I said to the dial tone.

I figured that Kathy first thing in the morning actually wouldn't be an awful sight at all, though her building—in fact the whole neighborhood, even this early—was a quaint spin through hell. I wasn't sure if the stench was actually stronger in her hall, or if I was just more sensitive to it in the morning. On the second-floor landing I passed a bum sleeping off some nightmarish bargain-basement hangover. By the time I reached the fourth floor, I felt like joining him for a nap.

When Kathy opened the door my suspicions were confirmed. She didn't quite look perfect, but not that far off. She wore jeans, and a baggy t-shirt that I was sure she used as a nightshirt. She looked pleasantly disheveled—no makeup, jeans hastily pulled on—but she'd combed her hair. She was barefoot, and between that and the faded blue denim, she looked like a different person. Like the one I'd gotten a glimpse of the other night. The one who didn't always dress in black. I wondered if this Kathy lived inside the other one, and how much of her I'd been allowed to see. How much more there might be yet to discover. The thought that she might put up fronts to hide behind was very appealing to me. It made me feel closer to her.

"It's good to see you," I said.

She studied me in the doorway. "You'd be a terrible stalker," she said. "You're wheezing too loudly. People would hear you a mile away. Perhaps you should take better care of yourself."

173

"Perhaps you should invite me in before my feelings are hurt and I abandon the stalking trade entirely."

"Heaven forbid," she said. "Come in."

Kathy turned and walked into the apartment, leaving me to follow her. I thought again about how comfortably attractive she looked, and how she hadn't been awake very long. Gina, by contrast, was one of those high maintenance girls who was never off-duty and could only look stunning after hours of work.

Whatever Kathy's sleeping arrangements had been, everything was neatly put away, and the sofa was just a sofa. I noticed again how old-fashioned the place looked, more strikingly so in the light of day. The sunlight that streamed in every window gave the apartment a yellowed, faded look. I didn't find it at all depressing. In fact, I thought it was warm, almost homey. I'd probably be pushing my luck if I asked Kathy to bake some cookies.

"Make yourself comfortable," she said from the kitchen area. She was filling a coffeepot at the sink.

I sat on the couch and picked up a flier from the coffee table. It was just one side of a single page that had been crudely mimeographed. It featured a black-and-white photo of a nude woman facing the camera and glaring defiantly. One foot was in what looked like a pail of water; the other was in a very high, spike-heeled pump. Her hands were at her sides, in fists, and one was holding the end of an exposed electrical wire. Written across her breasts in lipstick or light marker was the phrase, "Of course it hurts." The photo was captioned "Forever Victims," and under the picture, in slightly smaller print: "An Evening of In-Your-Face-Angst with Melissa Livingstone." There was a small note at the bottom of the page listing three or four "guerrilla theater" locations and dates. One of them was last night.

"Are you familiar with her?" Kathy asked, walking over with two empty white china mugs. When she placed them on the table, she scooped up two clear glass cups and saucers that I hadn't noticed until she moved them.

I felt that tug in my gut again and the instant hot flush of jealousy. In the space of a few seconds I thought about who she'd had coffee with, where they'd gone before that, how long she'd allowed him to stay, whether they'd slept together, and why the fuck he'd gotten a cup and saucer while I was having a plain chipped mug like you'd give an encyclopedia salesman.

I took a few deep breaths and was smart enough not to speak until I got it together. You have no goddamn claim on this girl, I said over and over to myself. Don't screw up now.

"I'm not familiar with her at all," I said. "I was just trying to figure out if she sings, paints, or just sets herself on fire."

"She's a performance artist."

"So it's the setting-yourself-on-fire thing."

"How very open-minded," Kathy said. "Actually, she was pretty bad. I mean, I think art should be provocative, but she doesn't have much going for her once you get beyond the shock. But I've seen a number of performance artists recently whose pieces were well-done and interesting."

"Does she perform naked?" I asked, looking at the flier again.

"Some of the time. Last night a couple of people sort of heckled her for a few minutes. She screamed at them to go back to New Jersey."

"Oh good," I said. "Someone else from Kansas telling people they're stupid because they live six miles from here."

"You weren't even there. You're not from New Jersey. Is there anything you aren't defensive about?"

I thought for a moment. "No," I said.

She smiled. "It's good that you're aware of it."

Kathy went back over to the stove and retrieved the coffeepot. She sat with me and talked for a while about trivial happenings in and out of classes at school. I'd been trying to come up with a plausible story for when she would begin with the real questions, but nothing credible was coming to me. I wondered if a version of the injured dog story from my father's lawyer would fly. Kathy must have read my mind.

"I'm running out of mundane things to talk about," she said. "And I get the feeling you're dreading that I'll ask you something. It's making me very tense. You called me at eight o'clock and woke me up. You're sitting on my couch having coffee. I'd really like to know what's up with you."

"I'm not quite ready to talk about it," I said.

"It's my couch," she said. "My coffee. It was my sleep."

"I know." I turned my head and looked out the window. Across the street was an abandoned building with sheets of tin over the windows. Someone had painted a half-drawn shade on the top half and a flower in a pot on the bottom, as though it sat on the sill. A meaningless gesture in terms of how the building looked, but I thought it was nice. If this was my neighborhood, and I was old, I wondered if I'd go around doing something like that. "I'm going to need a few days," I said.

"What do you mean?"

"The last couple of weeks have been very—I don't know—rough, I guess. A lot of changes. A lot of weird shit. I think it's over now. But I need a little time to let the dust settle and make sure that everything is all right. If you can bear with me, I'll tell you what I can soon."

"A lot of people go through changes," she said. "It's not the end of the world, even though it always seems like it at the time. If you're thinking about leaving school, maybe you should put off a decision like that until," she shrugged, "as you say, the dust settles."

"A lot of people go through changes," I said. "They have a hard time at school, or a teacher has it in for them, or their boss does. Or their parents get divorced. If it was like that I would have told you already. I'm not blowing you off. Give me a few days and ask me whatever you want."

"Even about girlfriends?"

"Even about boyfriends. Even about livestock."

"I always suspected that was what it was like late at night out on the prairies of Brooklyn. Okay, you can be mysterious for now. But can you tell me why you're really here this morning?"

"I'm not sure myself. I felt like I needed to see you. Right away."

"I see," she said. "Was there some deep spiritual reason for this, or were the livestock just busy?"

"Both," I said. "I swear I don't know. I like you; I like your company. I also think you're extremely attractive. But right this minute? Beats the hell out of me. Maybe I see you as my salvation."

"Then you're in much more trouble than I suspected," she said, as she rose from the couch and went to the kitchen. When she was seated again and had refilled her cup she looked at her watch. "My alarm would be going off just about now if you hadn't called. I don't give myself much downtime, because I grab all the sleep I can. What I'm saying is that I'll be throwing you out soon."

"Sure," I said. "No problem. I did barge in on you. So how soon should I come back? An hour? Two?"

"I don't know," she said. "I haven't thought about it."

"How about tonight?"

"I don't know. No. I have plans tonight."

"A date?"

"A friend. Dinner."

"I could meet you after dinner. Desert. Coffee. Drinks."

"You're pushing," she said. "I don't know what time will be convenient. Or if tonight is good at all. Besides, you don't have a really good track record. You didn't show up for the first date, and left in the middle of the second."

"I understand how you feel, but from my perspective that puts me a date and a half behind where I should be. I'm trying to regain lost ground."

"Starting tonight?"

"Well, starting in ten minutes was what I was thinking, but I can be flexible."

Kathy looked like she couldn't decide whether to be annoyed or amused. That ambivalence was better than I expected and more than I knew I deserved, so I practiced keeping my mouth shut and hoped I looked sincere. She glanced at her watch again. "Are you familiar with Bradley's? It's a jazz bar on University Place."

"No," I said. "But I'm sure I can find it."

"Okay. Do you want to meet me there at ten tonight?"

"I'd love to."

"Good," she said. "Now get out. If I don't start to get myself together soon I'm going to feel rushed and hassled all day."

I drained the last of my coffee and stood. I sensed that I was in the middle of one of those moments in life that I would look back on later, wondering why I hadn't left well enough alone. I decided to try that this time. Kathy walked me to the door, and I apologized about three more times for waking her up. She gave me a brief kiss at the doorway.

"When I finally figure out who you are," she said, "you'd better be worth it."

"Maybe the mystery is intriguing," I offered.

"The mystery," she said as she closed the door, "is a pain in the ass."

I'd been a little worried about someone fucking with my car on Kathy's block, but when I stepped out onto the street I was depressed to see how well it blended in with its surroundings. I drove away before anyone had a chance to make the same observation about me.

My father was out when I got home. It was still early and I figured he was making his rounds. As I sat in the apartment alone, the malaise I'd been able to shrug off for a while settled in on me again.

The short time I had spent with Kathy felt like a vacation, or what I'd always assumed a vacation would feel like. The longest trip I'd ever taken with my family had been a three-day weekend at a beach house on Montauk, back when we first learned my mother was sick. It hadn't been very restful, but it was all my father could swing. He made good money with the numbers, but there was no such thing as a day off. I sometimes thought that he'd set his life up like that—tied himself to the neighborhood so there would be no danger of being lured away. I wondered for the first time if maybe I hadn't been doing the same thing when I accepted the job with Tony.

It was something that I'd seen all my life, and had been consciously aware of since I was about ten. I'd always told myself that I was too smart to get involved in any of it, even on as low and stable a level as my father had. It had seemed to me that hooking up with the wiseguys was like becoming an actor. About one percent makes it big and everybody else hangs around doing menial embarrassing jobs waiting for the break that never comes. And as with acting, there was never any lack of enthusiastic wannabees. I used to think my friends and classmates were unique, but I knew better now. Everything worked today the way it had when I was sixteen, and, I assumed, when my father was sixteen. It probably worked the same way five hundred years ago when there were Indians hanging out on the corner where the fruit store is.

Around junior or senior year in high school, the first couple of guys drop out. Most get full-time jobs. The video store, a supermarket, or driving a tow truck. One or two just hang around. They begin dressing a little older than their age. A guy who's eighteen and starts wearing slacks and a sports jacket to hang out in the candy store sort of stands out. It was, I finally realized, a ritual not unlike shaping-up down at the Fulton fish market, where guys stand around all night with hooks slung over their shoulders until some vendor or driver is shorthanded enough to call them over. They can usually pick up seventy-five dollars for a night's work, and go home with a couple of pounds of nice fish.

Tim McLoughlin

The guy in the store just waits to get noticed. He can't hang around the social club because he's not old enough and he doesn't have any connections yet, so the old-timers will just heap abuse on him and drive him out; but sooner or later some low-level wiseguy with a scheme will need an extra hand. In his dreams it's to be a wheelman or, even better, part of a credit card or insurance scam. It never works out that way. After half a year of dressing like Bogart and perfecting a steely stare in the mirror over the soda fountain, it's usually: Hide in the men's room at Bloomingdale's, wait until an hour after closing, then grab an armload of good leather jackets and hit the fire exit on Fifty-ninth Street. Somebody's waiting in a van down the block, and if he makes it that far, he probably gets away. For his trouble, for heisting maybe five thousand dollars retail merchandise, the wiseguy throws him two hundred bucks. And of course now he has bragging rights; he's pulled a *job*. There are a million variations on it.

All goes well the first few times, until the stupid bastard gets caught. In the beginning that's no big deal either because, it's New York after all, and no one goes to jail here. But after the third or fourth arrest, the wiseguy only throws him a hundred bucks, and if he doesn't like it, well, fuck him, because, hey pal, take a look at that record, who the fuck's gonna hire you? So he takes the hundred, does a couple more small jobs, gets caught one or two more times, and finally ends up with six months or so off the street.

And that's it. He doesn't hear from the wiseguys anymore because there's always a new kid in the candy store who's never been pinched and every security guard and store detective in Manhattan doesn't know his face. So the guy with eight or ten arrests and a rap sheet that includes city time keeps hanging around, because, in fact, who the fuck *is* gonna hire him. And eventually the wiseguy that hooked him up in the first place, or someone just like him, will, out of the goodness of his heart, find something for the poor guy to do, like throw a windbreaker over someone's head and break his nose for fifty dollars. Or have him lift car radios or batteries at ten bucks a pop. Try getting caught doing that a few times and see where your friends are. Eventually even his family turns away in embarrassment. The same guy is hanging in the candy store every morning, but he doesn't bother dressing up anymore, and just after noon he drifts over to Peggy's or

179

one of the other joints and starts drinking with the old men and the other losers. He's probably picked up a couple of jailhouse tattoos— at the very least a little cross between the thumb and forefinger of his left hand—and he starts to look older than he should.

As much as I knew that in no sense had anything like that happened to me, I still felt a little bit like one of those guys. I'd agreed to work for Tony because of my father, and because I was afraid that he was right about it looking like I was running away if I didn't. But, deep down, was there some little piece of me that harbored thoughts of being a big shot, in contention someday to be made?

I was still feeling restless, and it would be a few hours until my father got back, longer if he hung around anywhere for a couple of pops. I was hoping he'd come straight home, and I wondered how the side of his face looked today. A shiver went through me as I recalled the previous day's events. For an instant I felt paralyzed with fear, certain that Todd and Edward would be back to kill both me and my father. It passed as quickly as it came, and when I was rational I knew that, as my father had said, the odds were it was over.

Thinking of Edward got me dwelling on Nicky, and the night he'd been killed. Then I thought of Louise, and remembered Joey shrinking back behind the corner, waiting until she'd gone down the block before he would move. I had intended to look her up and see how she was getting along.

I went to the kitchen and opened the refrigerator. I stood staring for a minute, and it dawned on me I had no idea why I'd gone there. It was one of the few adolescent things I still did that drove my father crazy. I'd look into the open fridge, or a kitchen cabinet, or even a clothes closet, and just go into brainlock, with no clue as to what I was after. I closed the door, grateful that he hadn't been there to see me, and decided to go out. I was obviously too antsy to hang around and pretend to watch TV.

When I got downstairs I decided to see about Louise. It was either that or stop in on Gina, and I wasn't up to having that kind of day. The feeling that it was over between us had been growing for me, but she remained oblivious. In my typically responsible way, I figured I could duck the whole thing by seeing her less and less often, until she got the hint. Realistically, there was no way that was going to happen. If I went off for five years, she'd scream blue murder when I returned, then go back to picking out our wallpaper. I would ultimately have to do something decisive, and right now that made checking on Louise look pretty good.

I drove to the apartment she'd shared with Shades. It had been Nicky's place first, and his had been the only name on the bell. The listing for their apartment now read Facchetti, and although I didn't remember Louise's last name, I was sure that wasn't it. Louise was Colombian, and her surname was distinctly Hispanic. I rang the bell anyway. There was no answer. After trying the super's bell with the same result, I turned to leave.

A tiny ancient woman with startlingly white hair approached the building, pulling a shopping cart full of laundry. She was wearing a faded housedress that displayed a sunburst surrounded by rainbow colors, white sweatsocks with red trim, and navy canvas sneakers with a hole cut in one to accommodate a very impressive bunion. I doubted she weighed more than seventy pounds. I stepped outside and held the door for her, but she stopped at the bottom of the stoop and didn't attempt to go up the steps. I couldn't imagine that she'd be able to drag the cart up.

"You don't live here," she said, regarding me carefully, one eye opened much wider than the other. "Who you want?"

"I'm looking for a girl named Louise," I said. "She used to live here with a guy named Nicky. They were in apartment 3B."

"3B's new people," she said. "Sicilians. Right off the boat."

"I figured she moved," I said. "I was wondering if you might know where."

"Dark as niggers," she said.

"What?"

"The new people. Dark as the ace of spades."

"Oh," I said. "Yeah. Do you know when the super's going to be around?"

"You looking for that girl got knocked up by the bum," she said.

"Yeah," I said. "Yes, that's her. Louise. She's pregnant."

"Nice girl," she said. "Always helped me with my bags. Ran to the store for a quart of milk if I needed it. She wouldn't take no tip, just enough for the milk. Now she's gone, no one offers."

"I'd be glad to give you a hand with the cart," I said.

She nodded and stepped back. When I took the handle she scooted around me and up the stone steps much faster than I would have thought possible. She opened and held the outside and vestibule doors, then led the way to a second-floor apartment and opened that door as well. She stood in the doorway and watched me approach her. She looked impatient. The cart must have weighed as much as she did. I was amazed that she was even able to pull it on flat ground; I was exhausted from lugging it up one flight.

"Do you know where Louise moved to?" I asked.

"Why you want to know?"

"I'm a friend. I was a friend of her boyfriend."

"The bum. She threw him out. Was his place, but she threw him out." She giggled like a kid. "Then the landlord threw her out cause it ain't her place an' he gets twice the rent from the wops off the boat. Dark as niggers. He'd love to throw me out, cause I don't pay next to nothing, but he's gotta live with me till I die. Rent control. Thirty-six years."

My eyes were starting to cross. "Do you know where she moved? I just want to see if she's all right, if she needs anything, how she's doing."

"Behind the hospital," she said.

"Excuse me?"

"Behind the hospital. The big one by the fort."

"Victory Memorial?" I said. "Over by Fort Hamilton? She moved over there? Do you have her address, or would the super have it?"

"Super doesn't know shit. Didn't know she moved till I told him. She went in the middle of the night." She giggled again. "She stuck him for some money cause he was throwing her out."

"The super?"

"No. The landlord." She glared at me like I hadn't been paying attention. When she squinted, even a little, she looked just like Popeye. "I don't know an address. Not like I visit anyone."

"Okay," I said. "Thank you." I started to leave, then turned back toward her as she hauled the cart over her doorstep. "What would you have done if I wasn't there to give you a hand?"

She looked at me blankly for a moment. "Sicily's only forty miles from Africa," she said, nodding. "Don't think some of 'em didn't take a swim." She pulled the cart inside and closed the door.

I went back out, but I didn't see anyone else, and I figured I probably wouldn't find anyone less loony who would be as cooperative, so I called it quits. I knew something, anyway. There was only one row of houses behind Victory Memorial, and they were all one-family, so if Louise was back there she probably had a basement rental. I'd check it out tomorrow. Right now I wanted to eat and take a nap, then get ready to shoot for a whole date with Kathy, whatever that would entail. On the way home I thought about Sicilian pizza and why it was square. I really should have asked.

21

With the exception of tormenting Gina on her holy acquisition pilgrimages, I was almost always on time for everything. It just seemed to make life easier. I'd gotten in the car to meet Kathy that night at nine-fifteen, allowing myself a generous forty-five minutes for the run to the Village and to park. So it was especially frustrating to be sitting in bumper-to-bumper traffic on the Brooklyn Bridge at ten o'clock, with no idea how long I'd be there.

When I'd returned from looking for Louise my father hadn't come in yet. I lay down for a couple of hours, and when I got up, he was in his room sleeping. I was beginning to feel like one of those immigrant stories where three Haitians rent one room and everybody sleeps in shifts. I ate something, and took my time getting ready. There was no way I expected any kind of traffic heading toward Manhattan at this hour.

Eventually the traffic began moving again, and as was so often the case in New York City, there was no visible evidence of what had caused it to stop. I took the streets to the Village, costing me another ten minutes, but insuring that I wouldn't get bottlenecked on the FDR Drive. When I got to Bradley's—which, thank God, was right where the information operator had said it would be—I discovered that along with my driving luck, my parking space karma had been exhausted. I finally got a spot three blocks downtown and ran to the bar. It was ten-forty.

Bradley's was dark, and laid out the way a proper tavern should be, with the long sturdy bar itself—backed by an ornately carved wood and gilt-trimmed mirror—the star of the show. A handful of tables lined the opposite wall, and in the back, a few more were arranged in a loose semi-circle around a small stage. The back-bar was strung with blinking Christmas lights, and several green cardboard wreaths were taped to the glass. It wasn't much, but it surprised me. I hadn't seen any decorations sprouting around the neighborhood yet, and I hadn't given even a moment's thought to the approaching holiday.

Two enormously fat black men were performing on the stage, one pounding a piano, and the other playing a huge standing bass fiddle. I'd never seen anyone play one of those except in old movies. The crowd was very much into the music, and it was, to be honest, pretty infectious. It sounded like real old-time jazz, big-band stuff or earlier, before everyone had to change their name to Zimbabwe and play songs of social significance that sound like a car wreck.

The bar was crowded, but never more than one deep, and there was a space here and there. All the tables were filled. I didn't see Kathy anywhere. Heartsick is such a corny word, but I swear that's what I felt. I made a quick tour of the room and was about to ask the bartender if he'd seen her when she walked through the door. She came right over to me and took my arm.

"I hope you haven't been waiting long," she said pleasantly.

Loaded question. If I was meeting Gina I would have paid hard cash for this kind of scenario. I'd rant and rave and look at my watch, and buy at least two broken dates from something like this. But so far, anyway, Kathy and I were on fairly equal ground, and making her feel bad wasn't really a part of my plan for making me feel good.

"I just walked in," I said. "I'm so goddamn relieved that I didn't keep *you* waiting. Everything that could have gone wrong did."

"Really?"

She smiled quickly, genuinely, and I realized in an instant that I'd been set-up. She had been in the bar before I got there. She had waited for me. She was pissed or went to make a phone call, and returned after I arrived. And she'd tested me. She wanted to know what I'd say.

I hadn't thought she was the type for that, but as my father kept pointing out, I was still young. I could almost hear his voice through the background music. Keep on your toes, it said. She may be the girl of your dreams, but that doesn't alter those XX chromosomes. The truth of the matter was I'd never felt more attracted to her. She kissed me briefly, and I felt proud. The tough ones might get me later, but I could still field the ground balls.

We signaled a waitress and told her we'd like a table whenever one opened. I asked Kathy if she'd like a drink, and she weighed the question far longer than was called for. When the bartender approached us, she was still agonizing over it. I went ahead and ordered Wild Turkey on the rocks, and she eventually asked for a screwdriver.

"Cheers," she said, lifting her glass.

"To vitamin C."

Kathy asked me if I knew the song that was playing. I didn't, but it sounded vaguely familiar. She hummed little snippets of five different songs until she hit one I'd heard before.

"They're all Duke Ellington," she said. "Each one's different, but unmistakably his. It's amazing, isn't it?"

"It's impressive," I admitted, "but what really amazes me is that you can hum one song while another song is playing."

"What?"

"You know, these guys are playing good rocking jazz, and you were able to hum half-a-dozen tunes at the same time."

"And that means more to you than Duke Ellington's songbook?"

"Actually," I said, "I've always felt that it was a sign of demonic possession, but I'm trying to be polite."

"Good job," she said.

A table opened up, mercifully far enough from the music that we could make conversation. Kathy talked some more about jazz, and though I had little to add, I enjoyed listening to her. She had a kind of intensity when she spoke that I suspected could make a lecture on Flemish architecture seem interesting. At the same time, of course, it meant she'd be a bitch on wheels in an argument. I filed the thought away.

We talked and drank for almost three hours. There were times when I was genuinely caught up in the passion of the conversation, and other times when I felt like I was barely treading water. She was sharp on music, mostly rock and jazz, but didn't know much at all about rap. I countered her suggestion that it promoted violence against women with several examples to the contrary, including lyrics by female rappers; and added the observation that she was judging from outside the cultural experience, and that just might be construed as racist. She backed off. The best defense really is a good offense.

She never slurred or lost focus, but when she got up to hit the ladies room I noticed that she was moving like she was negotiating the deck of a whaling ship in a nor'easter.

"Are you okay?" I asked when she returned.

"You could tell, huh?"

"You seem fine. It's just the way you were walking."

"I know," she said. "It's a curse. I can talk about nuclear physics with four drinks in me but don't ask me to pass the chips. Do you get like that?"

"No. I'm pretty lucky. I just get stupid, so no one can really tell."

"I'd be able to tell." She leaned forward and kissed me.

"Would you have done that," I asked when we finished, "if you weren't too drunk to pass the chips?"

"Yes, I'm pretty sure I would have. I've wanted to since we got the booth. Why? Does it matter?"

I shrugged. "Just curious. If it was the drinks, I wanted to keep count of what it took."

She smiled. "Give yourself a little credit."

"Vodka is more consistent. It doesn't have an off day."

"I hope you're not having an off day," she said. "I'll need you to pour me into a cab if we don't get out of here soon."

I told her that I had the car and I'd drive her home. After many assurances that I was still functional, she agreed. I left her in the booth and paid the check, then booked back to the car and drove to the front door. Kathy was waiting outside when I got there, and she looked noticeably better. Night air, especially cold night air, will either kill me or give me a second wind when I'm half in the bag. It seemed to be agreeing with Kathy.

We drove back to her place, and the parking gods decided to smile on me once again. I got a spot about two doors down from her house. She was steady on her feet and maneuvered the distance to her door better than I would have expected.

"Was the staggering a false alarm?" I asked.

"Not so much a false alarm. More of an early warning sign. As long as I see it when everyone else does, I stop before I wind up with a lampshade on my head."

"Pity."

"Trust me," she said as she opened the door to the foyer, "you don't want to carry me up these stairs unconscious. I'm not as light as I look."

Although I was sure Kathy was plenty light enough, I wasn't even crazy about dragging my own conscious ass up all those stairs. Considering how awkwardly she'd moved a short time ago, she navigated her way up pretty smoothly. I made myself keep pace.

When we got in her apartment I noticed that the morning's dishes had been cleared from the coffee table. They weren't in the sink, so I assumed she'd done them and put them away. The flyer for the performance artist was gone too, and the whole place looked pin-neat. Kathy tossed her jacket over the arm of an over-stuffed wing chair. I dropped mine on top of it.

"You can put some music on," she said, gesturing at the ancient stereo. "Most everything I have is still on vinyl, but there's a bunch of tapes on the bottom shelf. I still don't have a CD player."

"Me either," I said, scanning her collection. "I'd like to hear what you had on the last time I was here."

"Dire Straits?"

"Yeah. The *Sultans of Swing* guys."

"That wasn't the album." She came over and removed a record that was literally under my nose and handed it to me, then walked over to the kitchenette area. "What would you like to drink?" she asked. "Last time I offered you juice and you ran away. I don't have any bourbon. Would you like some vodka?"

"At the risk of ruining my reputation," I said, "cold water would be wonderful."

She opened and closed things and rustled and clinked while I figured out how to work the sound system. I don't know if deja-vu is the right term for something as set-up as this, but I realized that I'd managed to get myself back on the same sofa with the same music, and the same girl was only a few feet away. If I had to cut off the tattoo, change political party, religion, or gender, I vowed I wouldn't fuck it up this time.

Kathy brought me my water and sat across from me. "So," she said, "why Dire Straits?"

"I don't know much about them, but since the last time I was here I heard them on the radio a couple of times and thought of you. It was nice."

She shrugged. "Good thing I didn't play Thelonius Monk."

I stared at her.

"Never mind," she said. "You tried to hide your tattoo the last time I saw you. What's your game plan tonight?"

"Well, the last time I was here you put your glass on the floor, and I was able to suavely move in and kiss you on the way up. I'm sort of waiting for that kind of opening."

"Oh. It's a good thing you told me. Does it have to appear spontaneous?"

"That would be better," I said.

"Too bad." She leaned in and kissed me. It was across a fair distance, and I think she did it purposely to catch me off guard, but it was wonderful anyway.

"Not fair," I said when we stopped. "You didn't put your drink down."

"No, but if it makes you feel any better I did spill a little."

She put her glass on the floor and I slid along the couch to her. I was clearly a product of these twisted times to the extent that I was never sure whether I was going to have sex until I was in the middle of it, but I had to admit this looked pretty good.

We held each other tightly while we kissed. Her body felt absolutely perfect: soft, like a girl's should be. I was relieved. I'd never been an advocate of the great fitness craze that seemed to have most of the planet killing themselves or feeling like shit for not killing themselves. I thought that trim and toned was nice in a woman, but if you felt like you had your arms around the guy who just came off the lat machine at the gym, well, that made me feel queasy. Kathy was definitely trim and toned, but she was soft in all the right places. I was getting short of breath, and my erection was giving me serious discomfort due to the half-turned, stretched-out position I'd sunk into. We made out like two kids at a drive-in for a long time. Eventually I needed to sit up and re-align my circulatory system. I asked Kathy where she slept.

"This is it," she said.

"The couch?"

"Yes. It opens up. I don't usually bother, but I think tonight we should." She stood, scooped up her glass, and walked to the kitchen area. "Why don't you open that up?" she said, gesturing to the sofa. "I'll toss you the sheets."

Dire Straits had long since stopped playing, and I didn't really know the lyrics anyway, but I had to resist the impulse to hum the tunes that were still circling in my head. Kathy crossed the apartment, and I stopped her for another long kiss before she made her way to the bathroom. She stepped in, then right out, and threw two folded blue sheets over to me.

"I'll bring the pillows out with me," she said, and disappeared back into the john.

I got the cushions off the sofa and was thrilled that Kathy wasn't in the room to see me trying to figure out the mechanics of the pull-out bed. After eight or nine attempts some unseen mechanism clicked and the frame lifted up and out.

The bed opened easily from that point, and it appeared sturdy, though the mattress looked suspiciously thin. I had secured the fitted sheet and was tucking the top sheet in around one side when Kathy emerged from the bathroom. She was carrying two small pillows and wearing the same kind of white athletic undershirt she'd had on the last time I was up there. It seemed to be all she was wearing, but it reached just far enough that it was impossible to tell if it was covering underwear. She walked to the opposite side of the bed, tossed the pillows at the top, and began helping me with the sheet as though we were spreading a picnic blanket.

I finished my side while watching her as surreptitiously as possible. When she stretched to tuck the bottom corner her shirt rode up a little, just a couple of inches. I got a brief glimpse—the proverbial flash—of black fur. No underwear. It probably wouldn't be good if I came before I was physically in the bed.

When Kathy was done with her side she cut the light by the bed, pulled the top corner of the sheet down, and slid in. The kitchen light remained on, and it gave off a nice twilight effect. I felt a little awkward about her having changed in private, while I was being watched. I undressed quickly. Shoes first, then pants and shirt and shorts. I sat on the bed to get my socks off. I wasn't really drunk, but trying something like that standing up was just asking to be compared to Jerry Lewis. When I turned toward her I was naked, but Kathy was still wearing the white shirt.

"What happened to you?" she asked, gesturing at my bandaged side.

I'd changed the gauze after I showered, and the new dressing was half the size of the old, so it didn't look like much. "I got hurt working," I said.

"Driving?"

"Doing a messenger job. I had an accident."

When I climbed into bed she ran her hand over it lightly. "Does it hurt?"

"No, but if you promise to keep doing that I'll go bandage the rest of my body."

She traced the outline of the dressing with her nails. There was a moment when I was sure she was going to ask about it some more, then she changed her mind. Just for that instant, that one beat of time, she looked like Gina. It was the facial expression, the one that says *It's better that I don't know.* I hated seeing it on Kathy. It didn't belong on her face. That was not how I pictured us. But, as much as it disturbed me, I couldn't bring myself to say anything either, and the moment seemed to pass.

We kissed side by side, running our hands up and down each other's flanks. I cupped her breasts through the shirt, and felt her nipples harden against my palms through the thin material. I wanted to tear the shirt off her, to shred it. I reached under it and she stopped me, smiling.

"Not yet," she whispered. "I don't think just yet."

I slid my hand down her stomach and between her legs. She rolled half onto her back and parted them slightly.

That was it for me. I went from kissing her face and throat to a slow but steady slide south. I licked and sucked at her breasts, right through the cotton fabric like I was filtering a hit of strong weed. I kept moving down, and replaced my hand with my mouth. She gasped lightly, and cradled the back of my head with both hands, adjusting her position and pulling me in a little tighter. I was so horny I was starting to hump the mattress. This was what I loved. As far as I was concerned, women should be served on a plate. The smell, the taste, the feel, there was nothing quite like dining out. I usually dove down before I had the blouse open.

We had maneuvered ourselves over to lying diagonally across the bed now, and that was a good thing because otherwise I would have fallen off. I went at her greedily, and she responded to my movements by arching her pelvis up to push herself even more tightly to my mouth. Once we established a rhythm we went on like that for a long time.

I reached up again after a while, and slid my hands under Kathy's shirt while she rocked back and forth against my chin. She took one of her hands from my head, reached for my arm, then changed her mind and stopped. She raised herself slightly and pulled the shirt up to her neck. I laid my hands on her breasts and moved in small circles, pulling lightly in sync with the motion of her body. Dimly, far off, I was aware of the frame of the sofabed moving with us, swaying, squeaking a little. It didn't matter. Nothing mattered. Someone could have shot me again. Kathy was breathing fast and her movements quickened. She began pushing so rapidly that I released her breasts and reached under her with both hands, holding her ass to anchor her to me. As soon as we locked in that clinch she began to shake. Just a little at first, once or twice, then more frequently. The more she pushed the more I did. Kathy stopped moving suddenly, and was completely still for about five seconds, then grabbed my head in both hands and pulled herself hard against me. I sent my tongue forward as she convulsed two long times, then relaxed back into the bed.

I was right up against her, but no longer moving. I removed my hands from under her and rested one on her stomach. She caught my wrist in a grip normally reserved for handling poison reptiles and pulled my hand away from her. She let go, and I waited a minute or so, then wiped my mouth quickly on the sheet and slowly slid up the length of her body.

It had been stupid to try to touch her right away. She was still giving off little tremors when I got up next to her. We held each other for a couple of minutes, and when she'd unclenched enough I sent my hands out over her again. As soon as she reciprocated, I rolled over like a dog and she swung herself up onto me. Memories of lovemaking often tend to be warm and romantic, but the truth was we humped like lab rats on crack. I'd been half-mad from going down on her and now that I was getting off it couldn't possibly be soon enough. The bottom legs of the sofabed raised off the floor and thumped down with our movement, and although that should have quieted us, it only seemed to spur us on. I felt challenged, like we needed to make enough noise to drown out the bed.

I came quickly. It felt quick in sex-time, and real time is about half of that, but I couldn't hold back. When we stopped moving I felt like I didn't have the energy to blink. I decided that I'd been correct the last time I'd been here. Kathy was going to kill me.

She rolled off to the right and lay next to me. The mattress felt like a sponge. After a couple of minutes she pulled the top-sheet over us. I was starting to feel cold and damp, and I assumed she was too. When she didn't move after another minute, I excused myself and went to clean up and dry off. When I returned Kathy was back in her undershirt, and waiting to get in the john. I noticed that she'd removed the fitted sheet from the bed. It was rolled in a ball on the floor. She'd replaced it with the top-sheet, and tossed a light green cotton blanket over that.

I got into the bed, and almost immediately felt drowsy. The evening—the drinks and the sex—had finally caught up with me. Maybe it was the whole day, or more to the point, the last several days. I felt like I could sleep for a week. More. Twenty years. I fought to remain awake until Kathy came back. I managed, barely, and was still conscious when she returned. She walked past the bed and over to the kitchenette.

"Do you mind?" she asked, pointing at the overhead light. "I'm really exhausted."

This was the sort of sign that could send me back to the Church. "No. Not at all. If you're tired turn it off; we can go right to sleep."

She hit the switch and the room was plunged into total darkness. I couldn't even make out her silhouette. Kathy must have memorized the layout of the apartment, because I heard her navigate her way to the bed. She didn't hit anything. She got in, slid across, and curled up next to me.

"Isn't this a great way to spend a Friday night?" she whispered against my neck.

"Yes, but I think I would have had a good time even if it was a Tuesday."

"You're an idiot," she said.

I didn't have a response, and it was just as well, because she was asleep in about a minute. I nodded off shortly after, but for a little while I lay there thinking about how this was the first time I'd stayed with a girl after sex; the first time I stayed over; the first time I was falling asleep in someone else's bed.

I woke about two hours later with a vicious piss hard-on. I slipped out of bed without waking Kathy, and hit the john. Once the immediate problem of my bladder had been addressed I found myself back in bed, wide awake and with another erection. Kathy was sleeping like a stone. My judgment is rarely at its best at moments like that. We had been sleeping curled into each other, spoonlike. I returned to that position, and after squirming in as close as possible, shifted myself downward a little and went from rubbing gently against her ass to actively seeking shelter from the storm.

Kathy had barely stirred when I first moved. Now she rocked back against me steadily, still asleep. I was quiet, and tried to be as even as possible in my movements, but the sofabed started making noise again, swaying with us, and in spite of my efforts to control my breathing, I suspected that I rasped a bit in her ear. I couldn't see what I was doing, but when Kathy woke up, it felt like I was almost in. She stopped moving, and it was as shocking as my oxygen supply being cut off. Her body frozen in place, she turned her head to look at me.

"What are you doing?" she said.

"Nothing. Why do you ask?"

"I'm sleeping. You can't be looking to get laid now."

"You were doing all right for sleeping," I said.

"I thought I was dreaming."

"You are. None of this is really happening." I began prodding her again.

Kathy shrugged her shoulders once, slowly, elaborately, and squinted her eyes closed tight. "Jesus Christ," she said, pushing back hard against me, "I really need to sleep."

"Go ahead," I said. "I'm Irish. You won't even know I'm here."

She rolled over to face me, and reaching down, grabbed my dick firmly in both hands. I maneuvered myself on top of her, and, still holding me, she steered me in.

"Must be Black Irish," she said.

"An erection," I said, "is a terrible thing to waste."

"Shut the fuck up," she said, a little more harshly than I thought necessary. But it hardly mattered. I was breathing like a steam engine in no time and couldn't have uttered another complete sentence on a bet. I did have the presence of mind to consider the number and diverse nature of women who preferred my company when I didn't speak.

We moved smoothly this time, and remained in that position, without the somehow instinctive sense of urgency we'd both displayed earlier. I felt comfortable with her, as though this were our tenth or twentieth time together.

I kept pumping, slowly, long after I came. I felt like one of those wooden birds that, once you push it, dips its beak into a glass of water forever. It didn't even feel like sex anymore. I just didn't want to stop.

Eventually I collapsed, but even that felt like slow motion. I slid down a few inches and rested my hips mostly on the bed and very little on Kathy. I propped myself up on my elbows so my weight was off her ribcage. She nuzzled into my neck and shoulder. As good as it all felt, and it felt very good, I knew that I could only remain like that for a couple of minutes before my muscles started to cramp.

"All right," she said. "I forgive you for waking me up."

"I was making good time while you were out. Consciousness kind of put a crimp in things for me."

She shoved me over, sparing me the embarrassment of having to move on my own. I went back to what I was already optimistically thinking of as my side of the bed.

We lay half-entwined and drifted in and out of sleep for about the next hour. I would doze off, and it seemed she would too, but if I spoke she answered immediately and coherently. It was as though whenever I was awake, she was too. Or the other way around.

I got up with the sun, which meant I'd had precious little sleep. My watch read seven-twenty. I washed up and dressed in Kathy's tiny, ancient bathroom, and when I came out she was sitting up in bed.

"Did Batman beep you?" she asked.

"I'm not allowed to tell," I said.

"It's still dark out."

"That changes in a little while. It gets light. You'll see."

She nodded. "Obviously you can go whenever you want. I'm not saying you should stay. It just seems a little strange."

"These are my kind of hours," I said. I was embarrassed to tell her that I was afraid my father would worry if I wasn't home soon. "Staying here at all felt a little strange to me."

"Why?"

"It isn't something I do."

"What do you mean?" She was leaning forward, giving me that anthropology major stare.

"I have a difficult time sleeping away from home. Not in my own bed. Do you know what I mean? It's just a neurosis."

"Do you fight it?" she asked.

"No. Like most of my fears and phobias I think the healthy thing to do is surrender to it right away."

"Sure," she nodded. "I can see how that would be the way to go."

I declined Kathy's offer of fresh coffee, and she looked relieved. The offer had been made while she was still prone, and it appeared that she intended to remain that way for some time. I kissed her and told her I'd call her the next day, after she'd had some sleep. When she told me to pull the door closed tight I realized that I wasn't being escorted out. I was aware of my temples throbbing a little and my eyes burning as I'd gotten dressed, but that was about it, and it wasn't all that different from most mornings. I'd probably nap in the afternoon. I had no idea how Kathy was feeling, but I figured it was a little rougher for her.

"Will I actually be seeing you any time soon," she asked, "or should I just expect a call at five in the morning about a year from now?"

"You don't know?" I said. "No. Now that we've slept together this relationship has escalated into one of those *Fatal Attraction* things where I really do stalk you and terrorize and drive off any man you speak to until I've made you mine."

She nodded again. "I don't know how much you're joking."

"Then my work here is done," I said. "I'd like to see you again. I'd like to see you soon."

"Is that what you really want?"

"I really want to see you often. I really want to become your boyfriend, but I'm trying hard not to push."

"What about your girlfriend?" she said.

"Did I say I had a girlfriend?"

"No," Kathy said. "In fact, you specifically said you didn't. But what about her?"

"You asked me what I wanted. I told you. I'm still sorting out a lot of things and my personal life is one of them. Can this conversation wait a little while?"

"Why not," she said. "Everything else has."

Chapter

22

Our apartment looked exactly the way it had when I left. Which meant the way it had for the last three years. Which meant, I supposed, absolutely nothing. My father was already up and out, so I could have hung around with Kathy for a while longer after all. There were two notes on separate pieces of tissue-thin bookie paper taped to the television screen. One was, "Bed not mussed 7 o'clock— Shame Shame." The other just read "Gina 4X." It must have gotten on his nerves. He usually didn't bother to tell me at all when she called.

I went to the kitchen to see if there was anything salvageable in the fridge. There were four blue magnets in the shape of rabbits at play, holding a handful of papers to the outside of the door. My mother had purchased them at a gift shop on Eighty-sixth Street shortly before she got sick. One of them still secured a three-year-old Sunday Mass schedule from Regina Pacis that she'd placed there. The newest addition was my father's notice to appear in Criminal Court on the return date for his case. It was fastened by a leaping bunny and half-covering a page from a magazine that featured a recipe for rice-crispies squares.

I opened the fridge and the phone rang as though I'd tripped an alarm. I got it on the second ring, leaving the refrigerator door ajar.

"Hello."

"I finally got you, or you gonna tell me this is your fucking machine?"

"What's up, Gina?"

"What's up? Did your father tell you I called?"

"I haven't seen him yet today," I said. "You know the way our schedules are. He could go to Alaska for six months and I wouldn't know."

"I called you eight times," she said.

"Yesterday?"

"No. I mean, yesterday too. In the last couple of days. Where the hell have you been?"

I crouched down, sitting on my heels on the kitchen floor and staring at the bare bulb in the mostly empty fridge. "I've been running around," I said. "I've been busy as hell between school and helping my father out with a few things." My temples started to throb again. I swung the refrigerator door back and forth with one hand to fan myself.

"We gotta talk," she said. "Remember when you told me to pick out a ring? I think I found one, but you have to come with me to see it again. That's why I been trying to reach you so much. I don't even know what price range we're in. I really have to go over all this with you."

It sounded like she was calling me from Tokyo. I pictured the telephone cable stretching five thousand miles across the ocean floor to that house on Twenty-first Avenue. Maybe Gina and her mother were in kimonos. My head was pounding seriously now. I'd had a good night, which had capped a hideous week. I was feeling a little dizzy, and my stomach had tensed when I first heard her voice. I'd had too much to drink, not enough to eat, and a negligible amount of sleep.

"I'll be right over," I said.

It was a very short hop to Gina's by car, but I swung by Sixty-fifth Street and stopped for gas anyway. I gave the small, sleepy-looking Middle-Easterner in the bullet-proof fishbowl a twenty and told him I was topping off the tank. He didn't acknowledge me.

As I stood beside the car watching the numbers move silently on the newly installed pumps, I tried to focus on what I was going to say to Gina, but the gas fumes were causing my headache to escalate dramatically and I couldn't seem to concentrate. I knew I had to turn this thing around. There was no way I could let her buy a ring.

Everything cut in on my thoughts. Kathy. My father. Passing traffic. I could not articulate, even to myself in my own head, what I would tell Gina. I also knew that I should eat or sleep before I saw her, probably both, but there was no way I could rest with the specter of that ring on her hand floating before my eyes. My sense of urgency was disproportionate to the problem, of course. This had been an ongoing tug-of-war for several years, but the ante was being upped now to stakes I was unwilling to match.

The pump clicked off and I got my change from the terrorist under glass. I pulled out onto Thirteenth Avenue and was across from Gina's house five minutes later.

She opened the door when I was halfway up the stoop, which meant she'd been watching at the window for me. I hated that. She wore black jeans with a dark blue denim shirt, and powder-blue boots with enough of a heel that I barely had to bend at all to kiss her. The tops of the boots folded down. She had makeup and lipstick on, and her hair had been done. It was barely nine o'clock in the morning.

"Shopping?" I hazarded.

"In a little while," she said. "Victor's gonna take me and Mom to the Staten Island Mall, then we're going out to eat with him and Phyllis. You could come."

I shook my head. Gina led the way into the house, talking to me over her shoulder.

"I wanted to go to Alexander's, but Victor says Kings Plaza's all niggers now. He's got Mom scared to go."

"Where is your mother?" I asked.

"She's at the beauty parlor. She had a nine-thirty. Vic's coming at eleven." She sat on the sofa in the living room and turned on the small white and gold table lamp next to her. The room was already flooded with sunlight. She looked up at me and smiled. "So anyway," she said, "Victor has this friend. On Canal Street. That's where I saw the ring."

"Victor's a sweetheart," I said.

"Yeah. He is. Anyway, the ring books for five thousand. The guy will let us have it for thirty-five hundred. Victor says he might come down another hundred or two, but that's about it. And all this is only if we're talking cash. You gotta see the ring, Mike. It's really beautiful. I don't know from carats and clarity and all that shit, but believe me, you gotta see it." She was leaning forward on the couch, and her eyes were getting misty. She looked like she was describing the Shroud of Turin. "You should hear David, too," she said. "That's Vic's friend. He knows all that technical shit; the kind of stuff you'd want to know."

I stood and walked over to the windows. I looked out at my car across the street and pictured myself behind the wheel, starting the engine. "Thirty-five hundred's a little steep," I said.

"He'll come down some."

"Thirty-three hundred's a little steep."

"Maybe you can do better," she said. "You're good at that."

"I don't know." I was still looking out the window.

"How much?" she snapped.

"What?"

"How much? How much wouldn't be 'a little steep'?"

I turned to face her. "I'm not sure," I said. "I don't even know how much I've got."

"Three thousand?"

"I don't know."

"Two? One?" She was getting angrier.

"I don't know."

"Five hundred? Fifty?"

"Knock it off," I said.

"Give me a hint," she said. "A clue." Her voice was rising. "Do you want me to pay for it? Just tell me. Because I want this fucking ring."

I looked at her for a long time without saying anything. I was off my feed and not functioning at peak, but I didn't see how even being on top of my game would have helped me out. I'd been dodging this bullet for longer than I cared to figure, but I was out of excuses. I'd told her to find a ring and she'd found one.

Suddenly I got very calm. My head still hurt, but not with the jackhammer pain I'd been feeling. I suspected that this was what it felt like to let go when drowning, or freezing to death. To stop fighting.

"No," I said.

"No what?"

"You can't get this ring."

"I'm getting the goddamn ring," she said. "Why shouldn't I have it?

Why are you doing this?"

"Because we're not getting married," I said.

"We are. You said we were. You said it upstairs the night you were like an animal with me. You said it." She was rocking back and forth on the sofa and she'd started to cry. "It's time; don't you see that? I don't want to wait anymore. I told my friends you asked me. Why won't you even look at the goddamn ring?"

I walked over and sat next to her on the couch. I still felt oddly calm, like I was talking to the TV and Gina wasn't in the room. Like I was rehearsing for what I'd say when she got there.

"We're not getting married," I said. "I know you don't want to wait. I understand that. I don't want to wait either. I just don't want to do it. You know that. You've always known it."

She picked her head up, and the expression on her face threw me. She looked annoyed, but only mildly, as she did when I guessed the wrong perfume she was wearing, or I couldn't identify an outfit by designer in a store window on Eighteenth Avenue. "My mother will be home soon," she said. "You made me cry and fuck up my makeup. I have to fix it again." She stood up. "If you don't want to see the ring, I don't care. I thought it would be nice. I thought maybe you'd want to. It doesn't matter. I don't want to hear shit about it later if you don't like it." She turned and walked out of the room.

"We're not getting married," I said. I remained seated on the couch.

The sharp clicking of her heels echoed off the hardwood floor of the dining room as she made her way through the house, the sound diminishing to soft thuds as she hit the carpeted hallway. The bathroom door creaked open.

There was silence for about half a minute, then the door crashed back open, slamming fiercely against the porcelain towel rack. Her steps coming back sounded like those of a galloping horse. She stopped herself in the living room doorway with one hand on the doorjamb. The eyeliner or whatever had been removed from her left eye, but her right was still made-up, and the stuff had continued to run. She looked like Alice Cooper, and she was crying again.

"You. Are. Going. To marry me," she screamed. It was the loudest I'd ever heard her yell. "Do you understand? I've been waiting four fucking years. You come and go; I don't say anything. You don't call; I don't say anything. You run around; I never said anything." Her every phrase was punctuated by her fists pumping up and down at her side in sync, as though she was cross-country skiing across the living room. The volume of her voice had dropped but the tone still sounded like a scream, and she was hoarse, as if she'd been smoking unfiltered cigarettes for sixty years. "Everybody thinks I'm an asshole," she said. "My friends, my mother, Victor. They all say you won't marry me. That if you were gonna, you would have done it already. I'm gonna be twenty; most of my friends are married. Half of them are on their first kid. And I'm still spinning my fucking wheels with you."

I didn't have the slightest idea what to say. It didn't make any difference. I don't think she would have heard me. I was afraid to move an inch, for fear that it might set her off again. She leaned against the doorjamb, weak from the outburst, drained. I felt the same way. The zenlike composure that I'd displayed walking into this conversation had deserted me. I felt that I'd been betrayed by it, but worse, I felt bad. Everything that she'd said was true. It didn't matter how insane it sounded to say that she was almost twenty. It was the same insanity she'd had when I met her, and I had in fact let her spin her wheels for four years.

"If you knew you weren't gonna marry me, why did you string me along all this time?"

"I didn't feel like I was stringing you along," I said. "Not until lately. I just liked things the way they were."

"Sure you did. Who wouldn't? You do whatever you want; make your own hours; break dates. And when you get lonely or horny you come over and get laid. And now you found somebody else."

I looked up at her, not really sure what she was talking about.

"I never bothered you about seeing other people," she said, "cause you didn't get involved or rub my nose in it, or keep a gummada like Victor does. But now you met someone and you told her you're free. Well, you're not."

I was afraid to breathe. I was quite literally afraid to open my mouth to take a breath. I had no clue where Gina had gleaned her information. I'd never even suspected that she knew I'd cheated on her, or that her brother had a mistress. And I couldn't begin to guess how she'd figured out my situation with Kathy. My mind couldn't process the information fast enough. I couldn't make sense of anything. I wanted to run. I wondered if she'd followed me, or if she'd had Victor or someone else do it. I couldn't figure anything out.

"Four years," she said.

"There's no one else," I said, frantically trying to think of something to add.

"You wouldn't tell me flat out unless there was someone else. You'd bullshit me. You'd find some reason not to get the ring, or you'd get it and then we'd be engaged for a thousand years. But you wouldn't do *this*."

"Isn't it about time one of us did *this?*" I said, raising my voice. "I mean, obviously I'm not doing you any favors by hanging around, and you think you're hip to all my moves, so why are you still with me?"

"Because I love you," she said.

"You love the idea of us," I said. "You love playing house. Think about it. You want your life to stay the same as much as I do. Where would we live? Right here, upstairs. Are you gonna get a full-time job? No, not with mom for a landlord. You won't have to. And how about dinner? Will you cook, or do you think maybe we'd be dining down here six nights a week?"

"Not six nights," she said.

"That's as much of a compromise as you'll commit to now. If we got married you wouldn't even have to pretend. Fuck that."

The tone of her voice shifted again, to almost conversational, but it was still tinged with that raspy edge. "If you don't want your life to change," she said, "and I don't want my life to change, then let's get married and keep doing what we do now."

"What?" I said. "Live separately?"

"No. We'll live here, but you can keep doing whatever you want. I won't break your balls. I don't now."

"Gina," I said. "That's fucked up. That's not being married. That's being roommates. No."

"Listen to me," she said. "I'm sticking to my schedule. I'm gonna be married in a year, and I'm gonna have my first kid in two. I always thought it'd be with you, but if it's not, it'll be with someone else. Plenny a' guys come looking. If you don't commit, I'll find someone who will."

"Don't threaten me," I said.

"I'm threatening. I'm fucking threatening you. So what?"

"So go ahead. Marry someone else." I stood up and went past her in the doorway.

When I drew abreast of her she screamed in my face. "Four years. Why? I gotta start from scratch again. From nowhere. After four years."

I moved by her and was halfway to the door.

"You're wrong," she yelled. "This is wrong. You did the wrong thing." She was pointing at me from the doorway.

"I know," I said. I turned to the apartment door.

"It's gonna tear your heart out," she said.

"What?"

"When you see me with a kid. When you see me pushing that carriage with a baby down Twentieth Avenue. It's gonna tear your fuckin' heart out."

There was something there, I don't know what, that made me pause. She couldn't have been more wrong. I didn't even want to get married, let alone have kids. But she spoke with a sense of confidence that I normally didn't hear from her unless she was talking about clothes or interior design.

"If you leave," she said, "it's gonna be someone else. It's gonna be someone else and it coulda been you." Her face was a mess. She'd smeared the mascara from the still made-up eye across her cheek, and her nose was brutally red and running.

It coulda been me, I thought. Evading that fate was like receiving a last minute reprieve from the governor. But I still hesitated. I couldn't open the fucking door.

Gina seemed to know it. "Well," she snapped. "What are you gonna do?"

Somehow the situation had been turned around so that I was being given an ultimatum. And the depressing thing was, that was what I wanted. Don't ask me to act; ask me to react. I opened the door.

On the other side stood Gina's mother, six inches from my face. Her hair had been tightly permed and colored so black that it looked blue. At her feet was a small bag of groceries, a half-gallon of ninety-nine percent fat-free milk protruding from the top like a new skyscraper amidst neighborhood tenements. If she'd had to put the bag down, I thought, she'd been there a while.

"Hi," I said. "Have a nice day."

"She's right," she said. "It'll tear your heart out."

I took a step back from her, into the apartment. She picked up the bag and stepped in after me. As soon as she cleared the doorway I walked around her and out the door. I could still hear Gina crying when I was in the vestibule, and her mother's muffled voice, either chastising or comforting her.

I had to keep moving. I felt like I'd die if I stopped. Like my feet would stick to the small white octagonal tiles of the foyer. Then I'd sink slowly, like a large, stupid animal in a tar pit. Archeologists five million years from now would mix and match my bones with those of all the other fucking idiots who didn't put enough distance between themselves and this house.

I went out the front door and down the steps of the stoop, and sprinted across the street to my car. As I started the engine I had the sensation that I was still in the house, watching myself from the living room window; standing there as I had a few minutes ago, but trapped, unable to leave. I put the car in gear and pulled out of the spot recklessly, almost hitting the car parked in front of me.

I drove straight for about ten blocks before pulling over, then sat there for a while and caught my breath. I felt like I'd run the distance on foot, and I could not explain the emotional swings I was feeling.

I began driving again, and more or less unconsciously pulled over at Lucky's on Thirteenth Avenue. I was, and had been, starving, and I could feel my stomach acids crashing in the surf of my empty gut more intensely now than before, but I knew I couldn't eat. I was still too upset—a nervous wreck, actually. I wouldn't even be able to swallow.

I drove on home, and of course everything looked the same. I could return here after a wave of plague, nuclear holocaust, or alien invasion and find our maple paneling and red brick pattern linoleum intact. A twisted kind of comfort.

I began to pace, then sat on the couch, exhausted. I felt exhilarated, and morose. I was free, and realized that until now I hadn't been conscious of feeling otherwise. But I felt sad too, and I felt guilty.

I'd had blowouts with Gina plenty of times. They were an integral part of our history. I'd cursed her mother, called her brother a piece of shit, and railed viciously at her every flaw, but I'd never told the truth before about anything of any consequence between us. Apparently neither had she. I was still reeling from her knowing about my running around. Had she done it too? Was I jealous? I really didn't know. What I couldn't deny was that I missed her; I felt that I'd lost something. I had never dreamed I would feel that. Also, she'd called me on things, and she'd been right. After catching her in pointless lies and stupid insignificant deceptions half a million times, she'd nailed me cold on matters that counted. And after stomping off righteously dozens of times in my dreams, I'd left as a scumbag in real life, called on all my sins.

I felt terribly tired, speed tired, like coming down from a crystal meth jag after a twenty-hour card game. The body still wants to run, nerve endings torqued to the pulsing tips of fingers and toes, but behind it you start to shut down. I coaxed myself off of the couch and went to bed.

Chapter 23

I woke for the first time about ten o'clock that night, got up and pissed like the last wolf on earth trying to mark all of Alaska, and went in serious search of food.

I located half of an eggplant parmigiana hero in the fridge, and noted that it hadn't been there that morning. My father's room was empty, so he'd been in and out. There were two dead butts floating in the bowl, so he'd spent some time grooming. That meant he was gone for the night. I heated and ate the eggplant, and chased it with some cold cereal. I was still a little hungry, but I'd live.

I put the television on, and of course everything sucked. I had an urge to call Gina and I almost did. It was odd to suddenly feel like I shouldn't. Then I figured I'd call Kathy, but if a guy answered I knew I might go somewhere and take hostages. I wasn't used to thinking of myself as someone who needed to have a girlfriend, but the truth was I'd always had one. I was going on twenty and couldn't remember not being in a relationship since before the eighth grade.

When I realized I didn't have anyone to call, I turned my attention back to the television. There was a movie with Steven Segall on cable, where he plays a tough Brooklyn cop whose family is killed by the mob, or the government, or somebody. Before seeing it I'd always assumed that anyone could do a Brooklyn accent. Midwesterners.

Aborigines. Mimes. I guess you never know. It was okay with the sound off.

After the movie I found that I was tired enough to lie down again, and after a few false starts I drifted gratefully into a deep sleep with dreams that neither woke nor remained with me.

I didn't know anything about telling time by the position of the sun, but I was familiar enough with the subdued light that came through my window when I woke up. It was well past my usual six-thirty alarm that had been the norm for car service or school. I couldn't say why, but waking up mid-morning felt somehow old, nostalgic. Maybe because it was what I did when I was a little kid and stayed home sick from school.

I got up and pulled on old jeans and a t-shirt without washing up, giving in further to the pull the late sun was exerting. I slipped on sweatsocks and headed to the kitchen, trying to conjure up my mother brewing tea and pouring me a bowl of Cap'n Crunch.

My father was seated in his usual spot at our abbreviated kitchen table. It faced out, down the length of the apartment, and he watched me approach him. He was wearing light gray trousers with charcoal stripes, the leg I could see moving up and down in time to the Muzak on the table radio. His black mesh hose descended into a pair of Italian loafers with tassels that cost more than my car. Only my father and Gina would be able to name the designer from a half-block away. It was all they had in common, but I'd always thought it was a lot.

He'd removed his shirt, and his V-neck tee was pulled taut over his ample gut. His chest, always formidable, was beginning to show that tired, bra-less girl sag. The mark on his face from Edward's swipe had blossomed into a blue-tinged bruise, stopping thankfully just low enough that there was no black eye. It didn't seem to bother him, but eating couldn't have been much fun. He was pushing the remains of over-easy eggs around a nearly empty tin with a corner of toast. There was a blue cardboard container of coffee next to his plate, and with his free hand he was quietly rattling a pair of dice.

"Anything for me?"

"Two hard-boiled in the fridge, o.j., toast in foil on the door."

"You'd think I could get a hot meal," I said. "I see you took good care of yourself."

"Like I know when the fuck you might decide to take your prima donna ass down the hall for a stroll," he said, getting the last piece of egg on a tiny bit of bread and popping it into his mouth.

My eggs were still warm and the toast wasn't really stiff, so he hadn't been home very long. His entrance might even have been what awakened me, but I didn't know. I gathered up my food and sat across from him.

My father had pushed his plate aside and was playing with the dice. He rattled them loudly, shaking them in one hand, then both, cupped, then passing them back and forth while he watched me eat.

"Sounds like you had a pretty good night," I said.

He nodded. "I had a decent night. Dinner at Embers with MaryAnne, the coat-check girl from Ernie Barry's. She's a nice kid. We saw a comic at Topper's and stepped out at the Golden Dove. After that, well . . ." He shrugged. "Let's just say I'm a gentleman."

"She's got two kids practically my age."

"They're with their father in Jersey for a few days. The asshole wants them to move out there with him an' his new wife. Seems it ain't safe here anymore. Little Marie caught lime-tick disease staying with him over the summer, an' they can't barbecue out in the yard, cause they got enough radon to make Staten Island look healthy. But otherwise it's paradise." My father shook his head, grinning.

"So you had a date," I said.

"It wasn't a date. We stepped out."

"It was a date. An actual date. I'm shocked. I'm really proud of you. When did you catch a game?"

He looked at me, still rattling the bones. "What game?"

"When did you play? After you left her place?"

He had both hands together shaking enthusiastically, like he was mixing James Bond's martini. "My only gamble last night," he said, "was whether I'd get my dick wet or be buying roses for my right hand this morning."

He opened his cupped palms and their contents hit the table, skidding in different directions. One landed directly in front of me, bouncing gently off my navy blue plastic plate and stopping at my napkin. I looked at it curiously for a moment without recognition. It was not a die, and that threw me. I started to reach for it, and, when I almost had it, I realized that it was one of the uncut diamonds I'd seen at the Parlor Car.

I pulled my hand back impulsively like I'd found a bear trap or a land mine, jerked out of my chair—pushing it to the wall with the motion—and looked around.

"Don't forget to check under the bed," my father said. He was still smiling.

"What did you do?" I yelled. "What did you do? Are you fucking nuts? Jesus, why can't you leave this alone?"

"You sure woke up fast," he said. "I shoulda had something like this to get you up when you were in high school."

I felt suddenly claustrophobic. I did want to check under the beds. My father was still grinning like an idiot. I paced the length of the kitchen, glanced out the window at the courtyard, and walked back. I put my hands in my pockets. "What is this? What did you do?"

"Sit down," he said, and he stopped smiling. "Go ahead, just sit."

I couldn't possibly. There were three of them, all diamonds, displayed innocuously around the plates like parsley. I couldn't sit.

"Shit, sit down, will you?"

"Not here," I said, shaking my head emphatically.

My father got up and walked past me into the living room. I followed him, and we sat on opposite ends of the couch. He leaned back, one hand resting on the arm. I perched on the edge.

"Calm down," he said. "Everything is cool."

"Where did you get those?" I asked. "Why did you take them? You know they're gonna know."

He settled in the way he used to before telling a story, or, more often, giving me a lecture. He hunched his shoulders and rolled his head around, closing his eyes. Then he stopped moving, looking asleep or dead, the back of his neck against the puffed vinyl headrest, and exhaled loudly.

"Who's gonna know?" he asked.

"Edward. Todd. I don't know, maybe Tony. Everyone."

"No one's gonna know," he said. "No one but me an' you."

"There were like twenty stones or so," I said. "You don't think those fucking guys will miss three?"

"These weren't there. They ain't part a' the twenny," he said.

"What do you mean?"

"Holy shit, an intelligent question. Lemme sit up so I can think." He melodramatically hauled himself forward, and angled to face me so that our knees about touched. "I mean what I said. These rocks weren't ever in the Parlor Car. Nobody's gonna miss 'em cause nobody knows they're gone."

I organized my thoughts so that my next question would be straightforward. My father was in his world-class ballbreaker mood.

"How did this happen?" I tried.

"It happened when I came here for the bag. I looked to see what it was, of course, an' it was that little sack locked with a master lock. But it was one of those real tiny ones. So I got a bolt-cutter from the super's workbench an' I snipped it up here. I took these rocks out—they're the three biggest but I don't know if that means anything—an' I split. I bought another little master lock at Bruno's on the walk back and," he spread his arms wide, "the rest is history. Those stupid fuckin' bastids are out three big rocks."

"What if it didn't work?" I said. "I was there alone with them."

"That's why I did it. It looked like they were playing us straight, but if they weren't, I had the three stones stashed for insurance. I got an excuse to get you outta there, to guarantee they let you go. It would have been you going to get them the second time. An' you wouldn't have been coming back.

"Then when that scumbag pulls out a pocketknife like he's in the freakin' Boy Scouts, I know we're in. See, if one of 'em had a key, we might have been fucked, but if they gotta cut it open, then it means they receive the goddam thing locked."

"Jesus. Then why'd you try to take two more in the bar?"

"You don't think we could use two more?"

"Tell me," I said.

"I still wasn't positive. I wanted to make sure I didn't tip my hand."

"So you let him hit you?"

My father smiled. "Shit, I'd love to tell you I let him hit me. I'd love to tell you I *made* him hit me. I had no fuckin' idea that was coming. But I was trying hard to act like an asshole, an' I guess it was easier than I thought. That monkey hittin' me was our get-outta-jail-free card. No question but that they bought it."

"Fuck," I said. "I bought it. Why didn't you tell me before? On the way back?"

My father shrugged. I stood up, walked into the kitchen again, and stared at the stones sitting around our empty plates. I felt like I needed to keep them in sight now to believe they were really there. They were unquestionably the largest of the diamonds I'd seen, but, like my father, I had no idea what that meant. I walked back into the living room.

"Now what?" I said.

"Nothing," my father said. "Now you leave 'em stashed. Put 'em away; forget they exist."

"Stash them for what? For how long? We don't even know what they're worth."

"You know what hurts?" my father said. "What hurts is that Todd was right. What the fuck good are these rocks gonna do me? I got no way to move 'em. The scumbag is right. I got no contacts outside the nabe. But later, years from now, you'll know what to do."

"I'm never gonna know what to do," I said, and it scared me a little to think I was telling the truth.

"I'm talking down the road, maybe ten years. Don't worry about it. When the time comes, you'll know."

"So, I'm still asking, why didn't you tell me before?"

"Before what?"

I sighed. "Now who's asking stupid questions? Before now. Before today. Like as soon as we left the bar. Why didn't you tell me everything was okay?"

He leaned forward and took his cigarettes and lighter off the coffee table. He didn't respond until he had one lit. "Why didn't you tell me you took the bag?"

"I don't know."

"That's it?"

"No, that's not it. There were a couple of reasons. I guess mostly because by the time I figured out how stupid it was, I didn't want to involve you. I didn't want you to worry."

"Looking out for me, huh? That's nice." He inhaled so deeply that I watched the paper burn along the cigarette like a fuse. "I didn't tell you cause I was pissed at you. You kept things from me. In fact, you lied outright. So I wasn't gonna tell you shit."

He stubbed out his half-dead butt and lit another one. "It's been so long since I was mad at you," he continued, "that I forgot the rules. If you ain't gonna hide shit from me sometimes, then who you gonna hide it from? You know what it is? Until this happened, I lost touch with just being mad at you like you were my son."

"I didn't notice anything like that."

"You weren't here. I walked around for almost a day feeling like that before I came around. After I decided to tell you, I had to figure out how. I was still thinking about it when you woke up."

I went into the kitchen again and I picked up the stones. I rattled them lightly in one hand the way my father had. I carried them back into the living room. "I broke up with Gina," I said.

"Who's the new girl?" my father asked.

"Why does there have to be a new girl?" I snapped.

"You wouldn't leave Gina unless there was a new girl."

"Why do you say that?" I asked. "You hate her."

"I don't hate her. She's okay."

"You called her a cunt," I said.

"Once."

"I don't believe you sometimes."

"I'm just surprised." He put his second cigarette out, sat back, and smiled. "So tell me about the new girl."

"She's not Italian."

"So?"

"That's it."

"She's not Irish, is she?"

"No."

"So you'll be okay then."

"You don't care that she's not Italian? You're probably glad she's white."

"I'm glad she's a girl." He stood up and fished another cigarette from his pack. "Got no Italian in her at all, huh?"

"None."

He shrugged. "Jesus."

The shortest day of the year is December 21st. It gets light pretty late and dark fairly early, and for exactly those reasons it's my favorite day. In my private universe it's a bigger deal than Christmas or New Year's. A nice nine-hour window of daylight. I would fare well in Sweden or Norway. I never understood the high suicide rate in those countries.

On December 21st at 8:20 in the morning I sat in my car parked on

Parrot Place, the street that ran behind Victory Memorial Hospital. I had a container of coffee, a walkman, and a pen and pad. Me and Joe Friday.

There were twenty-two attached, brick, one-family houses on that block. I had no idea how many had illegal basement rentals, so I had to assume they all did. I'd been sitting there for an hour that morning, and had so far counted six people emerging from such apartments for work, or shopping, or Mass. None were Louise. I conscientiously marked off each address. Six from twenty-two. Sixteen to go. Not bad for an hour's work.

I didn't know exactly what I'd say to Louise when I found her. For all I knew, she could have had the kid already. Would Nicky have a son or a daughter? I wondered which he would have preferred. And I wondered what Louise would tell him or her about Shades when the time came. Maybe I could have some input there, tell a few stories. I supposed that would be easier if it was a boy, but either way I'd think of good things to tell the kid. Nicky had been a schoolyard hero longer than he'd been a junkie.

An old woman emerged from a driveway with an empty shopping cart that had a bad left rear wheel. I marked the address off. Fifteen left.

I'd called Kathy the previous night and arranged to meet her later in the evening. She hadn't seemed surprised that I called, so I guessed that she was aware of how seriously I felt about her. I sipped some coffee and put the headphones on. The lead singer from Dire Straits picked up at a spot that couldn't have been better, though I'd already been playing the tape to death for two days.

and now I'm searching through these carousels and
    carnival arcades
searching everywhere from steeplechase to palisades
in any shooting gallery where promises are made

The guy was English. I guessed he was singing about England, but Christ, sitting there that morning, I felt like he was talking to me.

The three rocks were hidden in my room, where I assumed they'd remain nearly forever since I had no idea what to do with them. Obviously my career with Tony was over, and that was just fine. But I didn't know what my next move would be. I certainly wasn't going back to school.

I reached over and turned the engine on so I could pump a little heat into the car. I had almost a full tank of gas.

Maybe this was as good as it got, I thought. Maybe if you weren't curing cancer or perfecting time-travel, then there weren't any great callings. And maybe that was how it should be. Then the best to hope for was to find what you didn't want, eliminate it, and see what was left. Okay, I didn't want to be a gangster or a student. And I could probably scratch off cowboy. Beyond that, I was unwilling to commit.

Right now I just savored not doing anything. It was like waking up late this morning—a warm, cozy feeling. I wasn't working, looking for work, or in school. I hadn't been without some kind of job since I was fourteen. It felt luxurious. I had enough money to last a good while.

Ultimately I'd do something; it wasn't really in my personality to sit around too long. Maybe it was the knowledge in the back of my mind that this stasis was temporary that made it feel so valuable.

A few indifferent snowflakes drifted down and settled on the windshield. I raised the heat some more, then cranked the walkman a little higher. I had all the time in the world. Halfway down the block another door opened. I reached for the pad.

Also from Akashic Books

Adios Muchachos by Daniel Chavarría
245 pages, paperback
ISBN: 1-888451-16-5
Price: $13.95

"Daniel Chavarría has long been recognized as one of Latin America's finest writers. Now he again proves why with *Adios Muchachos*, a comic mystery peopled by a delightfully mad band of miscreants, all of them led by a woman you will not soon forget—Alicia, the loveliest bicycle whore in all Havana."
—Edgar Award-winning author William Heffernan

The Big Mango by Norman Kelley
270 pages, paperback
ISBN: 1-888451-10-8
Price: $14.95

She's Back! Nina Halligan, Private Investigator.

"Want a scathing social and political satire? Look no further than Kelley's second effort featuring 'bad girl' African-American PI and part-time intellectual Nina Halligan—it's X-rated, but a romp of a read . . . Nina's acid takes on recognizable public figures and institutions both amuse and offend . . . Kelley spares no one, blacks and whites alike, and this provocative novel is sure to attract attention . . . " —*Publisher's Weekly*

Michael by Henry Flesh (1999 Lambda Literary Award Winner)
with illustrations by John H. Greer
120 pages, paperback
ISBN: 1-888451-12-2
Price: $12.95

"Henry's the king. He writes with incessant crispness. Sex is reluctantly juicy, life is reluctant and winning-even when his characters lose. What's it all about, Henry? I think you know."
—Eileen Myles, author of *Cool For You*

Outcast by José Latour
217 pages, trade paperback
ISBN: 1-888451-07-6
Out of print. Available only through direct mail order.
Price: $20.00

"José Latour is a master of Cuban Noir, a combination of '50s unsentimentality and the harsh realities of life in a Socialist paradise. Better, he brings his tough survivor to the States to give us a picture of ourselves through Cuban eyes. Welcome to America, Sr. Latour."
—Martin Cruz Smith, author of *Havana Bay*

Kamikaze Lust by Lauren Sanders
287 pages, trade paperback
ISBN: 1-888451-08-4
Price: $14.95

"Like an official conducting an all-out strip search, first-time novelist Lauren Sanders plucks and probes her characters' minds and bodies to reveal their hidden lusts, and when all is said and done, nary a body cavity is spared." —*Time Out New York*

Once There Was a Village by Yuri Kapralov
163 pages, trade paperback
ISBN: 1-888451-05-X
Price: $12.00

"If there were a God, then *Once There Was a Village*, Yuri Kapralov's chronicle of life as an exiled Russian artist on the Lower East Side, would have gone to Broadway instead of *Rent*. Only the staging of this book, set amid the riots of the late '60s and the crime-infested turmoil of the early '70s, might look like a cross between *Les Miserables* and *No Exit*." —*Village Voice*

Manhattan Loverboy by Arthur Nersesian
203 pages, paperback
ISBN: 1-888451-09-2
Price: $13.95

"Nersesian's newest novel is a paranoid fantasy and fantastic comedy in the service of social realism, using methods of L. Frank Baum's *Wizard of Oz* or Kafka's *The Trial* to update the picaresque urban chronicles of Augie March, with a far darker edge . . ."
—*Downtown Magazine*

These books are available at local bookstores. They can also be purchased with a credit card online through www.akashicbooks.com. To order by mail, or to order out-of-print titles, send a check or money order to:

Akashic Books
PO Box 1456
New York, NY 10009
www.akashicbooks.com
Akashic7@aol.com

(Prices include shipping. Outside the U.S., add $12 to each book ordered.)